WHITE CATS CAN JUMP!
(BUT BLACK CATS ARE SCARIER ON HALLOWEEN)

WHITE CATS CAN JUMP!
(BUT BLACK CATS ARE SCARIER ON HALLOWEEN)

SHORT STORIES OF INTRIGUE, HORROR, HUMOR, AND MYSTERY

FREDERIC DONNER

Copyright © 2013 by Frederic Donner.

Library of Congress Control Number: 2013901314
ISBN: Hardcover   978-1-4797-8385-4
         Softcover   978-1-4797-8384-7
         Ebook   978-1-4797-8386-1

All rights reserved. No part of this book may be reproduced or transmitted in any form or by any means, electronic or mechanical, including photocopying, recording, or by any information storage and retrieval system, without permission in writing from the copyright owner.

This is a work of fiction. Names, characters, places and incidents either are the product of the author's imagination or are used fictitiously, and any resemblance to any actual persons, living or dead, events, or locales is entirely coincidental.

Edited by Jonathan Lim
Reviewed by Mark Nell Mendoza

This book was printed in the United States of America.

Marketing and Sales
CRex Marketing @aol.com
Carla Rexrode
970-682-2251
P.O. Box 271796
Fort Collins, CO 80527

Rev. date: 6/4/2013

To order additional copies of this book, contact:
www.FredericDonnerBooks.com
or call Xlibris book sales at 1-888-795-4274 ext 7879

To Q, my beloved deceased cat.
Hell, if Prince can change his name to a symbol,
I can dedicate stories to whomever or whatever.

ACKNOWLEDGEMENTS

A special thank you to the Xlibris staff including but not limited to; Sergio Lee, Faith Go, Tim Fitch, Cynthia Matthews, Miranda Mickish, Ariadne Vale and Ram Alturas who all worked so closely with my Marketing Manager, Carla Rexrode from C-Rex Marketing.

TABLE OF CONTENTS

Introduction xi
Once Upon a Diary 1
Love 11
It's All in Your Point of View.. 15
All Dogs Go to Heaven 33
I Will Have You, My Love...43
Vinny Plays God 53
'Shrooms...67
The Philanthropist...79
The New Wild West 103
The Lord is My Shepherd, I Shall Not Want......................................115
G-String 123
Finally, Flowers 143
The Story Teller... 151
What Do You Call a Copycat Who Copies Copycats? 169
Conclusion 177

INTRODUCTION

Once upon a midnight dreary, while I pondered, weak and weary, over many a quaint and curious volume of forgotten lore — While I nodded, nearly napping, suddenly there came a tapping, as of someone gently rapping, rapping at my chamber door. "Tis some visitor," I muttered, tapping at my chamber door — Only this and nothing more.

The Raven, Edgar Allan Poe

It was as if someone had slung a medicine ball right into the soft, vulnerable flesh of her breasts. She could feel them push out toward her ribs—it hurt—and then she had the dog by the throat, her fingers sinking into its heavy, rough fur, trying to hold it away from her. She could hear the quickening sob of her respiration. Starlight ran across Cujo's mad eyes in dull semicircles. His teeth were snapping only inches from her face, and she could smell an unclean world on his breath, terminal sickness, senseless murder . . . Somehow, using all her strength, she was able to fling him away, and then his back feet left the ground in another lunge for her throat.

Cujo, Stephen King

One is a snippet of a poem, and the other is a paragraph from a novel. Each penned by two of the most accomplished fearmongers of any generation. The emotions evoked by these brief passages are strong.

The writing of fiction and, in particular, horror and suspense, is truly art. Allow the pundits and critics to praise novels like *Shogun* and poems from Robert Frost. I have no complaints with the great works of fiction and nonfiction. Yet it is not every day (or month) that a reader has the intestinal fortitude to digest a multithousand-page epic. Instead, allow readers to be thrilled, scared, or shocked by a brief foray into the dark side. When one finds a long-term lover with talent and ability, a permanent partnership may be in the offing, but who amongst us has not enjoyed a brief and heated, but nonetheless doomed, short-lived affair?

The tales I have written in this book are divergent and strange. Some readers will enjoy many of them, others may only locate one story of interest, but even if only one idea strikes a reader's fancy, my job has been a success.

When I was a younger pup, I devoured the fiction publications containing short stories from Ray Bradbury, Isaac Asimov, and Stephen King. Fiction with twisted endings, heroes transformed to villains, with every reader unsure of the outcome. There are no easy outcomes in the repertoires of these stellar authors. I do not claim to have these writers' skills, savvy, or flair for drama, but I do believe there are periodic insights and surprises in the stories you will read here. If even one of you is entertained, then my job is accomplished.

"Enjoy the feast," as an author colleague of mine would say. Just be wary of where you left that turkey carving knife and the long-handled—and sharpened—fork.

ONCE UPON A DIARY

Many diverse and unique people write detailed diaries. Others hide brief notations and keep these spontaneous tidbits in scrapbooks as remembrances. Others are so important that secretaries, aides, and hangers-on keep the recordation of their accomplishments and failures.

This story will examine the diary entries of seven entities for days surrounding April 7, 2011.

#1: I had a wonderful time last night with Kevin. He took me to the Top of the Triangle after he made me dinner at his apartment. Dinner was fresh sea scallops sautéed in butter, thyme, scallions and accompanied by linguine. We drank two bottles of sweet spicy wine that tasted like soda pop. Kevin said it was Gewurztraminer. I said, "Goose me where?" And he replied, "Anywhere, any time." He made a decent effort for there right on the carpet next to the table, but I pushed him off and said no way because he had promised to take me to the Top of the Triangle which overlooks the city and is my favorite spot for a drink and dessert.

I drank two cosmopolitans, and he sipped on a chocolate martini. He said that chocolate was a well-known aphrodisiac. I told him he didn't need any help in the sexual-enhancement department. As we left, we hailed a cab.

His apartment is near the spot in Pittsburgh where the three rivers intersect. I still love the thrill of asking visitors to Pittsburgh to identify the rivers for which Three River Stadium is named. All natives know the answer is the Ohio, the Allegheny, and the Monongahela. The junction of the rivers has special meaning for Kevin and me since he proposed to me there at Point State Park.

Our wedding is coming up in two months, and while burdened with details, I'm so EXCITED!

Unfortunately, the night did not go off as scheduled because, outside the park, a black cat with the cutest white belly and a white-tipped tail was cruelly thrown into the river by a dark-haired, greasy-skinned boy. The poor cat was little more than a kitten, and the rivers run quickly there. A little black head bobbed up for just an instant but then was sucked back under with the current.

Kevin ran over to the punk, a mixed-breed street lowlife who had not seen a shower in weeks. He looked sixteen years old and was clearly high on methamphetamine. Kevin chased him down and, despite the grease in the hair, was able to hold him by the fur for a few moments and bitch slap him in the face five or six times.

While Kevin was holding him, I admit I kicked him in the crotch twice with my boots. The slime got loose from our grasps and escaped on foot.

As he ran, he screamed back at us, "Fuck you, you whitey scum. It was only a cat. All you whites are weak for animals, you treat them better than us niggers."

By then, the kid was gone, and Kevin only had a still-bleeding chunk of Afro in his hand to remind us of the little bastard's presence.

Neither of us said much on the remainder of the way back to Kevin's apartment. The romance had slipped away and been replaced by anger. I had to wake early for work and kissed him and left in a separate cab for my own condo. We had kissed good night a little longer than usual, and after I left, I thought of that poor white-bellied cat and that horrible little punk who killed it.

#2: I know I should never keep a diary because it explains the times I have killed. I'm compelled to author it though, and I relish rereading the details of my killings. How each person cried for their lives? It recreated the ecstasy I feel

after every single killing. This is especially true when my target is young. I often have hour-long erections as I reread my diary entries of my dismembering a young child or using piano wire to garrote a worthless old man living long past his allotted time.

I like the killings more than the mutilations. There is always a possibility of apprehension, but as the life and soul slip from the body, my excitement is fulfilled. It is a love affair—something God has ordained that I must do. Often God will point out who my next target of opportunity should be, but God does not control my actions. I decide. I'm more like God. I choose. Who lives, and who dies. Most importantly, I decide how, and if the target seems kindly or honest, probably just a severed neck.

Most people don't realize the razorlike sharpness a hunting knife can be honed down to.

When O. J. Simpson killed his wife, Nicole, OJ had used a very high-quality blade. The killing stroke had been so clean that it had almost severed her head entirely. The knife had sliced entirely through the throat, neck, and muscles and actually nicked the spinal column. That was good work. No doubt, the dirty bitch had deserved it. All women did. Most men deserved to die painfully also. And any nigger, male or female, immediately qualified as a target.

I am working at a higher calling by killing the undeserved. God has spoken to me, and he has told me the inferiority of the Negro race. So when I can select Negroes as victims, I do.

I just got into town a few weeks ago, and it's cold here. I don't much like Pittsburgh. But the train stops here, and Amtrak is how to move when you kill humans for pleasure. Here in Pittsburgh, the station is on Liberty Avenue, an area where a short cab ride can take you to prostitute hotels where victims are easily found. There are also numerous parks where I can do my hunting.

It is late in the evening of April 7, and I am walking

down the main drag of Liberty Avenue. A ticket vendor at the train station had said that if I walked directly down Liberty Avenue, there was a park where the three rivers converged. I have been to Pittsburgh before, and it is a little too cold for me, but wearing a jacket makes it easy to conceal an O. J. Simpson–sized cutting knife. I also have my miniature fire axe.

The axe is fifteen inches from handle to the axe head. The handle is nonslip, easily graspable, hard rubber. It never slips in my hand. The axe end has two parts, similar to a double-headed axe that a miniature Paul Bunyan might have carried. This beauty is built differently though. The axe side is curved and honed to razor sharpness.

Each night in my room, I spend at least an hour sharpening my tools.

The other side of this tool has a three-inch curved spike point, also sharp and solid. It is this spike that I use to inflict deep blows, generally to the temple. When struck with precision, it has never failed to leave my chosen one decidedly dead. Blood splatter is relatively minimal. As I contemplate the weapon's dimensions, I feel the heft of its weight in my oversized right internal jacket pocket. I smile as I stride down Liberty Avenue.

The road is quiet, and in one alleyway, I see a figure slumped behind a dumpster overfilled with garbage. No other people are visible. The figure stirs, and I see that it is a nappy-haired nigger with some type of recently inflicted head injury seeping and oozing blood from the wound. I carefully scan the entire area, see and hear nothing, and I carefully loosen my jacket.

"Excuse me, young man, but I'm a bit lost. Could you direct me to a park? I believe it is called Liberty Park. It's where the three rivers converge."

The nigger slowly regains some semblance of consciousness and was clearly extremely high on some mixture of drugs.

"Fucking leave me alone, you white cocksucker, or I'll beat your ass until you're as black as me."

"I'm sorry to have disturbed your slumbers, my young friend, but it is unlikely I will be going quite yet."

I raise the axe and, using the pointed end; quickly and efficiently plant it in his temple. He is twitching and writhing on the ground and partially propped up by the dumpster. Because I had not particularly liked this youngster's language or attitude, I flip the axe over in my hand and, with two strong chopping motions, completely sever his head. I grab his nappy, greasy hair and toss the head into the dumpster. I move the body out of sight and see my clothing is relatively blood free.

It is dark, so I return to my hotel and take a long hot shower and clean my tools. I need to get some sleep because I am scheduled to take the Amtrak to Philadelphia early the next morning.

It is another city and another opportunity.

#3: It is Friday, April 8, 2011, and it has already started out poorly. I have not yet finished my Sunday sermon, and now I only have two days to complete it. I am exhausted.

Late last night, I had received a request from Saint Francis Hospital to provide last rites.

Last rites? He'd only been dead four hours; some psycho chopped the poor young man's head off with a battle sword of some type. It was surprising that the boy's crucifix stayed on what was left of the stump of his neck. Last rites, my Lord God Almighty! I bowed my head, made the sign of the cross over his body, and prayed for his everlasting soul.

I did not even know what prayer to use. The doctors were speaking in hushed tones, but obviously, the poor child had been crazy high on meth. Meth was the true scourge of today's inner-city youth.

As always, the hardest part was dealing with the young boy's family. His mother and father and a sister and brother—all were crying in their anguish at this moment of torment.

I recognized the family from church, one of the few black families that regularly attended. Most of the blacks went to non-Catholic churches, but these folks came every

Sunday, dressed in their finest. The rest of my predominantly white congregation adored the Styles family. What a horrible shame.

I will work hard on this Sunday's sermon and attempt to find considerate and heartfelt words to ease the family's misery. Yet only God can truly show light and assist in our greatest times of trouble. But there should be penalties and retributions for evil, as well.

As stated in Psalm 55:21, "His words were softer than oil, yet they were drawn swords."

Sometimes I am confused as a priest; God's way seems lost. I seek guidance and inspiration from the Bible and the unspoken word, but periodically I'm deeply troubled.

How could God allow a young sixteen-year-old child, Jason Styles, to be so brutally destroyed? I think of Jason's younger brother, Luke, now deeply grieving. Luke is only thirteen; how will he deal with these issues? I know young Luke so very well. He has acted as my altar boy and is devout in his religious beliefs. I have often personally counseled Luke on Catholicism and the path of the Lord. I believe my words have touched his soul and influenced his being.

I returned to the Styles family and tried to comfort them as best I could. Young Luke ran to me and hugged me and asked if Jason would go to heaven.

I pulled him closer to me, brushed away his tears, and said, "God loves Jason. He will find his just rewards in God's heart."

After Luke's mother and father quietly led the family away, I thought of what Jesus Christ had purportedly said in the Gnostic Gospels: "If you bring forth what is within you, what you bring forth will save you. If you do not bring forth what is within you, what you do not bring forth will destroy you."

As I left and went back to the church, tears fell from my eyes and onto my black jacket that covers my official collar and vestment.

Under my breath, I question God and ask why, as a ten-year ordained priest, why am I so weak? Why, God, why?

Why had I sexually touched Luke? And years before, why had I forced Jason to give me oral sex? Why?

I hurried back to church. I still had not finished my Sunday sermon. For my other sins, I would ask God's forgiveness later.

#4: Boy, my fucking head aches. Lost my ass at that shitty little harness track outside of Pittsburgh yesterday. I dropped two grand.

What day is today? Saturday. Yeah, it's Saturday, April 9. I need Tylenol and some scotch.

Thank God, I didn't finish off that bottle of Chivas Regal last night. My hand is a little shaky as I write this morning's entry, but the Chivas helps.

What kind of wiseguy writes in a diary? I must be the most fucked-up outfit guy in all Pennsylvania. Thankfully, I'm only an associate and not a made guy. They thought about making me, or giving me my button under Milano in Philly. Got lucky there. I'd have gotten busted with the whole family, from the capo on down.

I am fucked though. I owe Fat Jimmy Salerno forty-five grand. I been doing my Hail Marys all morning and counting my rosary beads. He's in Philly, probably eating Philly cheesesteaks, waiting for my return. If I ain't got the cheese—forty-five grand worth of cheese—him and the boys will stuff me into sausage casings. But I got's an idea.

There is a little scumbag named Ratzo Vaccarro here in Pittsburgh that runs a little heroin. I'll go jack him up and see what I can get out of that fuck. Maybe it'll be enough to take to Philly and keep Salerno off my back. I'll finish my diary entry when I get back—hopefully, with my pockets a little more full.

Saint Mary be praised. It's finally my lucky day. Now, after all my bad luck, I'm in

FAT CITY. OVER AT RATZO'S APARTMENT, HE IS ALL BY HIMSELF. NOT ANOTHER SOUL.

WE TALK BUSINESS FOR A LITTLE WHILE, AND HE SAYS HE AIN'T GOT NO "H" 'CUZ HE JUST SOLD HIS WHOLE LOAD TO LITTLE SQUEAKY (WHAT A PUKE LITTLE SQUEAKY IS). SQUEAKY PAID HIM SIXTY LARGE—SIXTY MOTHERFUCKING GRAND. RATZO'S ALL BRAGGING ON HIS BAD SELF, SAYING WHAT A GREAT OPERATOR HE IS, AND PULLS OUT THE CASH AND SHOWS ME.

SURE AS SHIT, SIXTY THOUSAND, MOSTLY IN BEN FRANKLINS. SO I SAY, "CONGRATS, BUDDY, NICE HIT." THEN I DRAW MY LITTLE NINE-MILLIMETER BEST FRIEND AND SHOOT RATZO IN THE FACE. THEN I SHOOT HIM IN THE HEAD, BEHIND THE EAR, THREE TIMES, JUST FOR LUCK. THE SAME WAY YOU PUT TRIPLE-ROASTED COFFEE BEANS IN YOUR SAMBUCA, WHICH YOU THEN ENJOY WITH ESPRESSO.

I'M HOME FREE; NOBODY IN THAT NEIGHBORHOOD WOULD EVEN NOTICE SHOTS BEING FIRED. I PACK UP MY SIXTY THOU. I'LL BE HEADING TO PHILADELPHIA TOMORROW TO REPAY FAT BOY SALERNO HIS FORTY-FIVE, AND I END UP FIFTEEN GRAND TO THE GOOD. AND RATZO VACCARRO ENDS UP DEAD AS A FUCKING BONUS. WHAT A BEAUTIFUL COUNTRY.

#5: ANOTHER DAY, ANOTHER SOUL. EVEN WITH ALL THE HELP I HAVE, BEING SATAN IS NOT EASY.

"DID YOU GET THAT DOWN, DEMON NUMBER 43?"

GOD IS TOO BUSY WITH WARS IN IRAQ, THE INTIFADA, AND FAMINE IN AFRICA. SOMETIMES WITH ALL THE BIG STUFF, THE MAN UPSTAIRS MISSES ALL THE FUN WE ARE HAVING WITH THE INDIVIDUAL HELLS WE WREAK ON EARTH.

JUST AS AN EXAMPLE, I AM LOVING LIFE (OR DEATH) IN A US STATE CALLED PENNSYLVANIA RIGHT NOW. AND IT IS NOT EVEN CLOSE TO OVER YET. I GOT AXE MURDERS, PRIEST CHILD MOLESTERS, DRUG DEALERS, MURDER, AND MAYHEM. TALK ABOUT A SOCIETY FALLEN FROM GRACE.

#6: It is in the early afternoon of Sunday, April 10, 2011. I'm sitting on a train, headed out for a well-deserved vacation.

My sermon this morning was sparkling. It was just the right mix between fire and brimstone and God as saving grace. I saw tears in the eyes of all the parishioners. I also saw the Styles family. I felt sorry for their loss, but I know Jason is in heaven.

I admit that, as I looked at Luke and noted his family's loss during my sermon, I was sexually excited under my vestments. Though I know it is wrong and evil, I will have him just as I did his brother. I will enjoy the pleasures of his soft, young, untainted virginal flesh.

The train is just leaving the metropolitan section of Pittsburgh and entering the countryside of central Pennsylvania. I look around at my fellow train passengers. Most are the normal executives destined for work in Philadelphia, the City of Brotherly Love.

No one looks overly interesting. I do notice a hard-looking man wearing a long overcoat. His eyes appear menacing, and he constantly keeps his hand inside his jacket. The only other person of interest is a man, obviously of Italian heritage, who is smiling like the cat who ate the canary.

Wow, that was a hell of a bump. We're going over a bridge, above one of the rivers outside the city. They are all tributaries of the three main rivers that conjoin in central Pittsburgh. What is that screeching? The train's wheels are locking up? My god, the train is derailing. God help me. Everyone on this train is going to die!

#7: Today is my birthday, April 10. I am seven years old. My parents gave me this diary today on my birthday to help teach me to write better.

We had cake for my birthday. Chocolate because I like chocolate best. Tonight I will probably get ham for dinner because ham is my favorite.

But the bestest present of all came from Daddy. He gave me a little black kitten with a white tummy. He said he found it out by our barn at the river. He's curled up by the fire now.

I am going to name him Lucky.

LOVE

Clarence is a writer, an artist of the pen. He understands that true writers have feeling, sense, tone, and touch.

His writings explain the dying burnt-orange embers of a setting sun partially hidden behind thunderstorm clouds. His skillfully grafted words are capable of striking emotional chords in readers.

Clarence is proud of his work and his talents. He continuously carries an elegant, slender Cross ballpoint pen. This pen is as unique as his writing and is ready, at the slightest provocation, to set down an in-depth treatise on all subjects and manners of beauty and despair.

Clarence looks and acts the way a writer should. Currently, he is wearing a stylish red-and-gold striped silk vest, with a black hat casually tilted sideways. He always wears gloves: buttery-soft black calfskin gloves. The rest of his outfit is just as immaculate, and some might consider him a DANDY, but he knows they are merely jealous of his good taste. His jewelry is just as tasteful. He always wears a Rolex Oyster Perpetual Datejust Two Tone 18kt Gold and Steel watch and a matching 10 karat gold Cat's Eye ring. Writers must look strikingly perfect. It is a prerequisite to their craft. He has been a lifelong subscriber to *Gentleman's Quarterly*. The magazine is the authority on good taste, good grooming, and perfect manners in all ways. He jealously guards his hope that, one day; he will be on the cover of that magazine. He is a famous author, known as much for his clothing as his pen.

As he strides down the street, he takes in the stares of both women and men. Though none will recognize him as Clarence Donnetello the author, most will be struck by the ascot and the crisply pressed black-tinted trousers. Obviously, the handmade black silk shirt is a tailored match. It is warm this morning; so unfortunately, he does not need a coat or a topcoat. Clarence has coats of every material and hue, all perfect in their sartorial beauty.

He notices a lovely light-skinned black woman in a sexy red skirt, eyeing him with an amorous look. Clarence returns a similar-minded glance and smiles broadly. Even if not on the cover of *GQ*, his perfect bone-white teeth could have landed him a spot in any toothpaste advertisement.

He waves to the young beauty and crosses the street and introduces himself as Clarence Donnetello. She says her name is Marrisa. He explains he is an author and, while dismayed that she does not recognize his name, he beams his brilliant smile again when she agrees to join him for a drink at an exclusive local cocktail lounge, Entrepreneurs.

He lightly clasps her hand, and she does not shy away or pull back in the slightest. Clarence looks into her lovely green eyes and realizes she is reminiscent of the talented singer and actress Vanessa Williams. Marrisa is, however, taller and much lovelier. He is certain their relationship will be exciting and erotic.

They pass by a newspaper vending machine, hand in hand, and both are so involved in their warm aura of potential that neither bothers to note the newspaper headline and article.

STALKER STRIKES AGAIN

The body of a woman was located strangled in the southeast downtown section. It appears to be the fifth person to fall prey to the so-called piano-string strangler. The police have located few clues and are requesting help from all citizens.

The victims have all been black females. Psychological profilers are confident the perpetrator is a black male, likely between the ages of 20 and 35. Further information, released just yesterday by Police Lieutenant Jackson Udall, confirmed that each victim was marked with a blue-ink pen on the upper thigh. The markings appeared to be brief Haiku-stylized poetry.

Any information concerning these crimes should be forwarded directly to the homicide task force and Lieutenant Udall.

The potential lovers continued their hand-in-hand stroll toward their appointment with two glasses of wine and some conversation. Clarence believes they make a striking and lovely couple as he casually fingers his pen in an inside pocket of his vest.

Once inside Entrepreneurs, Clarence catches a quick glimpse of himself and Marrisa in the bar mirror. She cannot be a day over twenty-five, and he looks much younger than his forty-five years—not even one of his naturally blond hairs has a touch of gray. They both smile, and he casually brushes her cheek with the briefest of kisses. She smiles glowingly because she is looking forward to seeing more of this handsome older man.

They will have quite an intense time together. Clarence knows there will be other lovely women he will meet after Marrisa.

Criminal profiling is a very inexact science, as any profiler will admit. Clarence Donnetello reads the newspaper every morning, and he is certain they will not be searching for the piano-string strangler near a blond-haired middle-aged white male ascot aficionado.

If Marrisa had looked closely, she might have noted that his elegant leather belt was rimmed on the lower edge by a hint of gold, or perhaps bronze. This rim could be easily and quickly removed if need be. Clarence enjoyed having such easy access to his piano string, which had brought him such joy.

He realizes what a beautiful woman Marrisa is and how lucky he is to have met her. As he casually rubs his belt, Marrisa looks at him and suggests that maybe they could go somewhere with more privacy.

Yes, her place would be just fine.

IT'S ALL IN YOUR POINT OF VIEW

No one likes a know-it-all. More pointedly, everyone despises a braggart who is arrogant and does not possess the actual knowledge and experience they claim.

Many humans are unrecognizable behind the facade they put forward to the public eye. Everyone has idiosyncrasies, flaws, and imperfections of character, which they hide from the world; and few have the strength to gladly, and openly, display themselves without their figurative suit of armor.

There are, however, some who hide nothing; they are exactly what they appear to be. Good or bad, evil or saintly. No bullshit. It is time to sort through some of these types of personalities.

[SECTION 1 - WHO'S YOUR DADDY?]

Brian Sundra was a know-it-all, inexperienced in the ways of the world. He was weak, relatively talentless, and what some in the new generation would derogatorily refer to as "my bitch." Brian Sundra was also incomprehensibly wealthy. Of course, it had come via no personal talent. His father was a Texas oilman who had earned the family fortune. His father had earned hundreds of millions through risk, fearlessness, and strength of will. Brian was his only son, and via some genetic mutation or switch at birth, he was the exact opposite of his dad.

The father, Julius Sundra, was dark, hulking, and spoke in monosyllabic grunts; but people listened to those grunts. He had a nose for oil, and his wells spewed Texas black gold. Julius had been a hard-drinking, womanizing brawler. Even after he had made his third or fourth million, he would go to San Antonio, or into Mexico itself, to compete in bare-knuckle-fighting expositions. Once, after winning one of these competitions in Ciudad Juarez, Julius had bought tequila and beer for the celebratory fiesta at the local bar.

At that party thirty-five years ago, Julius swooned into an extended sexual relationship with a local green-eyed seductress who claimed direct lineage from the Spanish conquistadors. Her beauty, jet-black hair, massive breasts, and narrow waist immediately attracted attention. Angelica's fiery, flaming temperament and sexual fury had been a perfect match for the explosive and intense passions of Julius.

He had immediately snatched her willingly away from Juarez and made her his wife in the United States. During the day, Julius managed exploratory drilling on his landholdings, and these wildcat holes were successful beyond measure. Angelica shopped the border towns for clothes and exquisite furniture for their ranch. At night, they had rabid, sweat-drenched sex fueled by tequila. Later, they would temporarily calm their fires with icy cerveza, but only for as long as it took to regain their strength. Two creatures of the wild had found the pleasure of a perfect relationship. Angelica and Julius enjoyed every moment in a fullness of explosive living that was almost greedy in its lustful success.

Fifteen years of marriage and lust can pass quickly, and it did for Julius and Angelica. Their wealth was nearly as thick as their love for each other. On one of the rare days when the dust storms brought rain, Angelica ran into the parlor and squeezed Julius in a hug that bears would be proud of.

"I'm pregnant, you prong- horned stud."

They smiled, laughed, and tried a two-step through their elegant furniture. While Julius had good footwork as a fighter, as a dancer, he was clumsy as a three-legged mastodon. They tumbled in a heap on the carpet, rolled onto one another, and had sex. They were so loud it caused their hound dog to cower, and he fled to the safety of the kitchen.

They had had so much sex through the years, both had assumed one or the other was incapable of having children. But it was true, and as the months passed, Angelica began to widen near that narrow waist.

X X X X X

Nine months after her first hints of pregnancy, Angelica gave birth to Julius's son, Brian.

The delivery was a nightmare. The best doctors money could buy were at the hospital in San Antonio, but everything went wrong. As the birthing process began to quickly unravel, Julius was instructed to leave the delivery room. It took four orderlies and two nurses to forcibly separate him from his beloved Angelica.

"We will have to restrain you, Mr. Sundra, if you don't calm down." one doctor yelled.

"Fuck you! If Angelica is harmed, I'll fucking rip your throat out and shove it up your fucking asshole."

One of the doctors cavalierly turned away and made the comment that difficulties during pregnancy occur sometimes and waved Julius away with his hand. Julius saw this, and broke the grip of the orderlies under and freed one fist. One quick straight-arm jab with his off hand, and the doctor was missing five teeth and flat on the floor.

Through the agony, Angelica was able to piece together a weak smile and say, "Julius, I'll make it and be fine. Let these doctors do their work."

Julius looked at the only person he had ever cared for and slowly left the room. A short time later, a stretcher brought out Dr. Ruthless and Toothless, who was still completely unconscious. Julius was able to smile slightly.

X X X X X

Four hours later, one of the secondary doctors exited the delivery room and, with extreme caution, approached Julius.

"It was a breach delivery, which means ..."

"I know what a fucking breach birth is, doctor. I'm not as stupid as I seem."

The doctor, who was visibly shaken and covered in Angelica's blood, took a small step back. Julius noted the blood-covered operating scrubs and, while a single tear dropped from his eye, contemplated whether it was worth scrambling this physician's facial features to match those of his mouthy coworkers'.

"It was a breach delivery, and the umbilical cord was twisted and wrapped around the child's throat."

Julius's eyes glowed and had a strange color. His eyes were jaundiced yellow, and the normally brown iris of the eye was virtually black.

As the doctor backed away one step further, he continued, "During the delivery, or perhaps slightly before, your wife Angelica had a massive internal hemorrhage within the uterus and the surrounding tissue. We performed a radical hysterectomy. There also appeared to be necrotic tissue in various other areas in the region, and the loss of blood was extraordinary. She should have died immediately from multiple causes, but she survived."

"I want to see her."

"She is under intense sedation currently. It is possible, if we attempt to awaken her, she will die or enter a permanent comatose state. We must give her fluids, monitor her, and keep her medicated. This may take a few days, or even longer. It is also possible she will never become alert, or worse, that she has incurred significant cognitive damage due to the seizures she experienced during the operation."

The doctor expected Julius to ask about the baby, but he just stared at the pointed steel-tipped toes of his shiny black rattlesnake-skin cowboy boots. A moment passed, and the nurses wheeled out Angelica. There were wires, tubes, and monitors attached at every open spot of skin. Julius could not help but notice the crimson stain on the bed and sheets between her legs.

Julius stood. "I am sorry, doctor, and I know that you and your colleagues have done everything in your powers. My anger runs so deep, but she is the only thing I have ever loved. I will pay for whatever damages I caused, even for Dr. Fuckhead's teeth. Do all you can to save Angelica."

"Don't you want to see your child, your son?"

Julius flashed a flame-tinted glare at the doctor. "No."

XXXXX

Angelica was as steely as Julius, and she held on for almost two weeks. Julius was constantly at her side, lightly clasping her hand, and he could feel the inconsistent pulse. She regained consciousness only once, very briefly. Angelica somehow mustered all her remaining power and will to speak final commandments to her only, and forever, love.

"Julius, don't say anything. I have little time left on this rock. They must have needed a tough bitch for some duties in hell. Take care of our son, and give him love, but make him strong like you and me. I will have no weakling offspring. Name him Brian, after our friend who is strong and a hunter and a survivor. My love is yours forever, mi toro gringo."

With those words, she slipped back into her medicated slumber. Julius pulled her gently to him and whispered that their son would be stronger than any bull—white, brown, or black. He kissed her and sobbed. She died two days later, quietly, as Julius cradled her head in his thick, sinewy arms.

✕ ✕ ✕ ✕ ✕

The day after Angelica's death, he asked the doctor to see the baby. The child was still in the incubator and was many pounds underweight and could easily have fit into either palm of Julius's enormous hands. He had decided to name his son Brian Torito Sundra: the little bull. He believed Angelica would have been proud.

As he stood peering through the glass window of the incubation chamber, he felt a strong hand fall heavily on his shoulder. Julius turned and saw his closest friend and the only man he had ever completely trusted, Brian Olafson. They hugged, and there were tears in both sets of eyes. Nurses walked by silently, understanding that even giants can cry if the sadness is great enough.

Olafson dwarfed even Julius; he was six five and weighed close to two hundred eighty pounds. His blond hair was so closely cropped and so white, his head almost seemed shaved. There was no extra lard on the massive frame, and his eyes were a steely blue, which were menacing even behind his heartfelt tears.

"I'm so sorry, Jules. Losing Angelica—I can't believe she's gone. I'd have been here sooner, but some shit-for-brains general decided my continued presence overseas was absolutely essential."

Julius knew Olafson must have called in every marker he was owed by the marines to come home while the conflicts were still ongoing. Julius told Olafson that at the request of Angelica, the baby would be named Brian, and he also requested that Olafson act as godfather.

"I would be honored to be godfather and am more honored he is named after me. I will do all I can to help with his growth."

Julius explained the infant's full name was Brian Torito Sundra, and perhaps with the child's gene pool of Angelica and Julius, and with help from Olafson, he would grow to be a strong, honorable man. With luck, the little bull would strengthen into a full-sized toro.

[SECTION 2 - EL TORITO FAILS TO RISE TO THE LEVEL OF EL TORO]

Brian Torito Sundra proves he will likely never be a strong bull, but more a lamb. He was no bull, nor was he noble in any way.

He was a sickly child, prone to every childhood illness conceivable. He was stricken with measles, mumps, whooping cough, scarlet fever, and every minor virus that swings within a hound's howl of the Texas ranch. More disturbing was his lack of urgency and common sense. He broke one arm and a leg while on horseback. No, that would be incorrect; he was not riding the horse, merely sitting on its back and fell off to incur the injuries. He simply fell off a horse standing immobile—not once but twice. After that, he refused to be in the vicinity of the barn.

He had no drive and failed miserably in school due to laziness more than stupidity. Utilizing terminology his father might have used, to add horse piss to a shit sandwich, young Brian Torito Sundra was also a prolific liar who delighted in hurting helpless small animals and used his father's rifle to purposefully wound rabbits and prairie dogs to watch their sufferings before their death.

Julius had an impossible task to successfully raise his son. Everything was attempted. He tried love, generosity, and kindness; and his son took inappropriate advantage by stealing, using drugs, and shooting the hound dog with buckshot. That friendly hound did subsequently bite young Brian in the face, permanently scarring the right side of his already ugly maw.

Good dog.

Julius also tried corporal punishment and used the strap on Brian's backside. Brian, at thirteen, placed a 911 call to the police and alleged child abuse and sexual abuse against his father. No charges were filed because the police were well aware of Brian's propensity for lies and devilry, since a number of neighbors have complained that their pets had been tormented and tortured by the boy.

Julius hired a full-time nanny and housekeeper, Louisa, but she had no better luck with Brian. At fifteen, when he believed his father was at a far-flung oil well, Brian attempted to rape Louisa as he held her at gunpoint with Julius's Colt .45 revolver.

The fates intervened on this one, and the old man came home early. Louisa was naked in the kitchen, crying uncontrollably, as Brian was dropping his trousers. Julius entered screaming, and Brian foolishly fired one shot in his father's general direction. The round tore away the top of Julius's right shoulder.

Some mistakes are big errors; some mistakes are unforgivable. As Louisa cried pitifully, writhing, naked on the kitchen-floor tiles, she described in Spanish that this was not the first time Brian had tried to rape her. She had escaped before because he was weak, but this time, he had a gun. Brian does not speak much Spanish—hell, he cannot even speak English very well—but he got the gist of it and sobbed.

"Daddy, it ain't so. She came at me with gun and was force me to have sex with her. Why would I fuck some Mexican whore like Louisa?"

And then, there are some mistakes that are much worse than unforgivable. Julius moved, catlike, to within an arm's length of Brian and tore the gun away from his hands. Holding the gun flat in the palm of his gigantic paw, Julius struck his son full force on the side of the face. The entire cheekbone and nasal passage caved in.

Julius was not even seeing forms as his anger was overwhelming rational thought. As in many high-danger or high-stress situations, his focus narrowed, and his vision tunneled. All he could see was Brian's face as he pummeled him with lefts, rights, uppercuts, crosses, and body shots. The tile was covered in blood. The blood did not show too much on the brown Saltillo tile, but the grout was whitish gray. Or it had been, until Brian's blood colored it almost the same hue as the tiles.

Louisa was screaming and, despite being naked, was struggling with Julius, pleading for him to stop before he killed the boy. She was switching between Spanish and English, English and Spanish.

Perhaps it was the mixture of the languages, like the fans from the bare-knuckle matches in San Antonio or Ciudad Juarez, but Julius regained some level of control. Brian lay unconscious, with his body limp. His entire face was shattered. One piece of the left cheekbone jutted through the skin, and an eye socket was completely sunken, and the eye itself pointed almost backward into the head.

He tried to calm himself and told Louisa that it was okay. He knelt by Louisa and helped her up as he covered her nakedness with his jacket. She fled into the living room. As he looked at Brian, his anger returned, and he flashbacked.

Why would I want to fuck some Mexican whore? Mexican whore. Mexican whore. Mexican whore. Mexican whore.

Julius realized he still had the .45 in his hand. His wife, Angelica, his own Mexican angel, Brian's own mom . . .

Mexican whore. Mexican whore.

He took two steps toward Brian and pointed the .45 at his temple. He placed his finger inside the trigger guard and slowly began to draw back the trigger.

No. He would not kill Angelica's son. The son she had fought so hard to bring into this world. The son she had died for as he came into this existence.

Julius looked at his son, who had now regained some semblance of coherence. Brian puled in a high-pitched whine, crying and speaking gibberish. Julius again contemplated killing him but decided against it. Not because of Angelica this time but because Brian was unworthy of neither the bullet nor the effort it would take to pull the trigger.

Louisa came back into the room. He asked her to call 911 to ask for both the sheriff and an ambulance.

X X X X X

[SECTION 3 - WITH A WILL, THERE'S A WAY]

Things calmed somewhat after the incident involving Julius, Brian, and Louisa. Immediately after the situation, the sheriff's office reluctantly took Julius into custody for endangering the welfare of a minor. Once the facts were sorted out, it was clear that regardless of Brian's age, he was likely guilty of sexual assault and possibly even attempted murder when he fired the .45 toward his father. Louisa did not desire to have charges filed but did demand that Brian be closely supervised and she also stated she no longer wanted to work for the Sundra family. Julius paid Louisa $100,000 but said it was not enough. He vowed to her that he would closely scrutinize every move made by Brian and guaranteed he would never injure anyone ever again.

Eventually, all criminal charges concerning the beating and shooting between Julius and Brian were decided as self-defense actions. Brian was in the hospital for five months. Broken bones healed, facial injuries were largely repaired via plastic surgeries, and vision partially returned to his right eye after a trio of restorative cornea operations.

Brian moved back into the Sundra ranch, though temporarily in a wheelchair or on crutches.

There was one additional occupant of the ranch—a three-hundred-pound, long-haired, mountain-like blond man. Brian's godfather, Brian Olafson, was helping his closest friend Julius manage the oil and ranch affairs. Olafson had retired from the marines years earlier, and when he read in the paper of the incident involving his godson and best friend, he offered assistance, which was greatly appreciated and instantly accepted.

One cold breezy November evening, as the winds roared across the Texas plain, Olafson and Julius shared a few beers and a bottle of Cuervo 1800 tequila. Brian Sundra was upstairs in his room, smoking crack cocaine and listening to an old Black Sabbath CD at full volume.

Julius and Olafson had already spoken in depth about the night of the shooting incident and fight. Yet the beer and good tequila loosened their lips, and the subject reared into view once more. Julius began, "Brian is a lost cause, a bomb waiting to explode—and I know no way to defuse him. He is a blight of evil darkness that will bring destruction to some innocent soul. I should have killed him that night. God rest her soul. I think Angelica would have agreed."

"Jules, we're both here to watch over Brian now. Perhaps with both of our insight, we can help him to a better, more harmonious, less destructive path. I don't want him to hurt himself because I'm his godfather, but I will never allow him to hurt an innocent person."

They talked of many things. Julius missed Angelica and was terrified that if something happened to him, Brian would be heir to the entire Sundra estate. They both knew that with that amount of money, he could cause havoc on innocents everywhere.

The bottle of tequila was almost empty. At least, there were no worms to polish off in Cuervo 1800. Olafson—who was a native Norwegian originally from Kristiansand, a southern port city—could drink all night with little or no effects. Growing up on shots of Aquavit would harden anyone's drinking tolerance. Julius was drunk, so a strong piece of honesty fell from his lips. A slur was almost imperceptible, but its presence did not minimize the honesty and sincerity of what Julius needed to say,

"I know that Brian will try to have me killed, so I have amended my will. If I die, all of my assets will go to you, Brian Olafson—not my son, Brian Torito Sundra. Better a good Brian than an evil one. There will also be a large sum of money set aside for you to care for my son. You will get what you deserve for being an honest friend, and he receives more than enough to live his sordid evil lifestyle far from your view. I only ask that you look in on him from time to time. I will leave him the home here in Texas. I had not intended to have anything disclosed until the reading of the will, but seeing you, or drinking this bottle of tequila, changed my mind."

"Julius, are you sure? If you do decide it this way, I will forever watch over young Brian."

"You'll probably watch him go to hell. But no worries. Anyway, I'm not planning on dying anytime soon. I am as healthy as ever, though you can outdrink me, by God. I am straight to bed."

Brian Olafson watched his best friend stagger back into the warmth of the ranch house, opened another beer, and considered all that his friend had said. Olafson did not need any money from Julius's estate. He lived nicely in a cabin near Pagosa Springs, Colorado, an Alpine mountain-pass town near the continental divide. He also had over two million dollars in real estate, stock, and various investments. He had spent much of his younger days in the marines and gone to Vietnam when he was fourteen. Fake birth certificates were not difficult to obtain then; besides, he had been six feet two inches tall and two hundred ten pounds at that age. No one ever questioned him. After such success at this young age in the arena of war, he had seen no reason to drastically alter his career path.

It was quiet now, and the ranch house looked ghostly in the swirling patches of ground fog and mist. Olafson did not particularly like to think about his past, but it was what it was.

His past had not allowed him to have any real friends (only acquaintances, casual contacts), but it did allow him to have enemies. All those old enemies had been eliminated. The final one was extinguished just four weeks prior to his arrival at Julius's ranch. Olafson could now consider himself officially retired.

Retired from a forty-year career as a CIA caseworker, he had conducted operations in Mogadishu, Somalia; Mosul, Iraq; Karachi, Pakistan; Mazar-el Sharif, Afghanistan; and dozens of other more obscure locales. The agency was purportedly prohibited by law from conducting specified targeted assassinations and killings, but that had been Olafson's job. Someone had to do the "wet work."

He had hoped not to kill again, but after speaking with Julius, he believed one more killing might be necessary. Julius knew nothing of Olafson's true past; he believed him only to be a retired marine who had subsequently signed on with an overseas consulting firm. Yes, it could be called a consultation organization.

A *termination group* would be better phraseology. Olafson went to bed with a twisting, uneasy tightness in his gut. It was not the tequila.

Early the next morning, the house was hammered awake by a shotgun blast. The business end of the shotgun was in the mouth of Julius Sundra. His long arms could easily reach the trigger. When Olafson arrived at the scene, it was clear that the shotgun had been loaded with rifled slug. The back of Julius's head was gone. He had been lying supine, and after exiting his skull, the round had lodged in the padded oak arm of the couch. The brains had splattered only on one wall, and the cleanup would be relatively minimal.

Olafson knew that in the major cities (New York, Los Angeles, Houston, etc.), there were specific companies that came in and contracted to clean up messy crime scenes. He doubted if there was such a service in this area. Young Brian came downstairs next and shed crocodile tears; he seemed out of breath and was decidedly scared.

The sheriff's office arrived, cordoned off the area, and told everyone to leave the house. The homicide investigators came next, asked the typical questions, and said an autopsy would be conducted within the next few days.

X X X X X

The autopsy indicated that the cause of death was a self-inflicted shotgun wound. The pathological verbiage was redundant. Basically, Julius Sundra had gotten drunk, sucked on the barrel of a shotgun, and fired one rifled slug round through his brain and out the posterior section of the skull.

Olafson was impressed that the city did have what he had always termed a slop crew. Within two days, a group of plastic-suited cleaners washed the living room walls, carpets, and furniture. It was spotless, without a drop of blood to be seen. Once the couch was discarded, even a close examination of the room disclosed no reminders of the body.

The settling of the estate and the reading of the last will and testament would need to be delayed for two weeks because Julius Sundra's attorney was litigating a wrongful death case in New Mexico.

Brian Sundra was very unsettled. One moment he was crying, the next drinking heavily from his father's stock of tequila and laughing at nothing in particular.

Olafson took Brian aside and suggested that, during this difficult time, perhaps they should get away for a few days. Leave the Texas ranch and spend some time talking and getting to know each other better. It was what Julius would have wanted. Brian was his godson, after all.

Brian seemed initially reluctant, but Olafson suggested they go hunting in Colorado, near his home in Pagosa Springs. It would be cold but beautiful there now, and the elk were plentiful. When Brian learned that hunting and weapons were involved, his mood shifted quickly, and he became excited to go on his first big-game hunt. No prairie dogs and rabbits this time.

They drove Olafson's four-wheel-drive Ford Bronco and would camp along the way. They travelled Interstate 10 through Texas and intersected with Interstate 25 north. That would take them through New Mexico and into Colorado. At State Route 160, they could travel directly to Pagosa Springs and the lodge at Keyah Grande.

They took their time getting to the lodge and had plenty of time to talk during the travel. At first, Brian attempted to sound remorseful and saddened by his father's death, but eventually, it became clear there were holes in his cloak of despair.

"I will miss your father, he was my best friend. We went through martial arts training together in Dallas. Nine months of training. Your dad was a very talented fighter."

"Yes, I respected my dad's skills. I will miss him so much. Even when he punished me, I may have deserved it. Would it ruffle your feathers if I smoked a little weed? I'm kind of on edge."

Olafson told Brian to feel free to blow a little smoke. Olafson was not surprised the kid needed a little come down; the night before, Brian had been making love to his crack pipe endlessly when he did not believe Olafson was watching.

After a few tokes and a ham sandwich eaten in Raton, New Mexico, the kid fell asleep as Olafson drove.

He had learned much during the drive. Brian had never hunted big game like elk and had no experience with higher-powered or scoped rifles like the .30-06 Springfield or the Remington .308 heavy barrel. Olafson had brought two rifles, one for himself and one for Brian, and both were .30-06. He would utilize his original Springfield model 1903, with a K25 weaver scope. The .30-06 round had served the military through two world wars and countless conflicts and is used in various rifles, but most famously the weapon he himself would carry—the model 1903 Springfield. Olafson would use 165 grain Winchester Supreme Fail Safe factory-load ammo, with a muzzle velocity of 2,800 feet per second.

The other rifle he would provide to Brian would be a Beretta Mato with Leupold 2.5-8X VARI-X III sight—a fine newer model .30-06 weapon. The ammunition for this second rifle had been specifically hand loaded by Olafson himself at the armory within his home in nearby Pagosa Springs.

Upon arrival, both were impressed by the lodge, which had soaring wood-beam ceilings, with fireplaces in all the correct spots. The icicles were hanging from the lodge's eaves, but the fire indoors was crackling and providing an orange-tinted glow to the entire lobby. The lodge conducted guided hunts, but Olafson knew the area extremely well and would be driving away from the lodge property to a nearby private acreage owned by a deceased associate.

Both went to their respective rooms early that night. In his adjacent room, Olafson could hear Brian repeatedly firing up his crack pipe late into the night. This was good. He would be exhausted in the morning.

X X X X X

The plan was to rise at first light, eat a hearty breakfast, and head out. Olafson pounded on Brian's door, and eventually, a pale, shaky Brian answered and asked for a few more moments to get ready. Olafson returned to his room and could hear Brian violently retching in his bathroom.

In the restaurant, Olafson ate a large stack of syrupy buttermilk pancakes, three pork sausage patties, and a thick slab of ham. Brian nursed a cup of coffee, and his greenish skin was reminiscent of someone debarking from a rough ocean cruise.

They headed back to the vehicle, and Brian was wearing a light parka, jeans, and gloves. Olafson was wearing neoprene undergarments, a wool sweater, neoprene socks, and heavy waterproof boots. Olafson also had thermal pants, a waterproof parka, and a beaverskin hat which covered his ears. He had two sets of gloves, an inner acrylic pair with the right index finger cut off and full-weather mittens.

They drove approximately twenty miles, and then four wheeled ten more, and lastly hiked in two additional miles into fairly thick underbrush. While Brian shivered, Olafson set up the camouflage netting hide they would sit in until prey arrives. The hide is non-glare and largely waterproof and was set against a tree, which Olafson cut notches into, and then placed the equivalent of benches and steps into the slots. In this manner, they could climb to a higher level for a better view. From his pocket, Olafson also removed a spray, which he spritzed on himself and Brian.

"What the fuck?"

"It's scent blocker, young man. Now the elk cannot smell your human scent."

"Oh yeah, of course. I do that all the time when I hunt in Texas."

"I'm sure you do. Also, rub some dirt and snow on your clothing, and use this camouflage paint for your face."

Olafson removed a high-quality set of Swarovski Optik binoculars and scanned the surrounding region. No movement yet. Once nightfall arrived, he also owned a set of night-vision goggles, or NVGs, he acquired from the CIA, which would allow him to identify targets during anything but total darkness. It was a quarter-moon that night and there was cloud cover, so it would be perfect.

He had a perfect view of the entire grazing field. If an elk entered the area, he should have a wonderful shot.

The basis of any good killing shot is in your point of view. Olafson loaded his weapon and advised Brian to do likewise. Brian was shaking now and asked if Olafson would load Brian's rifle. Olafson smiled a wide grin and said, "Of course," and loaded the weapon with one of the rounds that had a crimped bullet end. In his own weapon, he chambered a 165 grain Winchester Supreme Fail Safe round. Now they sat, waited, and hoped for a quality elk to wander through their icy slice of heaven.

XXXXX

It was growing dark, and Olafson switched to his NVGs. In the distance, he saw a single large elk. It was still too far away for a killing shot, but it was huge. From the size of the rack, it must have weighed over a thousand pounds—one of the largest he had ever seen. Brian was crying now, and he was swigging from a bottle of Jack Daniel's. All the better: the alcohol would seem to warm him but would just dilate his blood vessels and increase the effect of the cold.

It was beginning to snow, and the wind was blowing the fine powder into bluffs. The fineness of the snowflakes told Olafson that it was now much below zero. The snow was like confectioner's sugar in Brian's hair. The dumbass was not even wearing a hat where 75 percent of body heat is lost. His skin was beginning to turn gray, pink, and blotchy—signs of imminent frostbite. Brian took another large swallow of Jack Daniel's.

While Brian has whined and whimpered, Olafson has watched the elk slowly move into range. He removed his right glove and stretched his hand and index finger. Luckily, the elk was on the right side, and as a right-handed shooter, he was in the perfect position. He looked through the scope, knows the bullet is designed to break heavy bone and give reliable penetration. He slowly squeezed the trigger. There was a loud, shrill bang, and then a metallic hissing sound, like sticking a superheated branding iron into water. He chambered another round, and he looked through the scope.

The elk was dead. A pool of blood in the snow confirmed the heart shot was successful.

"Can we go now?"

"No, we must field dress the elk and carry it back to the truck."

"I'm cold. I want to go now."

"Not until we get the animal. Bring your rifle in case we see another elk. I'll leave my weapon here in the hide."

It had been a good shot, maybe two hundred fifty yards; not bad for the old .30-06 Springfield. As he was gutting the elk, Olafson noticed Brian drunkenly using his own weapon like a cane or a crutch. He was shivering, his teeth chattering, and the blotches on his skin were much more pronounced. He was weak, and it seemed as good a time as any.

"Brian, why did you murder your father at your house last week?"

"I d-d-d-d-didn't d-d-do anything. He killed himself."

Olafson lied and said that he knew what happened because he had seen it from the upstairs landing.

"That's a lie. There was no one on the landing. I looked."

"You did kill him. You killed your own father."

"Fuck my father, and fuck you too."

Brian raised the rifle and pointed it at Olafson.

"Don't kill me, Brian. I'm your godfather. I've always supported you."

"I'll kill you just like I did him." Brian just inched closer to Olafson, aimed, and fired.

A sickly *ffft* expelled from the muzzle as the blank went off.

Olafson stood up, and Brian realized how terrifying six feet five inches and three hundred pounds of angry man was. Brian's pupils were miniscule, just like a crack smoker's deserved to be. The fear coming from him was palpable.

The hatred coming from Olafson was crackling like the ozone in winter storms after a lightning strike. The lightning had not quite struck Brian, but it would soon. Olafson lifted Brian up by his jacket collar and slung him roughly back down to the icy ground.

Brian wet his pants.

"Please, please..."

"Don't beg me, you murdering puke. You are an embarrassment to your whole family."

From inside his jacket, he removed a small handgun and shot Brian Sundra once in the head.

"That's for your dad."

Olafson finished cleaning the elk and removed all the entrails. Then he cut the legs and arms off Brian and placed the entire body inside the carcass of the massive elk. He then sewed up the belly with fishing line. He hiked back to his Bronco, dropped it into four-wheel-drive low, and drove back to the location of the hide and the carcass. No, make it *carcasses*—plural.

He loaded the elk's entrails into a plastic bag, which he securely sealed. The elk body he strapped to the top of the Bronco. He hoped Brian was nice and comfy inside.

He dismantled the hide, located the expended cartridges and placed them in his pocket, and ensured he had all the gear he arrived with.

He headed out in the Bronco.

As he drove to his own small house on the other side of Pagosa Springs, his mind drifted to times past.

When he had utilized his specially hand-armored Remington .308 heavy-barrel sniper rifle to kill a terrorist in Afghanistan.

When he had utilized a fully automatic Colt M-16, firing .223 rounds to resolve a hostage takeover in Riyadh, Saudi Arabia.

When he had utilized a collapsible stock MP-5, firing 10-mm rounds to kill seven insurgents in Iraq.

And finally, he had just used a 9-mm Sig Sauer P226 to kill his best friend's son.

Of all the killings he had ever committed, this was the only one not "in the line of duty." Still, it felt the most right, the most justifiable.

Olafson drove to his own cabin and lit the potbellied stove and warmed the house. He fired up the industrial meat grinder to make dog food for his hounds and gradually tossed in pieces of the body of Brian Sundra and the innards of the elk. The clothes of Brian Sundra he burned in the potbellied stove. The fresh elk meat he took to the curing shed behind his cabin. The elk's pelt and antlers he placed in a separate storage room. He might decide to mount the elk's head and rack on his wall.

After all matters at his cabin had been attended to, he returned the next day to the lodge at Keyah Grande. He asked if Brian Sundra had returned and explained that they had become separated in the cold and storm of the evening before. Olafson said he had been forced to hunker down in a snow cave.

Olafson led the authorities to the area where he "believed" they had been, but nothing was found. That evening, a larger and more fearsome storm whipped through the area. The local police did not believe they would be able to go out again until the next morning. The storm socked the whole area in for not one but for three days.

There was never a trace of Brian found. The police said his body would likely show up in the spring. Of course, it never did, though Brian Olafson's hounds ate hearty for months.

Eventually, Olafson did return to Texas and was present for the reading of the will of Julius Sundra. He knew the estate's money was his now, and if Brian Sundra was not found alive, the ranch would be his as well.

Olafson hired a lawyer and gave him some simple instructions:

a. When the correct legal time period had elapsed and the ranch and its contents were Olafson's legal possessions, it was to be transferred in total to a nanny and housekeeper named Louisa. The lawyer knew Louisa's last name was Torres because of the prior sexual assault issue. The ranch would go to Louisa Torres.
b. The remainder of value of the estate would be donated to a charitable trust. A trust named in honor of Angelica, Julius, and Brian Sundra would operate a shelter for wayward and homeless children.

[SECTION 4 - CONCLUSION OR EVERYBODY DESERVES A DADDY]

So when all was done and over, the Sundra Trust provided homes for many young children who needed help.

Angelica and Julius Sundra definitely received an open invitation through heaven's gates.

Louisa Torres received a beautiful Texas ranch house, landholdings, and money she deserved.

Brian Olafson received the peace of no one trying to kill him and the joy of knowing his dogs will be fed for free for quite some time.

Oh, and Brian Sundra. That mean little punk got just what he deserved. Remember how cold he was in Pagosa Springs, Colorado? Well, it is always hot in the fires of hell.

ALL DOGS GO TO HEAVEN

Jasmine and Boats were sister and brother, but there was some animosity between them. They played rough and tumble, and usually, Boats got the best of it because he was much bigger and stronger. Still, Jasmine's claws were sharp and at the ready. Boats had a half-chewed ear and a number of scratches on his nose from their tussles. Jasmine owned a few nicks too. Her tail bent directly left about two-thirds the way down where Boats had accidentally broken it when it was caught as he slammed shut a closet door. Jasmine howled that day, and Boats felt bad.

Boats—whose full name was Boatswain due to his water-loving nature—was a shiny golden retriever. The name fit because *boatswain* is a nautical term for a navy officer in charge of rigging, anchors, and the like. Actually, *boatswain* is pronounced "boson," but *Boats* sounded better, so master made it *Boats*. He spent most of his days in the black-bottom pool, swimming for hours. Multiple times a year, Boatswain's owner would drive him in the Land Rover from Beverly Hills down south to Laguna Beach. A dog-friendly beach where Boats could swim for hours in the ocean surf. The saltwater stung his eyes, but he didn't care. He would run on the beach, roll in the sand, and have a joyous, sun-drenched holiday. After, he would get hosed down, jump back in the Land Rover, and he and his master would drive home. Boats would stick his head out the window, and the wind made his ears flop in the breeze. He always tried to stay awake the entire trip home, but the swimming and excitement wore him out. When they pulled into their long circular driveway, Boats was always fast asleep. He would be dreaming happy dog dreams, and his paws would be running in place on his own imaginary dream beach.

Jasmine—a mixed-breed, long-haired calico—had her own special days. There was a special ray of sun that shone through a skylight in the mansion, and on certain days, the ray warmed a small alcove about eight feet off the floor. The alcove was designed for a small statue or piece of art. The master never placed anything there because he saw how much Jasmine loved her personal sundeck. Her bright colors glowed as she lay sprawled in the sun. The spot was too high for Boats to jump at, so Jasmine was safe, warm, and at peace.

Though they never would have admitted it to outsiders, Boats liked Jasmine, and vice versa. On the rare occasions when other dogs or cats might visit the home, both yowled and barked at the other to fake dislike. Yet it was an act, and often when no one was around, they chased one another around the mansion and played.

They had both come to the house ten years ago—one a puppy, and one a kitten. The master's wife had died in a car accident, and the master's brother had given them to ease the loneliness. It worked as well as possible under the circumstances. The master, a famous screenwriter, spoiled them both constantly. If he was ever gone, a hired animal nanny doted on them and gave them treats.

Truth be told, other than being with their master, Boats and Jasmine enjoyed when they were alone. It was a huge place, with hundreds of spots to explore, and often they would play hide and seek. They actually loved each other too. Sometimes, just sometimes, when Boats was lying on his rug in front of the marble fireplace, and no one was there to see, Jasmine would curl up under his belly to stay warm. Then she would purr her loudest purr.

Later that year, Jasmine is curled up in a high-backed wicker chair on its gold-striped cushion. Boats is snoozing on the leather couch, which he's not supposed to be on, and their owner is peacefully snoring in his recliner. The flat-screen television displays ESPN *SportsCenter*, and the announcers are explaining how the Los Angeles Clippers recently were blown out by the Sacramento Kings. Other than the TV, everything is quiet. It is late—3:24 AM, to be exact.

An almost inaudible clicking noise comes from the front door. Jasmine does not notice the sound, but Boats' keen ears hear it. He opens his eyes and jumps down from the couch so he will not be caught in his current inappropriate furniture location. Slowly the front door eases open, and a large man clad in a black flight suit, gloves, and full-face hood enters. Jasmine is awake now, but their owner continues to snore over the volume of *SportsCenter*.

In his right hand, the man in black holds a wooden baseball bat. Boats growls, and the man notices the golden retriever and perceives him as a minimal threat. The man raises the bat over his head with both hands. Boats moves quickly and charges at the man, but he is agile and sidesteps the dog while simultaneously kneeing Boats in the chest. Then he raises the bat and crushingly slams it into the face of the homeowner. As the bat is raised for another blow, Boatswain lunges and clamps down on the intruder's forearm. The man hurls Boats down, shattering a glass end table.

"You fucking mangy mutt. I'll smash your head too."

The man again lifts the bat, but Boats moves quickly, and the blow only shatters bone in his shoulder and rib cage. Boats cries in pain but keeps coming at the man and bites down hard on his wrist. Instead of chewing on wrist tendons and veins, he clamps through the flight suit onto the man's black scuba diver–style watch. The watch is torn off, but the man is strong and raises the bat again and swings it downward into Boats' neck. There's a loud snap, and Boats falls, shuddering with death convulsions. To ensure the dog is dead, the man rears back and delivers a final blow to Boats' head.

He returns to the recliner to ensure the owner is also dead. From the corner of his eye, he glimpses a multicolored brown-and-white blur and feels Jasmine's claws tear at his mask directly at eye level. Jasmine grabs through the mask, holds, and claws away a hunk of eyelid. Jasmine tries to bite, but the man is too fast. He clutches the cat by the fur and hurls it against the wall. Jasmine hisses and avoids the man's vicious kick.

The attacker decides too much noise has been made and quickly returns to the reclining chair and smashes the bat three times into whatever remains of the head of Boats' and Jasmine's now-very-dead and blood-spattered owner. The man quickly exits the house, silently leaves the grounds, and escapes in a waiting vehicle.

X X X X

The next morning, the maid arrives, screams something in Spanish about Satan in the City of Angels, and calls 911.

Beverly Hills Police homicide detectives arrive and cordon off the entire estate. After the requisite photographs, their evidence team examines the scene for clues.

Blood, gore, and a dead dog beside a shattered coffee table stand out as the most likely items of interest. During hours of work, the crime scene is fine-tooth-combed by the response team. Finally, the body is taken to the coroner's office for an autopsy.

Detective Tailbott asks the on-scene lieutenant, "What about the poor dog? Are we going to leave him here?"

"We are, for a while, to keep the scene completely secure. I don't need a fucking O. J. Simpson scenario with somebody screwing with evidence. Leave a marked patrol unit and two uniformed officers to keep it all exactly as is."

Jasmine hides, and the police do not find her hidden under blankets in the attic.

Autopsies make murder scenes look like a playground. During old-time autopsies, there was a blackboard where an assistant wrote notes. Today, most pathologists use tape recorders, which are then transcribed. The information includes body weight, markings and puncture wounds, condition of internal organs, and various other pertinent details.

A partial summary of the transcription reviewed by Detective Tailbott went thus:

> *The standard Y-shaped cut is made from each shoulder, meets at the bottom of the ribs, and then runs as a single cut to the pubic region. Skin and muscle are peeled back. The ribs are then cut open, revealing the heart, lungs, and abdominal region. Separately, the stomach, liver, kidneys, spleen, intestines, and other organs are studied.*
>
> *Internal organs of the subject appear normal in all respects, with the exception that his appendix appears to have been previously removed via a routine operation. The scarring in the region is consistent with a surgery having taken place at least ten years ago. Genitalia, skin, limbs, and all other regions appear unremarkable.*
>
> *Generally, at this point in the autopsy, the scalp would be cut, the skull cap would be opened, and the brain removed. This is not feasible here due to the blunt-force trauma to both the frontal and posterior regions of the skull and brain. Both the areas have been largely destroyed by the use of a non-sharpened blunt instrument. The wound appears consistent with impact from a heavy pipe,*

club, or baseball bat. The remaining skull fragments and brain matter will be retained and sent for further laboratory and trace analysis.

Absent toxicology reports to the contrary, this subject's cause of death was due to his head trauma, was non-accidental, and is a homicide.

Detective Tailbott did not need medical analysis to know it was a murder or that it was a baseball bat that caused it.

Now it is his job to find out who committed the crime. A cursory review of friends, relatives, and acquaintances fails to hint at a perpetrator. Basically, the victim was pretty well liked and, as a screenwriter, had not pissed off anyone that would want to bash his head into mush.

Perhaps an even more in-depth review of the crime scene was warranted. Tailbott returned to the scene, which was still sealed and undisturbed. He saw Jasmine lying on the rug near Boatswain's body. He spoke aloud, "I didn't know there were any pets other than the poor dog. Here, kitty. It's okay."

Tailbott had a cat of his own. Homicide detectives didn't have dogs because they were never home on time to let them out. Most cops did not have wives either—or at least, not for long. Divorce was just another job requirement. Tailbott had a Siamese named Scooter who had a liking for Fancy Feast food and milk she drank from a fancy cut-glass bowl.

With a little coaxing, Jasmine came to the detective, who read her name tag. The tag was aluminum and in the shape of a small mouse. It also contained the address and phone number for the house. As Tailbott stroked Jasmine, he said, "Pretty little girl. You've had a rough couple of days. Lost your owner, and probably saw the poor dog get killed too. I wish you could tell me what happened and who did this. I don't think I'll mess up the crime scene if I try to find you some food or milk."

Tailbott carried Jasmine into the kitchen and saw four pet bowls side by side. Each was labeled with a name. The cat's food dish still had some dry food in it, but her water bowl was empty. Tailbott opened the refrigerator and found some milk, which was still fresh. He set her down, and she lapped halfheartedly at the liquid.

The two larger bowls were marked *Boatswain*. Tailbott did not need to be a detective to figure the dog's name had been Boatswain. He was reminded to reexamine the dog's body for evidence. He returned to the living room and saw the mangled dog. As he reached down to examine the animal, he heard a hiss behind him.

"It's okay, Jasmine. I won't hurt your brother. I'm just trying to figure what happened."

As he carefully rolled the dog's body over, he saw a glint of glass. A scuba-diver watch with dog teeth marks on it. He called for the uniform cop. "Get the Evidence Response Unit back here ASAP."

The dog's collar also had a name tag in the shape of an aluminum bone, "Boats." Jasmine had returned to the area and was looking up directly into Tailbott's eyes. He keyed his handheld radio and said, "This is Detective Tailbott, badge number 1473, to HQ Central, do you copy?"

"This is HQ Central."

"When the Evidence Response Unit arrives on scene, have them purchase a new cat carrier and bring it with them."

"Ten-nine, detective."

"Just stand by. I'll give you a landline."

Tailbott laughed at himself. It did sound weird to ask them to bring a cat cage to a crime scene. Bet they never heard that before. He used his cell phone to call central dispatch and explain. "Yeah, this is Tailbott. Sorry, central. I know it sounded odd, but at this crime scene, both the cat and the dog may have trace physical evidence on them. Boats—I mean, the dog—is dead, so he can be examined by the evidence team here. But the cat needs to be moved to a sterile environment as quickly as possible."

✕ ✕ ✕ ✕

Not long thereafter, Jasmine took her first ride in a police car. Jasmine was none too happy, but somehow, she seemed to understand. The lab scraped her claws and clipped some fur for evidence. At the mansion, the watch with teeth marks was placed in an evidence bag and sent to the laboratory.

✕ ✕ ✕ ✕

Analysis showed that DNA on the watch matched that of Calvin Theotis, a thug with an extended rap sheet for theft, attempted murder, and extortion. The scrapings from under Jasmine's claws were an even more certain match. The blood under the cat's claws was a 99.5 percent certainty match to the same Calvin Theotis with a date of birth of April 17, 1962, with a listed address in Venice, California.

Tailbott obtained an arrest warrant for Theotis, as well as a search warrant for his apartment in Venice. Tailbott and a four-man team knocked on the door of the place, which was located in a bad area a few blocks from the weirdo section near the beach.

"Police, search warrant, open the door."

No response was forthcoming. Not surprising, since Mr. Theotis was in the midst of trying to hoist himself out the back bathroom window. However, the officer outside that window was aiming a shotgun in Calvin's face and was quickly able to discourage that means of egress. Within a few minutes, he was handcuffed and seated in the backseat of a police car. A search of the apartment turned up gloves, a ski mask, a black flight suit, and sixty-five thousand dollars in cash.

The Beverly Hills Police Department is an impressive building. It has jail cells just as any police department, but it is Beverly Hills. If you want coffee and a donut, you will likely get Starbucks and Krispy Kreme. Tailbott and a second detective named Hathaway questioned Theotis. He was offered neither a coffee nor a donut.

Hathaway read him his Miranda rights, and he agreed to speak to the detectives. Tailbott said simply, "I am going to tell you some things, and then I will ask you one question. One time only. Your only chance. You tell the truth, and I will ensure the prosecutor does not request the death penalty. With the prison overload here in California, maybe you'll only do fifteen years for the murder."

Tailbott then laid the overwhelming evidence that conclusively proved Calvin Theotis committed the brutal slaying. Theotis nodded his head, and Hathaway asked, "We know you didn't plan this. You just carried it out. The only question is, why?"

Tailbott added two more questions, and Theotis was listening and not counting the number of inquiries. "Who masterminded it? Who told you to target this house and how to carry it out?"

Calvin Theotis was no brain surgeon, but he knew the legal system, and he understood he was cornered without escape. He also gave the cops credit for having placed someone below his bathroom window; if he had made it out, he would have been in Tijuana by noon. As he scratched his swollen eyelid, Theotis said, "Yeah, I did everything you said, but I didn't come up with the idea. My cousin Darrell has been screwing this Mexican slut named Louisa.

She's the maid at the house. Darrell made a copy of the front-door key, and I used it to get in."

Tailbott asked, "Why commit a murder if nothing was stolen?"

Calvin laughed. "Nothin' stolen, fuck. We'd been robbing that house blind for the last three years. The husband had all kinds of women's jewelry he never even looked at. Guess it was his dead wife's stuff. She croaked over ten years ago. Every few months, Darrell and I would steal a few pieces. We always waited until the owner took the fucking dog down to Laguna Beach. Bam! We'd go in and take valuable swag piece by piece. The Mexican bitch never knew a thing about it."

Tailbott had interviewed many criminals and was certain Calvin was telling the truth. Calvin continued, "A week or so ago, the maid tells Darrell that she doesn't have to clean the house the next week 'cuz the five-year audit is being conducted. If they'd done the audit, it would have shown the missing jewelry, the maid would have been suspected, and then probably she'd have coughed up her connection to Darrell. Darrell already has a rap sheet for burglary, so we figured you'd grab him. So what we did was, while I was getting rid of the owner, Darrell secured an ironclad alibi. That way, he would never be suspected of the murder."

Tailbott asked what possible alibi could be that secure. Calvin laughed hard because even though the plan had gone wrong, it was a great idea.

"It was actually Darrell's idea. While I was killing the owner, Darrell purposefully got himself dead drunk and ran his car into one of your Beverly Hills PD cruisers. Not enough to hurt nobody, but he sure as hell was in jail while I was killing the rich old man. By the time the audit was done, you cops would have figured the robbery had been done at the same time as the murder. Great plan. Somehow you guys figured it out though."

Tailbott put Calvin back in his cell and had Hathaway get a warrant issued for the arrest of cousin Darrell Theotis.

XXXX

Darrell was charged with the same violations as Calvin, and both subsequently pled guilty to the reduced charge of second-degree murder. Tailbott argued with the prosecutor that the crime was absolutely premeditated and first degree. The prosecutor, who was old and tired of the system, agreed but said that with their criminal records, they would be forced to do the full fifteen. Nine months after the murder, each was sentenced to do those years at a maximum-security facility in Northern California.

The day after the sentencing, Detective Tailbott drove out to the Beverly Hills estate. The family had tons of money, and the property had been given via a trust to an elderly aunt who now lived in the house. Tailbott knocked on the door and addressed the matron of the house,

"Good morning, ma'am. I am Detective Tailbott. I handled the investigation of your nephew's homicide. I stopped to tell you the final outcome."

"Please come in, detective. Would you like some iced tea?"

Tailbott accepted and, once inside, relayed the sentences levied against Calvin and Darrell. Then he asked what had happened to the cat, Jasmine. He also explained the important roles that Jasmine and Boatswain had played in solving the crime and admitted he was an animal lover too.

The old lady grabbed her nearby cane, stood, and asked if he would like to see Jasmine. Tailbott nodded, and she motioned to have him follow.

"Usually, Jasmine spends her days in the garden."

They walked into the expansive backyard full of rose bushes, lilacs, and rhododendrons, all currently in full bloom. It was a warm afternoon, and Tailbott walked forward and saw Jasmine curled atop a granite gravestone. He reached out and petted the cat, which purred and nuzzled his hand.

The headstone's only inscription was a quote by John Cam Hobhouse.

Near this spot are deposited the remains of one who possessed beauty without vanity, strength without insolence, courage without ferocity, and all the virtues of man without his vices. This praise, which would be unmeaning flattery if inscribed over human ashes, is but a just tribute to the memory of Boatswain, a dog.

I WILL HAVE YOU, MY LOVE

The microphone drops a bit too close to Clint Bridges's forehead and brushes a single curly dark lock. Bridges smiles at the interviewer, but the producer of the *GQ* photo shoot halts the production and rips into the operator of the boom mike. "Clarence, you incompetent fuck. You just slammed a microphone into Mr. Bridges. The most famous professional ballplayer in California and you clunk him on the temple. I should fire you..."

Clint Bridges interrupts and, in a baritone suitable for a starring role in a Wagner opera, says, "No worries, it was likely my fault. I leaned forward too far."

Clarence nods a quick thanks to Bridges and is confident his job is safe for another day.

This portion of the interview is completed, and the photo shoot commences. *Gentleman's Quarterly*, or *GQ*, had selected Clint Bridges as its man of the year. As a men's fashion magazine, the photos must be perfect. Bridges is patient when photographers desire shots of him in his uniform, in a hand-tailored double-breasted suit, and shirtless in running shorts. For some of the photos, well-curved blondes, brunettes, and redheads fill out the pictures.

After this day's shoot, there will only be one final day of interviewing by the well-respected Lucy Kaitlin. Bridges reads *GQ* and is anticipating talking to Kaitlin. She is an honest reporter that only depicts an athlete as a dumbass if, in fact, he is one. Bridges returns to his dressing room and slips on a pair of pleated black slacks and a silk shirt. Clint dresses well and probably could give tips to *GQ's* editorial staff on what to wear. He leaves his dressing room and sees the boom microphone operator. "Hey, Clarence, don't sweat the little stuff, man. If producer Jack Shit gives you trouble, tell him to kiss off. If he fucks with you, call my office, and he'll be off your back for good. Be well, dude."

As Clarence stares in numbed silence, Bridges slips out a side door and into the bright Los Angeles sunlight. From his breast pocket, he grabs his Blues Brothers–style shades and walks off the lot. Bridges sees the limos waiting to retrieve other celebrities, athletes, and stars. When he walks off the grounds, he is glad to be away from glitter and glitz.

He walks because it is a gorgeous day. A block away from the photo shoot, he regrets his decision to fit in as a normal well-dressed dude from LA.

An ugly, toadyish woman that resembles a female version of Star Wars' Yoda grabs his sleeve with greasy hands. "Clint, you're my world. Love me. Touch me. We are soul mates forever."

Clint tugs his shirt away from Thelma Retrude.

"Goddamn it, Thelma, you're a loon. There are three restraining orders against you about me. Other than you accosting me on the street, I've never even met you."

"Meet me! Be with me! Love me, love me!"

Clint can smell the alcohol on her breath, and her eyes have that crazy methamphetamine look. As Clint pushes her away, she removes a pistol from her dirty trench coat and points it at him. "If I can't have you, no one will."

She fires once. He feels a burning in his chest and falls to the hot asphalt as Thelma runs away. She is babbling about God's will, soul mates for life, and the last thing Clint hears is, "My love is brighter than the golden orange of the California sun."

X X X X X

Clint wakes in a hospital off Centinella Boulevard, and the golden orange of the sun is blinding him through the open hospital window. A blond nurse is staring at him as if he was a piece of flank steak, and she a carnivore unfed for several weeks. "Mr. Bridges, it's an honor to be your nurse, and even though your wound is minor, I enjoyed washing and prepping you for surgery. I understand what Nicole Kidman saw in you, if you know what I mean."

Clint was groggy, and his chest was sore, but his arms and legs were moving, and from what Nurse Bimbo said, his other important attachments must still be intact.

He asked to speak to his doctor, and within ten minutes, Dr. Emily Brandenfels entered Clint's room. If God had made all doctors look like

Brandenfels, the entire male population of the world would find a way to become ill. Blond, blue-eyed, and well-spoken—even Clint had difficulty listening to her without imagining her sprawled naked across his water bed. He dragged himself from his reverie and listened to what she said.

"Everything is fine, Mr. Bridges. You're a very healthy man, and the woman who shot you did it with a .22-caliber, and it did not even pierce your rib cage. Your chest muscle mass and ribs protected you. The round lodged between two ribs, and we removed it without a problem. Within five weeks, you'll probably be pumping up a set of healthy pectorals, as Arnold Schwarzenegger might say. We'll release you tomorrow."

Clint looked at Dr. Emily's left hand and saw a gold wedding band.

"Is that a prop to keep the hordes of men away, or are you actually married?"

"I'm happily married, but your interest is flattering."

XXXXX

A Los Angeles police detective was Clint's next visitor. The detective was built like a fireplug and had a face that only a nearsighted bulldog could love.

"I presume you can identify the perpetrator. Going out on a limb, I'll guess it was Thelma Retrude."

"That pretty much sums it up, officer."

"We've got an attempted-murder warrant out for Retrude. She's a bag lady on the street, and be careful, but I'm sure we'll have her in custody soon."

At that moment, in her foul-smelling glory, Thelma Retrude walked into Clint's hospital room, waving her pistol at Clint, the doctor, the detective, and every piece of medical equipment.

"You're mine. You were saved to be with me. It is a miracle and a direct sign from God on high."

The detective efficiently removed the gun from Thelma's grip and tore away one of her fingernails and the tip of a finger in the process. As he wrestled her to the ground, she babbled, "Mine, mine, mine. I shall decide your path, and you shall heed my words. As uttered in Job 19:23, 'Oh, that my words were now written! Oh, that they were printed in a book!'"

The detective handcuffed her, slapped her in the face, and told her to "shut the fuck up"—in that order. He radioed for backup and requested a cruiser to take Retrude to jail.

"Heed me, Clint Bridges. There are more things in heaven and earth than in your philosophy."

Retrude continued with more incoherency, and eventually, Clint realized that she was quoting from the book of Genesis but speaking the words in reverse order from the way they were originally written. Clint was a member of the society of MENSA and not your typical dumb jock. He realized it was a reverse of verses 24 and 25.

"Good was it that saw God and kind its to according ground the upon creeps that everything and, kinds their to according cattle the and kinds their to according earth the of beasts the made God and so was it and."

Thankfully, two LAPD street officers arrived and forcefully escorted Thelma Retrude to jail.

The detective stated that Retrude would be in custody for a long time, possibly in jail, but more likely a mental health facility.

XXXXX

A week later, *GQ* writer Lucy Kaitlin arrived at Clint's home in the Hollywood Hills and conducted an interview. The questions were typical and concerned Clint's job as a professional athlete with the Los Angeles Dodgers. His most recent season had been something of a disappointment due to a hamstring injury.

"I'm getting a bit long in the tooth to play ball with these kids. I have loved playing for the Dodgers, but I think in a year or so, I'll retire and hang up my spikes."

She asked him what he intended to do in retirement, and he replied that he had many interests. He had done some painting and, through his connections with the high-IQ society MENSA, had developed some writing contacts. Clint intended to author a book about his time in Major League Baseball and equate how his training in Scientology allowed him to love his sport more passionately.

He answered her common questions about Scientology and explained it was not a cult but a means of viewing the world and endorsed a healthy drug-free lifestyle, but he admitted he cursed more than his Scientology brethren would appreciate.

"Yes, I know Tom Cruise and his wife. They're nice people, and yes, Lucy, Tom is twice as handsome offscreen as on. He should be your man of the year, not me. Though I believe I am a better dresser."

They discussed Clint's hobbies and outside interests. He had a black belt in two separate martial arts, was an accomplished ballroom dancer, and engaged in the rather odd hobby of taxidermy.

"Many people think taxidermy is unusual, but I became involved when my favorite dog Lil' Bit died."

Clint led Kaitlin down to his taxidermy lab in the basement. Lil' Bit was a pug who rested comfortably on a couch. He looked as real as any living dog and had a shiny coat and blue marbles for eyes.

"I was just cleaning his fur. Normally, he would be upstairs resting on the sofa where you were just sitting."

Clint explained that he had had three cats and another dog named Bowser. The cats were all calicos, and Bowser was a black lab. When they passed away, he had missed each so much.

The first cat he had taken to a taxidermist to have stuffed and maintained. He had been so happy with the results that he learned the skills of taxidermy, and when his other pets had passed, he had done the preservation work himself instead of hiring others.

"It makes me feel closer to the animals. All animals' souls go to heaven, but this way, I can enjoy some facet of their bodily presence, even after they are gone. My pets each are comfortable in their favorite spots throughout the house. Bowser was an eating machine, and so he and his bed are in the kitchen. The cats are all lying in spots where sunshine peeks through various windows."

They went back upstairs, and Lucy Kaitlin seemed happy to be in a room with more open air. She did note a calico cat resting in a sunny alcove and shuddered slightly. She felt the time was appropriate to ask about Clint having been shot by Thelma Retrude.

"Are you concerned for your safety? Even though she is confined to a mental hospital, she could escape and pose a danger to you."

"I just hope she receives the help she needs. She's a very disturbed lady, but perhaps with therapy and medication, she can be helped through her problems."

"So you would help her."

"If she can be a healthy contributing member of society, I would help her in any way I could."

The interview ended, and while she had received great material for her story, she was relieved to be leaving a house filled with stuffed creatures.

Lucy Kaitlin cried out, and almost wet her tasteful pantsuit, when the calico in the alcove stretched and meowed. Clint laughed.

"That's Sylvester. He's just a young cat, Ms. Kaitlin. I don't preserve them until they pass away. Come here, Sylvester."

Sylvester leapt into Clint's arms. As Sylvester purred, Lucy Kaitlin quickly thanked Clint and, even more quickly, exited the house.

Things go good, things go bad, and things go middle.

That is what happened to Clint Bridges, Thelma Retrude, and friends. Clint's Man of the Year issue had been the highest selling in the magazine's history, but his hamstring did not heal correctly, and the Dodgers traded him to the lowly Chicago White Sox. Part of his contract with Los Angeles had specific wording that if he refused a trade, he would receive one season's salary, and he could retire.

Clint did not need the money. Unlike other athletes that splurged on sports cars, drugs, and women, Clint had invested wisely and had international stock and bond funds worth millions. Besides, he liked his silver Ram 2500 truck, did not use drugs as a Scientologist, and women were readily available.

He made some speeches, tossed a pitch out at an all-star game, and enjoyed life as a wealthy single guy. He swam off Santa Monica's shores, disregarding the fearmongers' admonitions of toxic waste from the LA River, and lifted at Gold's Gym near Venice Beach.

Life was okay. He worked on his hobby of taxidermy and received some training in larger animals such as elks, bears, and lions.

The big cats always reminded him of his calico kitties.

There were difficulties in his personal relationships. Most women wanted him as an arm piece or as a consistent paycheck. The stars were worse, and he realized why their definitions of a sustained relationship were six months maximum.

He was lonely.

The world of Thelma Retrude was moving positively. Small baby steps turned to successful strides, transcended into leaps forward in mental health. Her counseling was constant, but more importantly, her doctor determined that a specific antidepressant—originally created for those afflicted with schizoid behavior and manic depression—helped greatly. Thelma could not even pronounce the drug's name, but her twisted, misty, and murky view of the world began to clear. Things made sense, and rationality was not an abstract concept involving biblical references. After two months that seemed eons to Thelma, she asked her doctor, "Dr. Winston, I feel much different. I understand it is impossible for me to have any dangerous items which might cause harm to me or anyone else. Yet may I have some children's scissors, a comb and brush, and conditioner for my hair? Perhaps some Nivea skin lotion and a safety razor to shave my arms and legs."

All these items were permitted and within the restrictions of the prison/health care facility. Changes proceeded rapidly, and Thelma Retrude was no longer a psychopathic, murderous troll of a woman.

One month later, Dr. Winston returned for his monthly visit. He called to the orderly, "Attendant, this is not my patient. Please bring in Thelma Retrude, immediately."

"Dr. Winston, I'm Thelma. It is just that your counsel and the medications have worked their magic. It is nice to speak to you on a more equal footing."

Dr. Winston was completely silent. As he looked closely, he saw that it was indeed Thelma. Her hair was in a clever sideways-snipped bob, and her slightly pointed ears were completely covered, and she had tinted her hair somehow. Well, the hospital prison did have peroxide, and her arms and legs were perfectly shaven, and the Nivea lotion had obviously been carefully stroked into those legs. Despite his usual strict professional demeanor, Dr. Winston was curious as to any other areas she might have shaved.

"Thelma, you look wonderful."

Thelma continued her therapy and her medication. A minor miracle had occurred. Now, she was passing her mental exams with ease, and the staff had snuck in makeup for her. She was the star of the ward and Dr. Winston's most prized pupil.

Three years passed, and Dr. Winston petitioned the California courts to permit her supervised visits outside the hospital. Long ago, she had been transferred from the prison hospital and was in a minimum-security facility, which was more akin to a dormitory than a hospital or jail.

In a state courtroom outside Los Angeles, the renowned liberalism of California spoke full force.

"Ms. Retrude, it is the order of this court that you be released on your own recognizance. You must report to your probation officer every third week, and it *is mandatory for you to consult with Dr. Winston every other day for the first six months of your release. After six months, you must visit Dr. Winston once every two weeks."*

As the judge was prepared to slam down the gavel, Dr. Winston spoke, "Your honor, I request one additional item from this court. I'm confident Ms. Retrude is a cured woman who will contribute positively to society, but I believe 100 percent confirmation of this can be verified by a joint consultation between me, Ms. Retrude, and the original victim, Clint Bridges. I'm aware this is an unusual request, but in a secure environment, when no animosity is shown between the two, the safety of Mr. Bridges will be forever secured."

The court was indecisive, and Clint Bridges' attorney threw a fit on appeal, but eventually, it was approved. Dr. Winston, Thelma Retrude, and Clint Bridges would meet at a halfway house, with police security standing by.

✕ ✕ ✕ ✕ ✕

Clint Bridges arrived for the meeting in jeans and a blue blazer; Dr. Winston showed up in his hospital white coat, looking ridiculous; and Thelma Retrude beamed in a conservative gray pantsuit. The meeting was very brief and productive. Thelma apologized for what she had done and promised never to cause distress again.

"You are a famous and handsome man, and I was a lost soul. Please forgive me."

They talked briefly, and Dr. Winston, in his white coat, is satisfied that the pathological fantasy his patient formerly possessed is gone.

An observant bystander would have quickly noticed that Thelma, while relaxed, was closely watching Clint's every movement. Clint also noticed that Ms. Retrude was no longer the toady he recalled and was, in fact, very attractive.

✕ ✕ ✕ ✕ ✕

Clint Bridges had hired numerous private detectives to investigate and watch Thelma Retrude. He obtained her personal phone number and knew her hangouts. The private investigators said she was behaving normally, and her only frequent hangout was the Santa Monica Library. Her books of choice were fantasy novels and love stories, but still, Clint was concerned and managed to coincidentally run across her at the library one windy Wednesday.

Thelma nearly bumped into Clint Bridges in the history section of the library.

"Clint, my Lord! What brings you here?"

"I'm a scholarly sort and love the library—in particular, the classics. I'm glad you're doing so well."

They discussed Homer's *Iliad*, and Clint decided to test her resolve.

"Thelma, I have a century-old copy of the *Odyssey*, Homer's other epic. Would you like to come see it?"

It was an offer Thelma could not refuse, and she rode back to the Hollywood Hills mansion seated beside the man she has desired forever.

At the house, he poured a gin and tonic and showed her the ancient book. She carefully and meticulously flipped the pages.

"It's yours, Thelma."

He looks into her eyes and grasps her shoulders.

She is pretty. He kisses her softly, but with passion behind the kindness. Expectant of her strong embrace, he is surprised when she recoils from him.

"I learned in my counseling, Clint. I did not want you, though your beauty is stunning. I needed to find my own inner beauty."

"You have learned, Thelma. You do have an inner beauty and an outer beauty also. I'm sorry you did not continue to love me. I am the sad one now."

From Clint's vest pocket, he removes a syringe and injects it into Thelma's chest, directly into her heart.

"I love you."

× × × × ×

Three days later, an LAPD officer arrives at Clint's home.

"I'm Detective Stone Smith. My apologies for bothering you, but a woman has disappeared. Her name is Thelma Retrude."

"Yes, she shot me once. I was told she had recovered with therapy, but she is a troubled young lady."

Clint allows the officers complete access to his home, including the taxidermy room downstairs.

"We were aware of your taxidermy skills, and *GQ* reporter Kaitlin said some of the dogs and cats bite, but others are sleeping the deep sleep."

"I always take care of those I love. I am truly sorry about Ms. Retrude, though she did harm me a long time ago, but bygones must be bygones."

"Thank you, Mr. Bridges, we have found nothing here. Though your cat Sylvester is the friendliest feline I've ever seen."

"Come back and visit anytime, Detective Smith. I'm sure Sylvester would love to see you again."

Clint poured himself a glass of wine and ensured the police were gone. He pushed a hidden button in the basement where he completed his taxidermy. As he finished his glass of wine, the hidden compartment opened, and he carefully gutted the internal organs from Thelma Retrude. He sewed the opening and discarded the innards and utilized the specialized taxidermy dust and fluids to complete the embalmment. He leans over and kisses her cool pale cheek. She looks beautiful and content; perhaps tomorrow he will switch out her blue eyes for hazel or green.

Quietly, and almost inaudibly, Clint can hear his CD player. A Warren Zevon song:

> "He took little Suzy to the junior prom then he raped her and killed her, and he took her home, excitable boy, they all said.
> After ten long years they let him out of the home, excitable boy, they all said.
> So he dug up her grave and built a cage with her bones, excitable boy, they all said."

Clint smiles; he has always enjoyed this song.

VINNY PLAYS GOD

Vincent Antonio Caci was known as Vinny to close associates, as "Vinny the Whip" to mob cronies, and as "Louisville Vinny" to the FBI. In that Caci was from Brooklyn, New York, his moniker as "Louisville" was not based on a hometown but for his preferred murder tool—a Louisville slugger bat. In the old neighborhood, he had been a pretty decent stickball player, and had times been different; perhaps he might have used a bat for the pleasure of swatting home runs out of Shea or Yankee Stadium. But times were not changed, and Caci made his living as a soldier—or "made man"—in the Lombardo crime family.

Caci was sitting with the Lombardo family boss Dominic Zito at a small trattoria, or Italian cafe, in Queens. Zito was finishing his osso bucco veal shank, and Caci had already eaten his linguine with red clam sauce. During the entire meal, Zito had not said one word, so it would have been incorrect Mafia protocol for Caci to do anything other than order food. Zito was two levels above Caci in the family hierarchy, and so it was unusual that Zito had contacted Caci directly for an in-person meeting. Initially, Caci had contemplated that it was a setup to have him whacked, but Zito would never have chosen such a public mom-and-pop restaurant like the trattoria.

Zito waived the waitress once and ordered another bottle of wine as he pushed away his now-empty plate. Zito had eaten all the osso bucco and the pasta; all that remained was the shank bone itself. Zito had also sucked the marrow from that bone, quickly and efficiently. He has felt no need to use the small fork specifically provided for that task. Caci knew that while Zito had not used his marrow fork today, he was quite familiar with forks.

Five years ago, while he was underboss, Zito had used a regular fork to kill Fat Tony Dioguardo by shoving it through his eye socket into the brain. Caci had helped discard Fat Tony's body in a grave they had both helped dig outside Monmouth Park Racetrack. Afterward, Caci and Zito had gone to the track and coincidentally wagered $200 on a horse named Tony's Lucky Day. The nag won and paid $36.50 for a two dollar win ticket. They had split the $3,650; that had been a good day.

As Zito took a drink of his Chianti, he finally spoke, "Vinny, I think of you as my son. There is an assignment of great importance that I trust only you to handle. We both know the Oath of Omerta prohibits you from repeating anything I say. Still, the circumstances here are special and unique."

Vincent Antonio Caci looked his boss in the eyes and instantly realized this was not a normal snuff job.

The waitress asked if they wanted after-dinner drinks or coffee. Caci figured he might need a drink, so he ordered a double espresso and a sambuca. Zito then spoke to the waitress, "Good idea. Honey, bring me an espresso too, and give us the whole bottle of sambuca and some biscotti to dip in it."

The waitress—Caci thought her name might be Teresa—knew who Zito was, and he could likely have asked for a bottle of fresh goat's blood, and she would have found a goat to sacrifice.

Within an instant, a platter of biscotti cookies, a bottle of sambuca, and two espressos were on the table. Zito winked thanks to Teresa, and she shyly smiled back. Zito and Vinny clinked glasses, and Zito said, "Cento anni, mio caro amico."

Caci took a large swallow of the licorice-flavored aperitif and smiled at the choice of Zito's toast. It was a common Italian saluté and figuratively meant "good life." Literally translated, it said, "Live a hundred years, my closest friend." Both were well aware that neither was likely to live fifty years, much less a hundred.

Over the remainder of the bottle, Zito explained what he required of "Louisville" Vinny Caci.

Two weeks ago, a soldier from the family had screwed up and got a sixteen-year-old named Marcella Veronelli pregnant. The made guy's name was Luigi Franceschetti, a.k.a. Louie the Rat. Caci had cringed just hearing the matter involved Franceschetti. "Louie the Pig" or "Louie the Butcher" would have been better nicknames.

Zito continued and explained what Louie had done. Louie was married and had a son and daughter, and because he did not want his affair with young Marcella discovered, he decided to kill her. He waited outside her apartment, and when she came downstairs, he slit her pregnant sixteen-year-old throat and tossed her body in a dumpster.

Because he was stupid, he did this all in daylight, and as he casually tossed his former lover in a trash heap, a passerby witnessed it and attempted to intercede. Some white-collar Wall Street type and his girlfriend came up to Franceschetti and asked what was happening. Franceschetti pulled out a .45-caliber and shot Mr. Wall Street between the eyes. He was dead on the spot. The girl tried to run, so he shot her in the back, middle of the spine, and she would be paralyzed from the waist down.

As the story continued, Vinny realized what an incompetent coward Franceschetti was. He took another swallow of sambuca, and this time it burned a little going down. Perhaps it was the bile in his throat as he thought of a pregnant sixteen-year-old left in a dumpster.

"I think I understand, boss. If you want me to kill Louie the Butcher, just say so. He's a scumbag."

"Normally, I would do just that because I detest Louie more than you, but there are complications I must consider. A few years ago, I made a foolish mistake and used Louie on a hit. For once, he did a decent job, and I paid him ten grand, but the Feds had a wiretap on his phone. They don't have much of a case, but they know he and I have a connection. If he turns up dead, I'd be a top suspect. I'll probably kill him later, but now it would put too much heat on me."

The bottle of sambuca was almost gone, and Vinny was someone who could hold his liquor as well as his tongue, but he was very confused. He told Zito that he did not understand what he was being ordered to do.

"I have no choice, Vinny. I must kill the female witness that's paralyzed at the hospital. She is the only one that saw Louie. If the killings are not tied to him, then I will never have any problems. I need you to kill the witness. The gal paralyzed in the hospital. She is in a coma now, but I have a contact at the hospital, and they say she is being kept in the comatose state only for a few more days because they want her immobile. In a day or two, they will allow her to regain consciousness. Once coherent, the cops will come in and question her. It is just a matter of time until she identifies Louie, then it goes to my previous ties to him, and I get roped in on some fucking racketeering charge. The girl must die, and within the week. Capisce? Her name is Laura Heinke, and she is in room 218, intensive care, Memorial Hospital on Queen's Boulevard."

Vinny looked at the bottle of sambuca, which was almost empty. The thought of his new assignment and another sip, both made him queasy. He looked at his boss, Dominic Zito, and simply said, "As always, I will do the right thing."

"I knew I could count on you, Vinny."

Mafia rules are sometimes absolute and often merely guidelines. One guideline is that the superior upper bosses never pay the check. Vinny said, "I know what I must do," and turned and walked out the door of the restaurant. He had left the check for Dominic Zito to pay.

The next morning, Vinny visited the hospital where Laura Heinke was being treated. The police believed the attack and murder had been committed randomly by some deranged psychopath. Since they did not deem it an organized and planned crime, there were no police guarding room 218 at the hospital. As he quietly, and unobtrusively, entered Heinke's room, he considered what the police thought of the crime.

They believed it was committed randomly by a deranged psychopath. Actually, the cops were not too far off. Franceschetti was a murderous deranged psycho. The killing was, however, not random.

Vinny made the sign of the cross as he walked closer to Laura. A good Catholic, Vinny motioned with his hand over his chest, head, to heart, to hands. Under his breath, he also said his Ave Marias. He was about to kill an innocent, comatose, paraplegic woman. The Mafia often put its members in unusual, unpleasant, and compromising positions, but this was the hardest task Vinny had ever been asked to complete. Vincent Antonio Caci—Louisville Vinny, also known as Vinny the Whip—was crying as he neared Laura.

She was on a respirator, which was taking in air and forcing it into her lungs. Her chest was rising and falling, rising and falling. He looked at the machines that were hooked to every conceivable area of Laura's body. Vinny's sister was a nurse, so he knew something about the machines, and he had been shot before in the chest by a member of the rival Columbo family. He had not needed a respirator, but he knew about vital signs and could understand the machine's readings on Laura. The pulse was strong, and blood pressure normal. Clearly, after she stabilized, she would live.

Vinny looked closer at Laura Heinke. She was brown haired, and as her eyes fluttered, he saw they were hazel. Even through the wires, respirator, and machinery, she was clearly very attractive. Soon Vinny would extinguish that pretty young life. He knew how to temporarily shut off the respirator without having the nurse alarm sound, and then a pillow over her face should effectively suffocate her. Once dead, he would restart the respirator, and it would seem she had died of a heart attack or an airway blockage. Laura would die, Zito would be happy, and the scum Franceschetti would be in the clear.

Vinny had been a soldier for the Lombardo family for over seven years. In that time, and before, he had killed or assisted in the killing of twenty-four people. Twenty-two had been men, and two were women. The Mafia myth that women were never whacked was also a falsehood perpetrated by fiction books authored by clueless authors and movies written by people who likely had never even met a real outfit guy.

While it was correct that some family guys played the part to the hilt, like John Gotti in his thousand-dollar suits, others were low-key like Vincent "the Chin" Gigante, who was a capo and walked around in his bathrobe on the streets of New York. Some in the families thought Gigante's whole bit was an act so the Feds would leave him alone, but Vinny had met "the Chin" a few times and thought he was someone who rightfully belonged in a loony bin.

Now Vinny was moments away from killing a beautiful, physically damaged young girl.

Was the Mafia way always the right way? Vincent Antonio Caci had always believed the Mafia way was the only way, but now he was unsure. She would not be revived for at least one more day. He needed some additional guidance and reassurance.

With one of his gloved hands, he carefully brushed away one of Laura Heinke's curly brown locks that had fallen out of place and was caught between her mouth and the respirator. *A pretty woman*, Vinny thought as he left the hospital room.

The monitors all showed that her life signs were strong.

He went to his church and did his confessional to his priest. Vinny was a devout Catholic that believed fervently in the church. After every crime he had committed, he confessed his sins to Father Emelio Sarducci. He was always told the bad path of sin and was instructed to do Hail Marys and to use his rosary beads in the traditional private devotion. After his hospital visit to see Laura Heinke, Sarducci again cautioned him on sin and the evil within all of us.

Now officially purged of evil and given the Catholic Church's forgiveness, he headed out to efficiently do what he was required to do. Vinny had no fear that the priest would go to the FBI or NYPD. Primarily, it would break his vow of hearing confessions only in confidence, but more importantly, Vinny had previously told Sarducci he was aware that the priest had sexually abused a dozen altar boys and forced them to engage in fellatio on him. After a previous confession, he had told the priest that if he ever disclosed any of Vinny's confessions, he would ensure the cops were aware of the priest's blow jobs. Vinny also indicated that he would have minimal emotional turmoil were he to be forced to kill a priest, or anyone else, to cover his crimes.

Vinny felt as if a leaden weight had been lifted from his shoulders as he pushed open the heavy oak doors of the church. The New York City air seemed crisper than before, and there seemed to be slightly more blue sky peeking between the monolithic buildings and the intermittent clouds. The breeze was almost unnoticeable, but pleasant. It was a wonderful and important day.

XXXXX

One of the greatest inventions ever developed for crime was the cell phone—specifically, a stolen cell. Vinny walked to a nice restaurant in the business section near Wall Street. The vacant land where the twin towers of the World Trade Center had stood was a few blocks away near Chamber Street.

Dressed in his nicest Italian suit and silk tie, he fit in well with the investment bankers in their three-thousand-dollar, hand-tailored Savile Row British suits. Vinny quietly sat at a corner table and ordered some high-dollar meal involving medallions of veal and baby squash. He tried to fit in by ordering a gin and tonic, and with his meal, he managed to choke down a chardonnay.

Italians, especially mobsters, do not sip chardonnays. They drink reds, Chiantis, and the big strong reds from Piedmont. Vinny liked the Sangiovese grape and the intricate taste different vineyards could produce. His grandfather had his own small winery in Calabria. Calabrese Italians were purported to be the toughest by eking a living from hard soil. *Calabrese stubborn* is the term. Vinny was Calabrese—strong willed and obstinate—but *hardheaded* did not mean "stupid" or "ignorant."

He had been born in the United States and knew this was an opportunity Calabria did not offer. Violence was effective in the States, but innovation and caginess presented larger options and higher profit margins. Here in the Land of the Free and the Brave, low-key was important, and the dollar bill ran the show. With enough Ben Franklins, an "Ital" like Vinny could find success and a way off the streets. Vinny scanned the room and ordered a second chardonnay.

At a table halfway across the restaurant, Vinny noted a drunken investment banker spouting off to a blonde and singing the praises of his most recent merger transaction. She looked at him blandly but seemed willing to scarf down her vinaigrette salad with shiitake mushrooms and glazed chicken. The banker was growing increasingly drunk on double martinis.

"Nothing but Grey Goose vodka, of course, garçon," the investment boy slurred to the waiter.

The banker was constantly on his cell phone, blabbing of some intricately woven owner buyout or a stock hedge fund. The beautiful blonde looked bored when she was not busy with her salad.

The man eventually consumed enough double martinis that the weasel had to use the restroom. As he staggered to the john, Blondie went back to her plate of rabbit food in earnest. Her dining partner had left his phone lying on the table. Vinny stood after leaving a C-note for his own tab, and as he walked by Mr. Martini's table, he pocketed the cell phone. The blond bimbo did not glance up or notice the theft. As drunk as Grey Goose boy was, he would never remember where the phone was lost, and Vinny was able to quickly slip out of the fancy restaurant.

As he left, he was thinking he needed a nice glass of red wine or a sambuca.

Vinny used his new cell phone to place a call to Louie Franceschetti. His son Louis Jr. answered, and briefly—but only very briefly—Vinny considered aborting his plan. Using a scratchy voice that sounded nothing like his own, Vinny told Louis Jr. to get his dad on the phone. Once on the line, Louie "the Rat" Franceschetti sounded tired and hung-over. Vinny used the common terminology of mobsters. Hopefully, Franceschetti would understand, but any Fed listening on a wiretapped phone would not.

"Hello, Lou, we must meet in person to discuss a friend of ours. All is being handled, but I need a moment of your help."

Louie the Butcher was not the sharpest cleaver in the utensil drawer, but he was a mobster, and he understood the terminology. "A friend of ours" meant the conversation would concern another fully-made member of their Mafia family.

Vinny continued, "Meet me in one hour in the place we usually talk."

Their typical link-up location was a warehouse in the meat-packing district in Manhattan. Vinny loved the location; a meager few blocks from Wall Street and billion-dollar investment banks was the meat district. Here, hanging on hooks, were the meat New York's fanciest restaurants, like Sparks Steakhouse, would purchase. It was the best meat available in the city. Sparks was also famous as the location of the most visible mob hit in New York history that left Big Paul Castellano gunned down on the sidewalk in front of the restaurant.

They agreed to meet in one hour. Vinny knew there was a slight risk that Louie might notify someone else—maybe even the Lombardo boss, Dominic Zito—but Vinny doubted it. Louie thought of himself as a tough guy and also felt safe because of the location of the meeting in the meat-packaging warehouse. Buscemi's Meat Packing and Rendering Plant was quietly dormant this late on a Sunday evening, and both Louie and Vinny had keys.

Vinny walked almost two miles to get to the plant. This was not a time to leave his car outside, and it would allow him to watch anyone entering the area to see if they came alone. Louie did come alone, arriving in his new black Cadillac Escalade. After he entered the slaughterhouse, both men hugged warmly, and Vinny spoke, "Louie, I had to speak to you without anyone else knowing. Did you tell anyone you were coming to see me here?"

Louie looked ridiculous in a powder-blue Nike warm-up suit with matching blue running shoes, and he slurred his response because he was obviously drunk.

"Hell no. I'm a stand-up guy. No's body's got no friggin' idea I's here."

If Louie the Butcher had been more observant, somewhat less intoxicated, or not quite as stupid, he would have noticed that Vinny was wearing a rubberized full-length butcher's coat and gloves. Louie was close enough for Vinny to smell the alcohol on his breath, and that was close enough. From a side jacket pocket, Vinny pulled out an ice pick and jammed it into the Butcher's temple. There was very minimal blood loss, and it was very effective and quick. Louie gurgled a bit and twitched on the floor, but within a few minutes, he was dead, and his soul headed directly south to hell's gate. Vinny had no doubt that Louie would be quickly welcomed into the warm confines of the underworld. Hopefully, they would make him spend a long time in purgatory.

Vinny looked at his clothes and saw no blood splatters. He reconfirmed Louie was dead and shoved him into a darkened corner, beneath steer carcasses hanging on hooks. No one would find him until Monday morning, and that would be more than time enough. He left the plant, relocked the door, and packaged up his butcher's coat and gloves into a small sealable plastic bag. Later he would discard those items in the gigantic Staten Island landfill.

Wiseguys are usually not very nice people, but just as in the broader spectrum of humanity, no single goombah epitomizes every WOP stereotype, or every evil. Vinny was an old-time guy, but he was not a 1940s old-time moustache either. He fit somewhere between the Microsoft computer age and the break-your-thumbs-because-you-did-not-pay-your-gambling-debt era.

Most of Vinny's friends were associated with crime, but some were not, and one activity he enjoyed was fishing. The water and the saline air eased his world. Two years ago, he had flown to Cabo San Lucas, Mexico, and gone deep-sea fishing for sailfish, marlin, and tuna. It had been a highlight of his life. While it was not Mexico, the East Coast of the States had some good fishing. Vinny was close friends with the captain of a small trawler, whose base of operations was the island of Nantucket, off the coast of Massachusetts. Perhaps from parental humor, the captain's name was William Blythe Smith, but everyone called him Captain Bligh.

Vinny went to a payphone and used a calling card to call the captain in Nantucket.

"Billy Blythe, how goes the fishing off your windy shores?"

"It's lobster season, and no one is going out. Fucking federal fishing regulations make it impossible for an honest fisherman to earn a decent living."

"I need a vacation and thought I'd charter your vessel for a day later this week. Even if I don't catch anything but a cold, just being out on the water would be a blessing."

It was agreed that Vinny would drive from New York to Massachusetts and catch the ferry to the island. The ferry transported vehicles, and in this way, Vinny would have a car on the island.

"Hell, you can navigate a trawler as well as me. If you want some quiet time, you can take her out yourself, Vinny."

"I might just enjoy a solo cruise, thanks."

X X X X X

Vinny used his stolen cell phone to call Dominic Zito. The conversation would have been confusing to an outsider but was clear to both. Vinny began, "My mother's sickness at the hospital will be eased by this evening. Following that matter, at your convenience, I'd like to meet you at Central Park at 7:00 PM."

"Thank you, I knew you would handle it. I'll see you at seven."

Zito now believed Laura Heinke was soon to be dead, and Vinny was to meet Zito at their usual spot at seven. That usual spot was a parking lot, not in Central Park but off the New Jersey Turnpike south of New York near the city of Hightstown. Zito would not be required to pay Vinny much for the killing since he was the mob capo, but a thank-you and a grand in cash was the norm.

Zito showed up alone at the appointed time and hugged Vinny and handed him five hundred dollars.

"It would have been more, but my bookie business is down. So she's dead. I'm sorry I made you kill a maimed retard."

"Not a problem, Dominic. Actually, she is not retarded, merely a paraplegic."

Zito looked confused, so Vinny took the opportunity to remove a stun gun from his pocket and push it into Zito's sternum. A small crackle was audible, and Zito was quivering and convulsing on the pavement.

Sometimes good things happen to bad people, and vice versa.

The parking lot was empty. Vinny wrapped a cord around Zito's neck and, with gloved hands, tightened the noose until there was not a hint of breath coming from Zito's lips. Vinny efficiently shut and locked Zito's car, leaving the keys inside. Vinny then dragged Zito's body to his own vehicle and opened his trunk. Inside was a hundred-gallon sealable metal barrel. Vinny shoved Zito's body inside the drum and filled it with quicklime cement and resealed it. It was heavy, but it did not leak and was placed in the vast trunk of Vinny's huge older Lincoln Continental.

If the New Jersey State Patrol had been very observant, they would have noted that the rear end of Vinny's Lincoln was low to the ground as he proceeded back north up the Jersey Turnpike, but the cops were busy with donuts or other more pressing matters. Vinny travelled the turnpike, which turned into I-95 back up through New York, Connecticut, and Rhode Island, and eventually from Providence headed east to New Bedford, Massachusetts. It was a long drive, but all was freeway driving, and at New Bedford, he purchased a round-trip ferry ticket to and from the East Coast resort town of Nantucket.

X X X X X

Vinny had been concerned that—with the terrorist attacks of September 11, and with out-of-state tags—his vehicle might have been inspected before the ferry ride to Nantucket. He need not have feared; a third of the people had New York or New Jersey tags, and with the exception of screaming children waiting for a beach excursion, his trip was quiet. He was exhausted and slept through the entire ferry ride. Undoubtedly, the package in the trunk could not enjoy the salt air, and Zito's dead body was equally as quiet. Actually, Zito was the only one silent because Vinny snored through most of the boat trip.

Nantucket is a beautiful and historical island. The ancient mansions were built for the captains of whaling ships, and most had widow's walks on the roof. From the walks, the captains' wives could watch their husbands return from the sea with their catch. Often the ships sank, and the women would look forever oceanward in vain. It reminded Vinny of the Mafia wives who stayed at home, tending to their children and family chores while the men committed murders, robberies, and drug deals. Much like the ancient whalers—when successful, money was plentiful, but often the wiseguys were killed in a turf war, a robbery gone bad, or whacked because higher family members ordered it. Just like the ancient mariners, Vinny did not mind the risk. It was all he knew how to do, and a job is a job.

Vinny drove along the cobblestone streets of downtown Nantucket and realized what a tourist trap the town had become. Most stores sold fancy preppy clothing, overprized antique furniture, or Nantucket memorabilia. The mansions and houses were impressive and expensive. Many places were rented out to tourists during the summer months, and many homes were merely a getaway for wealthy New Yorkers, Bostonians, and others. There was another side to the island, and that is what Vinny enjoyed. On that side, one could find the largely vacant beaches and protected lands and the inlets and cays that made boating peaceful.

Vinny drove to Captain Billy Bligh's house, which stood on a grassy promontory that overlooked a large expanse of panoramic ocean. Billy Bligh did not have a lot of money—merely two fishing boats and the house his deceased mother had willed to him. He could have sold the house for hundreds of thousands, but the captain liked his ocean view, and the meager fishing paid his expenses. Billy Bligh was very much at peace and near the ocean he so dearly loved.

"Hello, Captain. It is nice to see you on the island."

They spoke of old fishing expeditions and how the island was being overrun by tourists. In the house, the captain's pride was his bar. It was filled with all manners of seafaring equipment, anchors, floats, and a beautifully carved mermaid, which had been situated on the prow of the captain's first ship, the *Ocean Lady*. The bar also had every type of alcohol conceivable, including a brown liqueur in a Siamese Cat shaped Decanter. Both Vinny and the captain opted for the more simple gigantic pewter mugs of rum punch. It was decided that Vinny would take the captain's smaller sloop, the *Sea Witch*, and sail it wherever in the morning. It was docked in the main Nantucket harbor. They drank late into the night, and sometime past midnight, Vinny went upstairs to his small room overlooking the water after the captain passed out in his mug of grog.

XXXXX

Vinny awoke early, before dawn, to head down to the harbor. The *Sea Witch* was a smallish vessel, but it did have a winch system at the stern, which allowed heavier loads to be lifted onto the aft of the ship. With some effort, and still under cover of darkness, Vinny used the winch to haul a metal drum containing quicklime and a capo known as Dominic Zito onto the ship. Quicklime gradually eats away a body, and after a few years, there would be nothing left but sandy particulate in that barrel.

Vinny steered the *Sea Witch* out into the harbor and then east onto the open ocean. The ocean was rough, and it was bitingly cold, but he was exhilarated. Approximately twenty-five miles out into the Atlantic, he reinitiated the winch, rechecked the hermetically sealed can of mobster, and pitched it overboard. It sank to the bottom of the ocean floor without a sound.

Vinny said aloud, "Good luck in hell, Dominic. I'm certain I will see you there in due course."

Vinny returned to the island, docked, and drove to the captain's house. They shared a few more drinks, and within two hours, Vinny was back on the ferry to the mainland. He drove back to New York, and once there, stopped for a drink at a local mob hangout. Carmine Tommaso, the bartender and a Mafia wannabe, said, "Where you been, Vinny? You missed all the excitement. Louie Franceschetti took an ice pick to his temple. They found him on ice at Buscemi's Meat Packing. But more important, the capo is gone."

"Dominic is dead?"

"Well, we don't know he's dead, but he has not been seen in a few days. His car was abandoned out on the Jersey Turnpike."

"I guess I better make some contacts to see what went down."

Vinny met with a few soldiers: Impy Salerno, Tony Pasquale, Joey Three Fingers, and a few others. None had any idea where Dominic Zito was. The other New York families denied any involvement.

The underboss of the Lombardo family was an old moustache named Giancarlo Spagnolli. A week later, Spagnolli called Vinny in for a sit-down. Vinny was certain that somehow they had found everything out, and he was going to get snuffed. Spagnolli, with a Cuban cigar hanging from the corner of his mouth, spoke to Vinny in a heavy Sicilian accent, "Da capo gone, Vinny. As they say in Sicily, I think Dominic swimming with the fishes. The consigliore has spoken to most of the family, and they've chosen me to be the new capo of the Lombardo family."

Now Vinny was sure he was going to hear a bang behind his ear or feel a piano wire around his neck. "Swim with the fishes" damn straight, but it was a common Sicilian phrase. When nothing deadly happened for a moment, Vinny felt calmer, and Spagnolli took a puff on his cigar and continued, "Our family has three segments. The old boys like me, and the young guns like Impy, Three Fingers, and a few others. But you can bridge the gap between the here-and-now and the old ways. After consultation, I've selected you, Vincent Antonio Caci, Vinny the Whip, to be the underboss of the Lombardo family. You will report directly, and only, to me."

"I'm honored, Don Spagnolli. I will do my best."

X X X X X

Vinny tried not to stagger as he left the meeting. Perhaps God was looking down on him, so he left the meeting and met Father Emelio Sarducci. He gave the priest four thousand dollars as a donation to the church. The father asked if he needed to make any confessions to purge his sin. Vinny declined, saying he had been very much doing God's work recently.

"Well then bless you, my son, and this money will go to worthy causes."

Vinny hoped none of the money went to buy candy to lure altar boys.

From a payphone, Vinny called the hospital where Laura Heinke was recovering. He asked for her room, and a nurse answered, "Ms. Heinke is sleeping now, but I'll let her know you called. Sir, it's a miracle. She's regaining movement in her feet and legs. The doctors believe that with sufficient time and rehab, she'll be back to walking and a full recovery. Who should I tell her called?"

"I'm just a concerned friend. I'm glad she's doing so well."

Vinny hung up without providing any name. He did, however, stop at a local flower store to send Laura Heinke a huge floral bouquet. The card said: "Get well soon. From one who admires your strength."

'SHROOMS

Slowly the green man with bulbous eyes that shine with blue-tinted malice sneaks up on his unaware prey. The fear in the room is tangible in intensity. Everything moves in super slow motion, and colors transform from one to the next. Green swirls into red, twists into blue, spins into brilliant gold. The world is a Salvador Dali painting.

Suddenly, there are clocks everywhere. The clocks are misshapen, lying over pieces of furniture, draped haphazardly about the scene.

There is the incessant ticking of the clocks—hundreds of clocks, thousands, millions. There is a ticking, chiming, ringing, clanging—a cacophony of sound, louder, louder, and ever louder.

Suddenly, there is absolute silence, and no movement, no vision, absolute impenetrable blackness. There is warmth, like blood through arteries, rushing thick crimson blood away from the heart. The heat is oppressive, and the blood flows faster.

It is so hot, and the blood is pumping. He must run. Run as fast as possible through the forest. That will cool the burning. Running through the forest, it is damp, but warm enough. Running, cooling the engine, slowly the fire is passing.

There is clarity and rationality of thought.

Dr. Theopolis violently vomits, purges, and a mass of grayish-brown puke lies at his feet. He is alone, far away from campus, and is shivering, wearing only a light sweatshirt, shorts, and Mexican-style huarache sandals.

As a fully tenured professor, Dr. Amilcar Theopolis does not have to be in his office early every morning. This is quite a blessing when one is still recovering from a psychedelic mushroom overload of titanic proportions. Theopolis, known both on and off the Lewis & Clark College campus as Theo, sips a Starbucks triple venti latte with two sweet and lows and struggles to recall last night's specific details. Hell, for that matter, he struggles to recall the details of the last six or seven years.

Theo enjoys teaching at Lewis & Clark, a liberal arts college in Portland, Oregon. When he describes the school and his role there to those not from Washington, Oregon, or California, he summarizes by saying:

"I teach at a small liberal arts school, with the emphasis on liberal. *My classes are small, usually no more than twenty-five students. I primarily instruct in advanced history courses, most deal with the Middle Ages, and I also help the drama department with certain works of Shakespeare. My job is a 'Midsummer Night's Dream,' if I've ever had one."*

Theo is very familiar with dreams and hallucinations. He believes fervently that hallucinogens expand the brain's operational potential for introspection and increase higher-level consciousness. Theo has tried various hallucinogens, including mescaline (a powder from the mescal cactus), LSD, marijuana, heroin, and even PCP. All produced interesting effects, but Theo most enjoys psychotropic mushrooms, or 'shrooms, powered by psilocybin. Fortunately, some of the best 'shrooms grow wild in the areas of Northern California, Washington State, and in particular, Oregon.

Theo had been a brilliant high school student from the rich environment of Choate back on the East Coast. He had graduated from Harvard with a Bachelor of Arts in History. He then earned a master's degree from Harvard in physics. He was working on completing his PhD in astrophysics and microparticle subatomic properties when he had an epiphany or, at minimum, a mind- and career-altering experience.

Theo had initially been a bit of a boring sort at Harvard, and the highlight of any particular week was an inspiring lecture on the unique potentialities of neutrinos. Then something changed this perspective forever. A fiery red-haired vixen named Rosemary took an interest in him. No odder couple could be imagined than Theo, the astrophysics geek, and Rosemary, the seductress, but somehow, it was the perfect match. There were multiday sex fests fueled by tequila, marijuana, and cocaine.

Theo had been granted a leave of absence from Harvard, ostensibly to do independent research. In reality, the only research had been in trying more powerful drugs and utilizing the *Kama Sutra* handbook to explore exotic sexual positions with Rosemary. Theo was from an extremely wealthy Boston family, so money was no problem, and the debauchery was of Bacchanalian proportions. Every conceivable controlled substance was used and abused, from wine coolers to black tar heroin. All was good in their world of sex and drugs, and included orgies and group sex. Theo particularly enjoyed watching his girl get gang screwed by a whole chain of guys, one after the other. Rosemary did not care; she seemed to enjoy it too, and she was on too many different drugs to really notice.

This world had lasted for about two years, until one drizzly February day. After the routine drug and sexual rituals were over for the night, Theo had awoke from his stupor and staggered downstairs for a cup of coffee. There were naked and semi-clad folks throughout the house. He saw Rosemary's naked ass bent over a couch in the living room. There was a scrawny Asian dude lying underneath her. The guy looked vaguely familiar from the party last night, or was it two nights before?

He had known it was Rosemary's ass because it was damn nicely proportioned and because of the bright red rosebush tattooed on the right cheek. Theo gave his favorite ass a solid spank, square on that rose tattoo. She did not budge an inch, and neither did the guy sprawled beneath her. Theo had pulled her off, and her fair skin had a blue tint. Neither Rosemary nor her evening date were breathing, and had not been for quite a while.

The remainder of the party guests made halfhearted efforts to revive the two, as well as sweep the house for drugs.

Most left, and then Theo dialed 911. The cops arrived along with an ambulance, but it was over before it even started. There were still remnants of drugs everywhere, and the subsequent toxicology report showed that Rosemary and the other young man, whose name was Wu Tai, died of massive overdoses of PCP. The house was leased in Theo's name, so he became the primary suspect. Everyone interviewed by the police admitted drugs had been used, but no one admitted anything about PCP.

After an extended investigation, the police charged Theo with drug possession because he had a small bag of cocaine on him when the police first arrived. They never found any PCP, so Theo received probation for the cocaine and a harsh lecture from a DEA agent and a Massachusetts state trooper named Sinclair.

"Theo, you're a little dime-bag punk using your family's money to buy smack so you can get laid. You're scum."

Then the DEA agent, a soft-spoken Irishman named Fitzpatrick, spoke, "The toxicology report shows massive levels of PCP. That's angel dust, phencyclidine. That's some evil shit. My guess is, she would not have taken that much on her own, but I can't prove it. I think you gave it to her and Wu Tai, not aware it was uncut. I will not be able to do anything about it now. But walk away assured that your name is in our DEA computer database. You fuck up somewhere or get someone else hurt; you'll be taking it up the ass in a super max federal jail somewhere. I will be watching you wherever you go. Now go spend time with your rich family, you puke."

That was how it had ended. Theo received probation but was probably on every DEA and Massachusetts police computer system. He had applied for teaching jobs at a few Ivy League schools, and Cornell even gave him an interview. His drug arrest showed up though, and even though Cornell was considered the low-grade school of the Ivies, they would not hire him. Yet with all his baggage, he had still graduated magna cum laude from Harvard, with a master's degree. Lewis & Clark figured it was getting a bargain and the ability to brag that a member of its faculty had a Harvard master's degree—with honors, no less.

Theo's initial three years at Lewis & Clark had gone well. It was a liberal school with a liberal faculty, and they did not care he had gotten busted for drugs. He did carefully conceal that, while the official drug charge only involved cocaine, the case itself involved PCP and two dead students. He also told no one, not even his attorneys in Massachusetts, that he had purchased the PCP ingested by Rosemary and Wu Tai. He had never had the opportunity to cut the PCP with the baby laxative mannitol, or even powdered sugar. Rosemary and Wu Tai got 100 percent uncut pure angel dust. They believed it had been cut, and with the dosage they used, they were both destined for death the moment it hit their brain.

Theo had rationalized that incident away long ago. It had been their mistake, not his, but he was extremely careful now. He was off probation, he smoked a little weed, did a bit of blow now and again, but he stayed away from PCP, heroin, and LSD.

Theo did have a new drug of choice, and a very safe one: psilocybin 'shrooms. You can make them into tea, or you can eat them raw, and it gives a great high.

He enjoys the 'shroom trips and the wild rollercoaster ride which ensues. The euphoric state of semi-reality is a great escape from the daily grind of being a college professor. Psilocybin mushrooms are not addictive in the physical sense, and probably not even in the psychological realm. It is possible to get a bad trip, but Theo understands the dynamics and only uses them when in a good and confident mood. He also knows to use the 'shrooms in moderate amounts. The only other danger with psychedelic mushrooms is to ensure you never get poisonous varieties that often look remarkably similar to good quality 'shrooms. Based on experience, and the bad situation years back at Harvard, Theo is meticulous in picking his harvest and knows the right areas and which poisonous types to beware of. There are any numbers of wild poisonous mushrooms that are deadly and that grow in close proximity to good psilocybin varieties. The poisonous types include toadstools, death angels, and the amanita.

Theo is feeling better after having downed his Starbucks, and he returns to his apartment. He has a date this evening with a beautiful young coed that likes beer, sex, and 'shrooms. The future is bright indeed.

Theo picks up Charlotta Katz, or Charly, outside her dorm. Technically, professors are not allowed to date students, but Charly is a transfer graduate student merely filling in a few undergraduate credits on her way to a sociology master's. Accordingly, Charly is fair game for a prof to date. Charly stayed on campus to get the meal plan, which cost about seven thousand a year, and to receive housing. It also made it easier for her to receive financial aid, which she absolutely needed. The aid paid for most of her meals and housing costs. Unlike Theo, Charly Katz was Portland poor.

Portland is a city of divergent financial spectra. It is a city where the super wealthy live in mansions in the wooded hills overlooking the Columbia and Willamette Rivers. It is also where the less fortunate live in homes that overlook industrial parks and garbage dumps. There were still homes outside Portland proper that had dirt floors. They were red dirt floors. Charly's family had lived in a house with a dirt floor that her mother swept every morning—every single morning.

Charly's poor upbringing had made her a hard worker that craved success. She was an interesting match for Theo who, when not in a drug-induced stupor, had become slothful and lazy. His wasted time at Harvard, and his drug abuse, had folded in on him; and now he slid by, resting on his Harvard credentials and a great gift for bullshitting his superiors. Charly found his stories intriguing, having never been outside of Portland, and Theo made all his achievements sound grand, and the places he had visited were described to Charly in flowery phrases like, "The deserts of Saudi Arabia could never compete with the white sands of Egypt. And the pyramids are the world's greatest wonder."

Charly was spellbound even though Theo had never seen a desert or a pyramid. Perhaps Theo had seen them via teleportation during a drug hallucination.

Charly was attractive in that Northwest Oregonian way: no makeup, perfect white skin, and a physique kept in constant shape and tone from morning jogs up Portland's rigorous hills. While she constantly wore sandals and tie-dyed skirts, she was not so organic that her blouses were only green, and she did shave her legs and underarms.

A match made in heaven? No, but Charly and Theo enjoyed each other's company and had some fun. The sex was good too.

That evening, they ate at Atwater's, a seafood restaurant that provides a panoramic view of the downtown area of Portland. Theo had a nicely poached Chinook salmon with a lemon butter sauce, and Charly had a glass of chardonnay and a salad. Unsurprisingly, Charly was a strict vegetarian. During dinner, Theo commented between bites, "Since you're a vegetarian, you'll be happy to know I just obtained a new harvest of mushrooms. Want to sample a few this evening over a glass of champagne?"

Charly got the point, and she enjoyed weed and mushrooms. She felt it easily dovetailed with her image as an organic person who enjoyed the harvests of mother earth.

"Sure, Theo, nothing too strong though. I've got tomorrow off, but after that, it's back to the books. Anyway, next Tuesday, I'm running in a ten-kilometer race."

They returned to Theo's place after picking up another bottle of champagne. Theo popped the cork on the champagne and poured each of them a glass. He went into his bedroom and found his zipper-seal bag of 'shrooms. He had just located these the weekend before, and they looked potent. He believed that the condition of the mushroom cap, or head, was an indication of the potency. They looked perfect, with a grayish mud-like color beneath the cap. Charly was not a heavy user, so he wanted to make her dose lower, so he boiled one portion of the 'shrooms into a tea and added some mint for flavor. This he brought back out and served to her.

"My lady, here is your beverage of choice. I'm going to eat mine straight, but I believe I will start with a hit from my cache of hash. Then after I chill for a bit, I'll join you with the Alice in Wonderland mushrooms."

As Charly was drinking her psilocybin-laced tea, Theo rummaged around his bedroom and located a ridiculous-looking four-foot-tall translucent blue bong. He placed a couple grams of hash in the pipe and fired up his lighter and smoked it away in five quick tokes. The water in the bong cooled the hash smoke effectively, and he did not cough once. He went back to the living room and turned on the stereo to an old Atlanta Rhythm Section album, *Champagne Jam*. It was one he knew made Charly horny. The album was older than dirt and, to Theo's knowledge, never even was produced into a CD, but Charly loved the old tunes.

As he put the album onto the ancient turntable and selected the tune "Imaginary Lover," he decided it was time to munch on some 'shrooms and improve his high. First, however, he decided to see how Charly was doing and grab a quick kiss.

As he returned to the living room, he was scared as he saw Charly in the middle of the room, convulsing on the rug. She was vomiting and twitching, as if in the midst of a grand mal seizure. Her glass of champagne had fallen to the floor but had not shattered on the plush carpeting. Her cup of psilocybin-infused tea was empty and resting on a coaster on a teak end table.

"Charly, baby, what's up?"

She just looked toward him and continued to convulse. Her eyes were rolled backward into her head, and all Theo could see was the white of her lower eyeballs. She was twitching more rapidly now, and her breathing was labored. Theo reached for the phone to dial emergency, and then hesitated.

Even in his hash-influenced state, Theo understood the situation. This was a second-time offense for drugs, and worse yet, Charly was beginning to get increasingly pale. If she died, with his previous criminal history, he was in trouble. He also knew there was a DEA agent named Fitzpatrick back in Massachusetts who would quickly place an urgent call to DEA's Portland office, demanding that Theo be prosecuted as fully as possible.

"Fuck. Come on, honey, wake up."

Theo tried to force coffee down her throat, but she just reflexively vomited it back out. Tears ran down Theo's face, but it was no use. Within twenty minutes, she had stopped breathing and was dead.

He was sobbing, angry and scared. Somehow, he must have used toxic mushrooms and not psychedelic ones to make Charly's tea. He was thinking of returning to the kitchen and making more tea for himself and eating the 'shrooms he had already prepared for his own consumption.

But Theo was a coward, so he just closed all the shades, locked the doors, and cried.

⨯ ⨯ ⨯ ⨯ ⨯

The next morning, he hoped against all logic that it had been a hallucination, or somehow Charly would be sitting in a chair, laughing, getting her Nikes laced for a three-mile run.

It had been no hallucination; her dead body was still on the living room floor. He did the only thing he could think of. He began to meticulously clean the house. He flushed the remainder of all the poisonous 'shrooms and all his other drugs down the toilet. Next, he carefully vacuumed the entire house, but particularly the rug in the living room. He removed the vacuum cleaner bag and replaced it with a new one. All drug paraphernalia—such as bongs, pipes, and ashtrays—he enclosed in an oversized plastic bag. Theo then lifted the coffee table off the rug, and then inside the rug, he rolled up the body, the vacuum bag, the drug materials, and all his own clothes.

He stood naked, weeping and staring at the room. His apartment had an internal self-contained parking garage. He placed the large plastic garbage bags in the trunk of his Ford Crown Victoria and returned to the living room and carried the rug, body, and other evidence and placed it in his trunk. Still naked, he returned upstairs, showered carefully, and donned a set of running shorts, tank top, and shoes. He also packed a small bag with another set of shoes, shorts, and flip-flops. He returned to the garage and started the Crown Vic. It was dark now and one of those common evenings in Portland with complete cloud cover.

He headed southeast into the Mount Hood National Forest and arrived near the area where he had harvested the best 'shrooms he had ever discovered. The area, though deserted, was accessible by vehicle. He stopped, removed the plastic bags and evidence from the trunk. He pulled a shovel from the vehicle, and for six hours, he dug a grave—a spot to forever hide the evil he had committed.

After her body, he tossed in the clothes he was now wearing and his shoes, and he filled the hole in. He walked a hundred yards away, discarded the shovel, and then returned to his vehicle. Carefully, he slipped on the clothing he had left in the interior of the vehicle and headed back to Portland. In Portland, he carefully washed the vehicle inside and out.

X X X X X

Five days later, the police arrive at Theo's house. In those five days, he had done three things:

1. Continuously clean and sterilize his house.
2. Repeatedly consume a product designed to mask any usage of illegal drugs.
3. Place multiple calls to Charly's dormitory room, asking to speak to her. In each case, her roommate said Charly had not been seen recently.

X X X X X

"Are you Dr. Amilcar Theopolis?"

As Theo nods in the affirmative, the Portland police detective continues, "We are investigating the disappearance of Charlotta Katz. Would you mind answering some questions?"

"Not at all, sir. I am worried something has happened to her. I have not seen her in almost a week."

The detective reads Theo his Miranda warnings, indicating anything he says may be used against him in court. Theo agrees to waive his rights and answer any questions. He explains that he last saw Charly about a week ago when they went to dinner at Atwater's. Afterward, they returned to his apartment, but she did not spend the night because she was running in a ten-kilometer run a few days later.

"She felt sex weakened her legs. I told her it was nonsense, but that was her way."

The detective was not convinced and said he would be back with a search warrant to search Theo's apartment.

"No need for a warrant, officer. You and your people may search my home anywhere and anytime. I just want you to find Charly."

X X X X X

In the following weeks, streams of forensic investigators, homicide detectives, and narcotics officers searched Theo's residence with no success. He also consents to a urinalysis test for drug usage. This test comes back inconclusive.

"Obviously, as you can see from my record, I have used drugs in the past. But not recently."

The police have no clues, and the case becomes an unsolved missing-person matter. Theo offers money as a reward for clues and also provides monetary support to Charly's grieving family.

✗ ✗ ✗ ✗ ✗

For the next year, Theo stays clean from drugs, believing he is under police scrutiny, but some things are unchangeable.

Gradually, Theo relapses into drug use. Initially, it is periodic marijuana, but the psychological urge for 'shrooms becomes overwhelming. After two years, he finds himself foraging for mushrooms near the vicinity where he buried Charly's body. The area is a forest of psilocybin on what seems to be her actual grave location. 'Shrooms are everywhere.

Theo harvests some of the crop, and back at his apartment, he tries the psychedelic fungi. The results are surreal.

Orgasmic memories of Charly spin into sexual fantasies of red-haired Rosemary. They are spinning tornados of light, color, and fire. It is a descent into Dante's Inferno. The motion is stop, go, slow, churning. Sounds of laughter, sobbing, and screaming—all intermingled into a noise so horrendous it must be the mythological harpies.

The psychedelic trip is the most intense Theo has ever experienced. It is clear that, somehow, the compost created by Charly's body has increased the strength of the mushrooms. He falls into his former ways and uses these high-potency 'shrooms almost daily. His work efficiency is slipping, but most in management attribute it to Charly's disappearance and let it slide. At home, much of his time is spent in a growing cellar he has created in the garage area of his apartment. He uses hydroponic tanks to mold the ground into exactly the correct consistency. He infuses it with fertilizers, loam, and other soil types to increase the likelihood of successful fungi growth. He takes this soil and places it in garbage bags and then transports it to the site of Charly's grave. There, he mixes it with the soil from the slight mound still present over the location of her body. The condition looks perfect. In a few months, Theo will know.

XXXXX

Theo has consumed almost the entirety of his 'shroom stash. He is excited to return to the location for the next harvest, but due to the likelihood of a massive crop, he wants to develop a way of better preparing the 'shrooms for usage at his apartment. To limit visits to the grave site, he must be able to chop and then store the product.

Theo does research and determines that certain types of factories utilize flying cutter blades to quickly chop and dice. He purchases the equipment and sets it up in his garage. It operates perfectly. With one more trip to the 'shroom grave site, he should be able to process enough to last him for years.

He makes what he hopes is his final trip to the grave. The grave is not recognizable as it is now a mountain of psychedelic mushrooms. His trunk cannot contain even half the bounty. These, properly maintained, will last him forever. Upon his return, he unloads the final harvest and uses the chopper to cut them into manageable sizes. These he places into sealed mason jars. After he is done, he notices that one small pile of 'shrooms remains, and out loud, he says, "What the hell. Enough work for today, let's enjoy the feast."

He places a number of the mushrooms into his mouth and eats them. He vomits violently and realizes this is an extremely powerful load.

The world is twisting in his view screen. He sees a television, big screen, high definition. Scenes flash on the TV: mountain passes, water views, and panoramic sunsets. There is music in the background, classical—perhaps Grieg's *Hall of the Mountain King*. The vision swirls: gnomes, trolls, and centaurs.

Wow, what a trip! This is the best ever! He is even having physical sensations coupled with the visions. He is being tugged into the tunnel under the mountain. A maiden in chain-mail armor guards a circular-shaped door, almost like a Hobbit entrance. The woman is stunning, red hair with a warrior helmet. She is singing an aria, perhaps Wagner. What a beauty. She beckons him with a wave. Suddenly, her clothes and armor vanish. His interest deepens, and his fantasy is full force. She turns and displays an ass of perfect heart-shaped symmetry. There is a scarlet-red rosebush tattoo. Wow, it is Rosemary in a Germany fantasy land. She turns and beckons to him again.

"Follow me, and I'll fulfill. I'll fulfill. Fill me with your love."

This is a proposal he cannot refuse.

Rosemary suddenly morphs into a blue light. He feels a pleasant tug at his cock. The light is stroking his erection. The light switches again to green, and in a misty, foggy area, he sees Charly, covered in sheer lace. She's wearing running shoes. She waves, and then he is holding her tight, stroking her strong muscled legs. He feels another pull, as if he is controlled by puppet strings.

Fuck, this is an all-world high. He could market these 'shrooms and make a fortune. There is another push from behind, another pull toward Charly. Now Charly and Rosemary are both ahead—calling, wanting him. Suddenly they are both on top of him, touching him, licking him; his cock is in both of them at the same time. They reach orgasm at the same instant. There is a collective and violent moan. It is ecstasy.

X X X X X

The cops show up two days later. It is not ecstasy they find, though after a full search, they do locate a small stash of the date-rape drug ecstasy in one of Theo's upstairs closets.

The cops find the 'shroom room, and a female officer named Sheen motions to her partner, a burly, broad-shouldered black officer named Timmons. "Hey, stud, we better get the narcotics team over here and homicide too. Doubt any guy would commit suicide this way!"

Timmons intently stares at the body of Dr. Amilcar Theopolis. He also notes other residual clues lying about.

"Nah, Officer Sheen, doubt most guys would kill themselves that way; pretty damn painful, and tough on your sex life too."

Both cops look again at the bloody scenery.

There are piles of half-chopped psilocybin mushrooms.

There is one naked body, likely Theopolis. It is almost surely Theopolis. Was it a suicide? He must have had a lot of motivation.

A penis lays severed in the corner of the room. Almost looks like it was torn off.

Was a pretty well-hung guy, the female officer Sheen thinks but says nothing?

The other item of interest is a severed human head, settled next to the flying cutter blade.

Officer Timmons speaks quietly while unconsciously grabbing his own crotch.

"You're right. Don't care how stoned you get, no guy cuts his pecker off and then sticks his head under a guillotine. It would have been *thunk*, like a chef lopping off the cap of a mushroom."

THE PHILANTHROPIST

*Philanthropy, as defined by the Random
House Webster's Dictionary (fourth edition):*

*Philanthropy is "an altruistic concern for human beings,
manifested by donations to institutions and advancing human
welfare."*

Alvin Harding IV, known by most as Alvy, was merely twenty-four years old, but a philanthropist of extraordinary proportions. He went to cancer wards for children and dressed up as a clown and performed magic tricks. He worked for the Shriners to assist burn victims, and he donated time and money to dozens of worthwhile charities.

He operated a small company that sold computer servers, but the majority of his time was dedicated to the management of his charitable trust. The trust distributed millions of dollars to assist the homeless, the victims of tragedy, and the disease-stricken.

He perceived his job in life as helping the helpless and providing hope to those without it.

He had the monetary ability to assist. He lived in the rich and exclusive area of Seattle known as the Highlands, a gated golf and country club community of grand mansions and pools that rivaled small lakes in size. Yet most of his time was spent at homeless shelters, hospitals, and care facilities. What he had, he gave away—in time, effort, and money.

His ancestral family was wealthy, and each generation had bettered the previous. His grandfather had owned massive tracts of timberland eventually sold to Weyerhaeuser and their predecessors. These sales generated a small fortune. Then his father had done the family coffers one better by being a personal friend of Bill Gates, who began Microsoft. They had both attended the highbrow prep academy Lakeside High School. As Gates became a multibillionaire, Alvin's father had made hundreds of millions making investments in the stock of his friend's fledgling computer software company. Microsoft became the largest and most successful software company ever, and Alvin's father had morphed from a very rich son of a timber baron to an almost sickeningly wealthy major stockholder in Gates' Microsoft venture.

While Alvin's father's wealth was not incalculable, it was far in excess of five hundred million dollars. He was an honest, humorous man who taught his son the value of both charity and hard work. His grandfather, the timber man, had passed away years back, as had his quiet and stoic grandmother. With all the money available, it was a shame there were not more heirs; but Alvin's father had been an only child, and Alvin himself had neither brothers nor sisters. Eventually, the entire family fortune would descend to Alvin, but both his parents were happy and healthy, so the time that Alvin would run things was far away.

Alvin was only twenty-four and he still lived with his parents in their Highlands mansion. Hell, he had an entire wing to himself—why move out on his own? They left him his privacy, and he had recently graduated with honors from Princeton and returned to Seattle. In due time, he would choose a full-time livelihood, but it would likely be working for his dad. Trusts had been set up for him to manage on his eighteenth birthday. This was done to teach him responsibility and the ethics his family demanded.

So while wealthy from inheritance, Alvy worked hard and felt an overriding responsibility to continue his family's honorable name. He believed that he must provide a positive return to his community and wanted to be successful as his father and grandfather had been. Most importantly, he must contribute to the overall benefit of society in the broadest sense.

This perspective on life was wrenched on a dark and dreary fall day.

It was a typical November day in Seattle: foggy, a light misty drizzle was falling, and it was cold, perhaps forty degrees. Alvy was jogging through the gloom on his daily five-mile run through the Highlands. Smoky puffs of breath escaped his nose and mouth as he ran along the twisting hilly roads and paths through the mansions and quasi-castles. Alvy was running hard this day because he was training for a ten-kilometer run that would raise funds for breast cancer research. The *Race for the Cure* was a month away, and Alvy intended to win the race and then donate twenty thousand dollars to this worthwhile charity.

Alvy's legs were growing heavy, but his lungs felt clear and strong. He decided to go beyond his normal distance and complete some interval work up some of the Highlands' steep hills. When finished, the sweat poured from him despite the chill, and as a cool-down, he walked the last mile back to his parents' home. He felt uplifted and expected to do well in the ten-kilometer run.

He had been gone from his parents' house for over three hours.

Alvy entered the mansion through a side door that allowed him direct access to his section of the home. It was early, and this way, he would not disturb his parents, who were likely still sleeping in the master bedroom wing. He took a long hot shower in his Italian marble bath and then grabbed a quick sauna in his personal spa area, jumped in his indoor/outdoor swimming pool, and swam twenty laps. He completed his workout with twenty minutes of cooling down on his rowing machine. Alvy had been a varsity member of the Princeton Tigers' crew squad. While he was enjoying this oar workout, since there was no competition from a Harvard or Yale squad, he found the single practice scull somewhat boring. Finally he stretched, completed some yoga and Tai Chi movements, and meditated for a half hour. Alvy felt cleansed and at peace, and hungry.

The small kitchen on his side of the house was not well stocked. He had been a little lazy in his purchase of groceries, and a check of his refrigerator revealed only a dozen eggs, a bottled Dannon yogurt fruit smoothie, and some Miller Lite. He considered a beer but knew his parents' oversized Sub-Zero fridge offered better opportunities, so he walked into the main section of the house.

The artwork was mostly contemporary and included one Pablo Picasso painting that was his parents' joy. As he walked through the hallway, he saw that the painting was not in its normal position, but on the ground. The painting also had a small tear along the edge of its frame. Alvy was immediately concerned.

He walked down the broad hallway, over thick white Berber carpeting, and in one corner he saw a large rust-colored stain.

It was drying blood. Farther along, he saw another mark, a much larger one. The area looked as if a pig had been slaughtered, and the blood soaked into the white Berber. Alvy thought of the family's two dogs—Calvin, a purebred Weimaraner, and his mongrel pup named 'Nippy.

Farther down the hallway, he realized the blood was from the dogs. Calvin's body was intact, but his head had been severed just below his collar. The leather collar had *Calvin* inscribed in silver alongside the family's phone number. Calvin's head was casually tossed into the corner stairwell. It appeared his head had been severed with a chainsaw.

'Nippy's fate had not been much better; he was hanging from one of the exquisite crystal chandeliers. His leash had been used as a noose to strangle the dog.

Alvy was scared, but angry as well. Calvin was newly purchased by his mother, but Alvy had raised the mongrel 'Nippy from a pup and given him his name. 'Nippy had always playfully bit at Alvy's fingers and toes when younger.

Alvy knew the situation was dangerous, so he carefully and quietly walked along the Berber carpeting into his father's office. In the bottom drawer of the desk was a nine-millimeter semiautomatic pistol. Alvy ensured it was fully loaded with hollow-point rounds. He eased his way into the main living room with the gun pointed out at chest level. Alvy's father had frequently taken his son to the firing range, and Alvy was a quick and accurate shot.

Once in the living room, Alvy's anger dissipated and was replaced by despair. His father lay dead on the floor, the majority of his head blown away from a shotgun blast. His mother was worse; she was naked and handcuffed to a heavy wooden chair. She was not sitting in the chair but draped over its back so that her behind was flagrantly displayed. Blood seeped from both her anus and vagina, and she had been violently raped. A small-caliber bullet wound leaked blood at her left temple.

Alvy listened carefully for any sound to see if the intruders were still in the home. He heard nothing, dialed 911, and asked for the police department.

The Seattle Police Department arrived and found Alvy weeping on the floor, still clutching his father's handgun. As soon as the police entered, he handed them the weapon and, between outbursts of fury and tears, told the officers what he knew.

Their initial investigation and inspection of the house determined a number of things:

A safe had been broken into, and its contents stolen. Alvy explained that the safe had contained antique gold and silver coins worth over $100,000.

The family's silver Bentley had been stolen.

There were at least two perpetrators because bloody footprints were of different sizes.

The guard at the gated Highlands community did not recall any questionable entries or deliveries, nor did he remember a Bentley leaving.

The police instructed Alvy that an evidence response unit would arrive at the house within an hour, and until their work was completed, the home must remain secured.

Alvy provided all the details he could offer and then asked if he could sit outside while the police completed their duties. The police left a female officer named Candace to sit with Alvy. The home had a greenhouse where his mother had grown rosebushes and other flowers. Alvy and Officer Candace Swenson waited inside the greenhouse during the search. Candace did not ask any questions, but during the next few hours, she did sometimes put her arms around Alvy as he cried.

The next few months were a blur for Alvy. There were interviews with homicide detectives, legal issues involving the wills and family trust, and preparations for the funeral. Seven hundred people attended the service. Alvy's family had touched many lives with kindness and charity, and all wanted to pay their last respects. During the ceremony, the mayor of Seattle, a high school classmate of Alvy's father, gave a moving speech about the family's desire to give back to the world. The list of dignitaries who spoke was extensive and distinguished. Finally, just prior to the pastor's benediction, Alvy spoke and said how honored his parents would be have been to see all those in attendance. During his conclusion, while struggling against his emotions and tears, Alvy said, "I want to thank the Seattle Police Department for their dedication, but also their discretion and decency in this matter. I am certain they will find the evil souls that committed these atrocities. I intend to continue what my father and mother have begun regarding charity and service to the community. Despite my loss, I refuse to allow this to interfere with the good my parents would demand from me. It is not my job to punish the evil, that duty is in the holy hands of the Lord, but I will strive to honor their memory by continuing their example of kindness. I'm sure that now in heaven, my mother is dutifully working at providing love to every angel, and my father is making them laugh with his humor."

Alvy had a few more sentences to say, but he broke down in tears and was unable to continue. One of the pastor's assistants helped him back to his seat, and soon the service was over. After hundreds of hugs, kisses, and offers of help, Alvy went home to his empty house, got oblivious drunk, and passed out.

In the midst of a tragedy that involved murder investigations and financial issues that must be resolved quickly and efficiently, Alvy had minimal time to grieve. Still, there had been chilling moments of pain caused by necessity. The investigation had called for not only the autopsies of his mother and father, but veterinarians also had to autopsy both dogs. Alvy understood this but asked that the animals' bodies be returned to him so that he could bury them beneath a massive cherry tree on the family estate. He had two simple headstones made, which merely said *'Nippy* and *Calvin*. The dogs had always chased one another around that tree, and Alvy knew their souls would be at peace in the shade of the massive branches. He dug the grave holes and purchased correctly sized boxes.

Alvy rarely became angry, but he had been enraged when he had gone to the veterinarian's office. After the autopsies, he was handed one box containing one plastic bag. The animal's body parts had been mixed together after the vet's clinical review. His comment had been, "Sorry, I didn't know you wanted the bodies back. You can sift through the parts if you want. It is easy to tell a Weimaraner leg from that of a twenty-five-pound mixed breed."

Alvy had held his temper, barely. Back at home, Alvy had gone through the body parts and was fairly certain that, when finished, 'Nippy was in 'Nippy's grave, and the same for Calvin. He placed a rose he clipped from his mom's greenhouse on each headstone.

The lawyers and trust accountants were never-endingly at the house. "Sign this, review that." "Consider revamping investments." Everything was a timeliness issue and, according to the professionals, had to be done immediately or sooner than immediately, if possible. He fielded thirty calls a week from these types during the first months. Most were rude and obnoxious.

Each wanted their fees as quickly as possible. Alvy began to realize why there were so many jokes about lawyers. They were crass, obnoxious vermin. Finally, after months of turmoil, he had completed the required duties with these "professionals," and at least, it was over.

The only positive was, he learned a joke hopefully of auspicious truth. In this dark time, it brought a smile.

"A junior lawyer in the largest law firm in New York is killed in a car accident, and he finds himself in hell. The serial killers are there, the child molesters, and the rapists, but basically, 95 percent of hell is populated by lawyers. He runs into another member of his firm that had died years before and asks her if the entire squad of attorneys from his former firm *Steal, Corruption, and Graft* are in hell. She replied, 'No, not everyone. As with all lawyers, only the lower-level ones get sent to purgatory and hell.' 'Well, what happens to the head honchos?' 'They go somewhere worse.'"

X X X X X

Alvy's most difficult day had not been his parents' funeral, burying his dogs, or even dealing with lawyers; it had been when he found out about a unique group of cleaners. Much of the house had been covered in blood from the dogs and from his mom and dad. Once the police had finished their crime-scene work, the blood remained clinging with tenacity to everything, and particularly to the white Berber carpets. When he did try to scrub out the blood, he became violently ill and vomited; only making matters worse. The stains would not come out.

He called the Seattle police officer Candace Swenson who had been so kind to him on the day of the murders. She explained that there were certain companies that cleaned up murder scenes and knew how to deal with the problem. She gave him a number to call, and the next day, five women in red medical scrubs cleaned up the entire scene in a few hours. The house was spotless. While the blood had been horrible, its cleansing made Alvy feel worse. Now every vestige of his parents' physical being was gone, and he was alone. He had later called Swenson, sent her some flowers, and thanked her for her help and advice.

The day of the cleaning, he had gone into his parents' huge bedroom in the west wing of the house. It overlooked the rolling lawns, the cherry tree, and the greenhouse. Everything was tended immaculately, and Alvy would maintain the entire staff. He had hired someone to closely and carefully tend to the flowers in the greenhouse, and he still went there often because it brought back memories of his mother.

That day, he decided that he would move into the master bedroom because he was certain his parents would have wanted that. Over time, he carefully itemized his mom's and dad's clothing, jewelry, and personal items. He called in an appraiser and estate sale expert. Through this individual, he sold all the valuable items and donated the money to charities. After taking his cut, the estate sale expert gave him a check for $175,000. The next day, in the name of his parents, he donated the money to a local children's hospital.

Four months slowly passed, and his life was in some semblance of coherence and order. He ran every day, lifted, and went through his flexibility and rowing routines. He had heard nothing from the Seattle Police Department recently, and he was concerned about their investigation.

This made him wonder about Candace Swenson. Alvy had been too busy thinking about other matters, but he had not forgotten her kindness on the day of the murders. He also recalled her blue eyes, blond hair, a figure that showed even through a bulletproof vest and police uniform. During the investigation, he had found out something about her: she was twenty-seven years old and recently divorced.

Hell, he had smoked a little weed at Princeton, but he was no criminal. He decided to call her and ask her on a date. He was as scared as a high school freshman, but he got the nerve and pulled out her card and gave the precinct a call and asked for her.

She sounded official when she answered. "Candace Swenson, how may I help you?"

Alvy smiled as he thought of a few ways she might be able to help him.

"This is Alvy Harding. Hopefully, you remember me. You came to my house the day of my parents' murders."

"Of course I remember, but I'm just a patrol sergeant who assisted that day. The homicide detectives are handling that matter now. By the way, thanks for the flowers, but that was unnecessary. I'll get you the homicide detective's number who is handling your case."

"Actually, Candace, I have the detective's number. I called to speak with you. I'm feeling awkward as hell, but I was calling to see if you wanted to go out to dinner."

Candace was surprised, but she was eligible and had grown tired of dating other cops. Alvy was handsome, in a preppy sort of way. She also remembered hugging him as he cried the day of his family's murder. He was broad shouldered, trim, and strong. They agreed she would meet him at his house.

"I'll leave your name at the gated entrance of the Highlands. I'm sure you remember your way."

She arrived wearing a full-length leather coat, which Alvy offered to hang up for her. He was glad he did because, beneath, she wore a white blouse and a long, black hip-hugging skirt, and both accentuated her attractive body. They sat in the living room, and Alvy asked if she would like a drink. He was impressed when she wanted a beer and not something highbrow, like a martini or a cosmopolitan. He brought them both a beer and was even more impressed when she declined the glass and drank it from the bottle.

"I know you probably search a lot of houses and get bored with tours, but would you like a walk through the house?"

Alvy gave her the grand tour and, when back at the kitchen, handed her another beer. They then looked over the grounds and walked the paths outside the mansion. It was one of those rare warm March days in Seattle, and Candace left her coat inside as they went out. Seattle's weather is generally nice only in July and August, but this March evening was an exception—warm and no rain. When they passed the greenhouse, Alvy asked her to wait a moment while he went inside.

"Besides, you've already been in there."

He brought her out a long-stemmed red rose.

"Thanks for seeing me. This is for you, Candace."

She gave him a kiss on the cheek and a hug. He noticed her nipples were erect. Maybe it was colder than he thought, or maybe it was something else. As they walked back to the house, Candace saw the headstones for 'Nippy and Calvin and said, "They are resting in a beautiful place beneath the cherry tree."

"I come out here often. I miss them, Candace."

"You should get another dog, or dogs. And while I don't mind if you call me Candace, my very closest friends call me Candy. You should."

Alvy definitely believed that, while Candace sounded romantic, Candy seemed more right for her personality.

"Candy, we're going downtown for dinner on the water at Cutters. I hope you like fish."

Candace explained that with a Scandinavian name like Swenson, if she had not eaten fish, she would never have survived her childhood.

Alvy had hired a car to drive them from the Highlands to Cutters, which is adjacent to the Pike Place Market in downtown. During the limo ride, and dinner, they discussed their pasts. She explained that her father had been a Seattle cop, and her younger sister was married to a bank executive. Her dad had wanted boys so they could follow in his law enforcement footsteps.

"I guess the tomboy in me made it easier for him because he still got a cop in the family. It just happened to be a daughter."

"I'm sure he's very proud, Candy."

"He was proud. I have his badge now with SPD. He died of cancer six years ago. After he passed, they gave his badge to me."

Alvy tried to break the tension and ordered another bottle of wine—a Chateau St. Michelle white to go with the halibut and salmon each had ordered.

Like any police officer, she could drink like a fish, and Alvy was glad he had a limo to drive them home. They had a window seat and watched the sun glint off the waters of Puget Sound. Ferries moved in and out of the nearby port, carrying passengers to and from surrounding islands. As the sun began to set behind the Olympic Mountains, the sky glowed orange as the clouds floated past. Finally, they had after-dinner drinks and dessert.

On the ride back, Alvy realized how much he was attracted to her and, in the privacy of the limo, kissed her. She kissed back more passionately and, demonstrating flexibility and surprising sobriety after her drinking, arched backward in the plush limousine seats. The top button on her blouse popped off from the stress. That was just fine with Alvy because it made taking off her clothes that much easier.

When they arrived back at Alvy's Highlands's mansion, she looked exactly the same as when they left, buttoned up warm and tight in her leather jacket. The only difference was that now her large purse contained not only her police-issued pistol but also her blouse, bra, and skirt. She had started, and ended, the evening without panties. They left the limo and went directly to Alvy's bedroom and continued what they had begun in the vehicle.

× × × × ×

Their relationship was not some cheap one-night stand. They fell for each other, and they fell fast and hard. After only two months, Candy had moved out of her Capitol Hill apartment and was living with Alvy.

This bleak Tuesday in May, Seattle's weather had not yet turned summerlike. Sleet fell sideways through a swirly wind. Candace was with her partner, Leroy Jackson, after having arrested a fugitive child molester aptly named Piggingham. Jackson said, "That was a good job today, Candace. It's nice to get that scum off the street. You want to go for a drink?"

Candace was repulsed even by being seen with Jackson, who was renowned in the PD for hitting on and sleeping with anyone with a pulse.

"No thanks, Leroy. I've got a man, and we're getting pretty close too, but I'm flattered by your offer. You did a good job on the arrest also."

"Come on, baby. That rich high-society boy can't give you what I got. I know your first husband was black like me, so you know what I'm saying."

Candace considered keeping her mouth shut, but she was not a demure shrinking-violet sort. "Listen to me, Leroy, you fucking piece of shit. You could not shine Alvy's shoes. He's better in bed than you and my ex-husband combined. So be my partner and watch my back and not my ass. Do your job, and shut your fucking mouth."

× × × × ×

A week later, Candace received a message to see her captain, Cletus Potts. Potts was a respected fixture in the department. He'd been with the PD for twenty-five years and had risen from beat cop to street crimes, to vice, through internal affairs, and narcotics. Now he was captain in charge of homicide.

Ten years ago, he was shot directly on the shoulder blade. An inch higher, the perp misses; an inch lower, his vest would have protected him. Instead, the bullet went through the shoulder blade and collar bone and entered Potts's chest by ricocheting off the inside of the vest. The round bounced internally through Potts's body, nicked his heart, took out part of one lung, and lodged in his spine. The multiple paths of the bullet decreased its velocity, so the spine was not damaged. Yet there the round remained forever, because any surgery was likely to cause permanent paralysis.

Candace respected Potts, but she was not eagerly anticipating meeting with him. She entered his office and noticed there were no awards and pictures on the walls. Cletus Potts was likely the most decorated police officer in Seattle, and yet he chose to keep his awards away from public view. Candace was impressed.

"You asked to see me, Captain Potts?"

"Sit down and relax, Candace."

Potts stood and reached out and shook her hand. He looked like a cop that McDonald's had supersized. At minimum, he was six five and weighed two seventy. The weight was not fat, and he looked hard and mean, particularly for someone in their fifties. His skin was so black it looked painted, but somehow, his eyes were blue. Those eyes were now piercing directly through Candace's skull. His voice was deep, an octave lower than most men. He sounded like Darth Vader, and Candace doubted his next comment would be "Candace, I am your father."

"Candace, I know you have become close to Alvy Harding. He has done nothing wrong, and the loss of his parents was a tragedy. The *Seattle Times* is crucifying us on this case, a full-page article every week. It must be resolved, and I want you to help because of your contacts with Alvy. But you can do this only with the utmost discretion."

"I'll do whatever you need, sir."

The captain explained that the department believed they knew who committed the crime from an anonymous tip. The pieces fit, but there was no motive and no evidence.

Another high-powered philanthropist named Vincent Howell had become overshadowed by Alvy's family. Potts believed Howell killed Alvy's family to enable him to assume the mantle of Seattle's most charitable family. They had also intended to kill Alvy that day, but he had been out on his long run. The captain continued and explained that the PD's concern was twofold. One, Alvy was still in danger, and two, Candace was also threatened because of her proximity to a potential murder target.

"Sir, why don't you talk directly to Alvy? I'm certain he would help."

Potts looked downward and was clearly deciding whether to disclose something to Candace. After a moment, he very quietly spoke, "Vincent Howell is closely working with the teamsters' union. I believe he hired some of their more criminal types to commit the crimes at the house, and it was made to look like a brutal robbery and assault so that it would not appear tightly organized."

Potts continued and provided some interesting details and theories. Mrs. Harding, while apparently raped by the intruders, may not have been. No semen, nor hairs and fibers, were present on her body. The anus and vagina, while clearly penetrated, had only trace amounts of latex and a gel rubber compound. Potts surmised that she had been violated by a vibrator so that it would appear she was raped. None of the other valuable items in the house had been stolen. No jewelry or anything traceable, just the gold and silver coins which could be melted and sold without a trail. The bloody footprints seemed to have been left intentionally to confuse the investigation. The blood was from the Weimaraner. If the perpetrators had stepped in the animals' blood, they would have had to walk down the Berber-carpeted stairs into the main room where the victims were found, but no bloody footprints were on the stairs.

Potts believed the murderers had brought extra shoes with them and dipped them in the animals' blood and then placed footprints downstairs. If this were so, obviously the shoe size and type was another false clue, and the killers' shoes would be totally different in size and type.

Candace was shaken but, as an investigator, very intrigued, and she asked, "What lends credence to the anonymous tip? Any nutcase could make up a story to discredit a respected figure like Vincent Howell."

Potts agreed that that had been his initial response too, nothing but crap, but he had a detective check into Howell. An old-time acquaintance of Howell's is a man named Barney Quist, and Quist is the gate guard at the Highlands' exit gate, the one who does not recall a Bentley leaving on the day of the murders.

The PD had detectives speak to Quist, but he is cagey and obviously knows the routine. He admits knowing Howell, but nothing else. Evidence teams located the Bentley stripped clean to its frame in West Seattle, not a print or fiber to be found. The only other item of interest is that Howell previously worked as a legal consultant to the teamsters. One matter Howell handled five years ago was the defense of a union laborer on the docks charged with assault. That laborer was named Barney Quist.

Candace sat in stunned silence. After a few moments, she promised not to say anything to Alvy but added that she would be at the house as often as possible for his protection.

"I've taken care of that, Candace. You are on a three-month paid leave of absence. I asked your 'good friend' Leroy Jackson to file a harassment complaint on you. He seemed happy to oblige, scum that he is. In a few months, I'll ensure internal affairs drops the charges and reinstates you with a clean record."

Candace smiled and said, "Captain Potts, you are a very sneaky, smart man. I'll ensure nothing happens to Alvy, and it will be a bonus to spend the time with him."

XXXXX

Candace returned home and told Alvy she was on three months' paid leave.

"I'm sure we'll find a few things to do."

Candace said that the second thing they were going to do was buy a German shepherd puppy. They named the dog Fritz, and Candace said she would train it, with Alvy's help. She failed to tell Alvy that her second job for Seattle PD had been to train the department's K-9 attack-and-response units. SPD only utilized German shepherds.

XXXXX

They selected Fritz the next day, but he was not exactly a puppy. A year old and already in obedience schooling from a K-9 instructor frequently used by SPD, Fritz bonded to both of them quickly, and Candace began the initial steps to attack-train him.

Alvy conversely taught Fritz how to chase and retrieve sticks.

Candace and Alvy spent most of their time together. Alvy even convinced her to go on his long, arduous runs. She always carried a fanny pack with water. Alvy did not know, but it also contained a five-shot Chief's Special revolver.

Candace logically could not accept that multimillionaire Vincent Howell would try to kill Alvy and his entire family because Alvy was a more renowned "philanthropist." Did massive fortunes make men that petty and evil minded?

She completed extensive research in the microfiche files at the local library, on the computer, and in police files. There was a more obvious answer, and it did involve jealousy but was only slightly less bizarre.

Seattle is a liberal city by most American standards. Interracial couples are common and generally accepted. Candace herself had been married to a black cop, though she considered it one of her gravest life blunders. It did not matter he was black, but her becoming involved in a relationship with another law enforcement officer had been a mistake. When she was promoted, many felt it involved her ex, and when he got in trouble with internal affairs, some in the department blamed her. It had been a mess, and she was glad it was over. They were still on speaking terms and had both been involved in a street-crime task force following their divorce, and while tense, it worked out okay.

Seattle also has a high percentage of homosexuals. It is not San Francisco, but it is clearly not Des Moines, Iowa, either. There are frequent gay parades and AIDS fund-raisers. Many of these events are tied in to the University of Washington, which sits on an idyllic spot of land adjacent to Lake Washington.

During her research, Candace determined that Vincent Howell was bisexual. He hid it well and was married and had two grown children, but he had also had numerous closeted relationships with men. Howell had gone to great lengths to conceal these gay affairs because it would harm his business interests and charitable duties. Most importantly, teamsters do not deal well with "fags"—as they would term them. Howell's intricate, essential, and lucrative dealings with the teamsters would be terminated if his sexual preferences were known. They might have killed him.

This would have been singularly Howell's dilemma, except for one fact. Alvy's father, Alvin Harding III, was also bisexual and predominantly homosexual. His own father had forced him into a marriage to continue on the honored family name, and once the son Alvy was born, everything was perfect. The family name continued, and Alvy's mother spent her time shopping and tending to her greenhouse.

Things had become somewhat more complicated when Alvy went to Princeton. With his son gone, Alvin Harding III felt more comfortable bringing his gay lovers to the mansion and orchestrating homosexual love-ins which, while not quite orgies, were close. Alvy's mom turned a blind eye to the doings, and Alvy was kept completely in the dark.

Candace determined this information with good detective work outside the mansion and a close examination of the home's contents. Alvy's father had a secret room with a hidden entrance in the basement, and during the previous police search, the room had not been discovered. Extensive photo albums showed parties at the home, and while lampshades and dildos were not readily apparent, there were a lot of men hugging and kissing other men, and often Alvy's father was much in the mix. Very few photos existed of Alvy's mom and dad together and, if present, were usually official photos from fundraisers at the university or various hospitals.

One photo album hidden away contained more graphic homosexual photos of Alvy's father and various men. He had also made a few home movies of his sexual exploits. One morning, while Alvy was on an extended run, Candace decided she should watch these VCR tapes. Candace was no prude, but watching videos of older men fucking older men was not her thing. Still, the tapes might include individuals tied to the homicides. Candace poured herself a strong scotch and soda to dull the impact of what was on the screen. She hit the fast-forward button frequently and was down to the next-to-the-last tape when she slowed it to normal speed.

This tape showed Alvin Harding III giving it, and taking it, in numerous ways with another wealthy man in the Seattle community: Vincent Howell.

Fortunately, Alvy had decided to take a long run that morning, and while not typically a morning drinker, Candace drank about half the bottle of Dewar's scotch. How could she explain to Alvy that she had been snooping through his father's most private belongings? How, with any taste, could she explain that Alvin Harding III was a hardcore, full-time homosexual? Finally, how could she address with Alvy the possibility that Vincent Howell could somehow be involved with the murder? She heard Alvy upstairs in the shower and knew he would be down to see her soon. She took another swallow of Dewar's.

X X X X X

Alvy snuggled up to her on the couch and said, "Well, if you are going to have an AM cocktail, I believe I'll make myself a margarita."

While Alvy made a pitcher of strawberry margaritas, Candace decided that these issues must be addressed.

She loved this man and also feared for his safety, and she must tell him the truth. He returned with his margarita, and she continued with her scotch and soda, heavy on the scotch. Candace said, "I've done some investigation into the murders, and I have also discovered a hidden room in this house, which supports my theories. I believe I know who ordered the killing of your family, but some of the details are unpleasant. Worst, all of the information is circumstantial, which I do not believe we can prove in court."

Candace explained everything she knew and how she learned it. She concluded with the supposition that his father had been killed not because of money but due to the fear that his homosexual relationship with Vincent Howell would be unearthed. She admitted that the only clue eluding her was why now?

Alvy's father had kept his gay life hidden for years, and all his homosexual lovers were powerful men. Therefore, he was unlikely to disclose anything that would implicate Howell.

Candace was surprised at how calm Alvy was. He returned to the bar and made more margaritas and another scotch and soda. He kissed her and said, "Candy, I love you. Perhaps I also have not been complete in my disclosures to you. I did not believe there was any reason to air my family's sordid and dirty laundry to the person I love."

He continued and explained a number of things that fit more pieces into the puzzle. Alvy had known for years that his father was gay. As a child and when young, he only suspected, but he too had plenty of spare time to explore a mansion and look for hidden passageways and rooms. At age fourteen, he had discovered his father's hidden room of homosexual magazines and home videos, but he had never had any reason to connect his father's activities to the homicides. The police had stated it was a random break-in and that valuable items were stolen. Alvy had never considered any possible linkage.

"I felt you might find me less desirable if you knew of my dad's indiscretions, and I did not want to lose you."

Now, as both were hugging and crying, Alvy explained something that did drop all the pieces of the puzzle into place.

"With what you have told me, I can understand why Howell had my father and mother butchered and why they left me alive. My father told me two months before he was killed that he was tired of living a lie. He intended to come out with a public statement acknowledging his homosexuality in order to legitimize the gay lifestyle. He thought of it as another way to contribute to the community. Typical of my dad—help others at the cost of himself."

Alvy finished by explaining that his father had told his closest lovers and gay associates that they should come out of the closet also, but that he would never force them out. He also said that his wife knew some of his lovers' identities, but his son Alvy had been kept purposefully in the dark.

Candy's mind was racing. Her love for Alvy was confusing her investigative instincts, or perhaps it was the scotch.

So this is why Alvy had been spared and why none of his father's associates had any information of value to offer the police when interviewed. They were protecting their own homosexuality and merely repeating the mantra of "We have no idea who might harm the family. They are kind, generous, and wonderful." But what would happen now when Candace and the PD stirred up the pot, interviewed his father's gay associates, and in particular, the likely perpetrator Vincent Howell? If Howell was not the actual killer, he had ordered the hit.

The entire situation was a time bomb.

The immediacy as to the safety of Alvy was gone because Howell would feel completely safe. Candace and Alvy had time to weigh their options. What should they do?

Neither Candace nor Alvy cared that Vincent Howell was gay, but they knew that with his social standing and his position with the teamsters, if he was outed, he might be killed, which was fine, or he might retaliate against Alvy. The homosexuality was the problem.

The *Post-Intelligencer* would have a field day and have reporters dig, and dig deeper, until all Howell's and Alvy's father's gay companions were identified. The police would meticulously catalogue the photo albums, VCR tapes, and party lists. Innocent men that wanted to keep their lifestyles hidden would be forced into the glare of the media spotlights. Some would lose their families, social standing, and their jobs. All because one evil man named Vincent Howell had decided to become a murderer and end, and ruin, the lives of Alvy's family. The answer was clear, but complicated.

They must speak to Howell and get him to admit his role in the murder, and then an evil man must die.

Snuffed out like a foul-smelling demonic candle. He likely had many enemies within the teamsters, and the police would believe his death was related to his connections there. Candace was nervous, and this was far from her side of the law and right and wrong, which she had learned in life and at the police academy.

Their first step was to meticulously go through the entire mansion and destroy all evidence of Alvy's father's homosexuality. All photo albums, sex toys, and videos were carefully and completely destroyed—with one exception.

The tape of Harding and Howell was duplicated so that the only scene on it was the sex between Harding and Howell. The remainder of the tape that included Alvy's father's other sexual exploits was erased and then burned in a trash can behind the home. Now the only evidence of homosexuality was the single video of Howell and Alvin Harding III; they would need this for leverage when they spoke to Howell.

As a final tribute to Harding and his wife, Candace redecorated the secret room with photos of the Harding family and specifically included artists' renderings of Calvin and 'Nippy.

The room was transformed from an area dedicated to the worship of sex to a shrine of the family's positive works: commendations from the governor for public service, framed letters of thanks from charitable foundations, and awards the family received.

As a final touch, from a recent family photograph of Alvy and his mom and dad, Candace took the photo to an artist of great skill who created a life-size painting of the three together. The painting was exquisite and celebrated the family's life. Beneath it, Candace placed a bowl of floating lilies from the greenhouse. She intended to personally change those flowers whenever needed to ensure their vibrancy. It was the finishing touch on making the room a celebration of life. When Alvy first saw the completed room, he said nothing, but Candy saw the tear trickle down his cheek.

Vincent Howell was an avid sport fisherman who often made the trek from Seattle to the Washington Coast and fished via charter boat from a small community on the Pacific called Ilwaco. On a warm, clear day in June, Howell drove his Lincoln Navigator south down Interstate 5, waiting for the turnoff west that would take him to the ocean. As he pulled off into a rest stop to use the bathroom, he failed to notice the rented silver Cadillac that followed him.

The rest stop was empty—a fortuitous break for the occupants of the Cadillac, Candace and Alvy.

Candace walked up to Howell, shoved a shotgun in his face, and offered him a ride to Ilwaco. His fear was visible, but he saw there was no alternative. Candace said, "Get in the backseat."

Howell was shocked to see Alvy there.

"What the fuck are you doing? You'll be in jail for life for kidnapping me."

"I doubt it."

Alvy carefully patted Howell down and searched for weapons, as Candace had taught him. Howell was clean, and Alvy placed a pair of handcuffs and leg shackles on him. Once secured, Alvy reached into the front seat of the Caddy and retrieved a small black-and-white TV with VCR capability. The television was plugged into the vehicle's lighter for power.

Alvy pushed PLAY and enjoyed Howell's misery as he watched a replay of him and Alvy's father having sex. Alvy said, "Sorry the picture is not clearer, but you were there. You know how it all goes down, pardon the pun."

Howell looked like he was going to throw up and choked out, "Enough. Turn it off. What do you want?"

"I want the truth, and if you lie to me, I'll either kill you or I'll give this tape to your teamster buddies, friends at the country club, and your wife. Did you kill my dad because he was going to acknowledge his homosexuality, which might force you out of the closet?"

"I'm not going to say anything."

Alvy removed a stun gun and, on low voltage, stuck it into Howell's crotch.

"Actually, I thought you might enjoy the S&M touch, Howell. Now answer the fucking question."

Howell still refused to answer, but after the stun gun was amped up a few notches, he became more talkative.

He admitted that he had hired three teamster thugs to commit the crime at Alvy's house and make it look like a break-in. He confessed that he had even been there and watched. Alvy's parents had quickly opened the door when they saw him, and the heavies just followed him inside, and yes, he had done it to avoid the disclosure of his homosexuality.

"I couldn't let that info out. It would have ruined my whole life. I'll do anything, pay you any amount of money, if you just let me go."

"I'll definitely let you go. I promised you that, but you will have to remain absolutely silent about this. It will be our secret. I do not want to tarnish my father's memory."

"God bless you, Alvy. I knew you were rational."

Alvy placed a gag in Howell's mouth and cinched it tight. They continued their drive south on the interstate, but instead of going all the way to the turnoff for Ilwaco, they went half that far and turned west at Chehalis. They were headed to the port of North Cove. Alvy was somewhat worried that they might be stopped by the highway patrol, but then he remembered that a Seattle police officer was driving. In the unlikely event they were stopped, this caravan was nothing more than a "prisoner" transport.

A week earlier, Alvy had taken his father's yacht, the *Lucky Seafarer*, and moored it at North Cove. He had also brought a few special items with him on the boat. They wrapped Howell in a tarp, tied with rope and straps. He struggled some, but both Alvy and Candace were strong, and they got him on the *Lucky Seafarer* without anyone observing them. They left the harbor and headed directly out into the Pacific. It was one of those rare calm days on the ocean, barely a ripple. Alvy removed a medium-sized metal washtub, the size that would have been good to chill twenty or thirty beers. Candace steered the vessel.

Alvy had recently discovered that Candy loved the ocean and knew much about sailing and yachting. Howell was writhing and moaning through his gag, and Alvy told him to stop and kicked him hard. Alvy pulled out bags of cement and gravel and a water-cooler-sized bottle of water. These he mixed well with a shovel and trowel and poured into the metal washtub. He removed the tarp from Howell, and the gag as well. They were miles out at sea, and no one would hear the screams.

"Put your feet in the concrete tub now."

"Oh god, please no, help me. Don't do this, Alvy, for God's sake."

"God has nothing to do with this. I'm running this show. While in the car, I promised you a few things. I promised I would let you go and that you would remain silent. I intend to wait until the concrete sets, then I'll let you go—overboard to the bottom of the Pacific. And I guarantee you'll be silent."

Howell was sobbing and babbling about his kids and God. Alvy spoke, "I'm not sadistic like you or your murdering associates that defiled my mother. The pathologist said that the vaginal and anal tears were very severe and would have caused enormous pain and that she was conscious throughout. Put your fucking feet in that tub."

When Howell did not comply, he set the stun gun on maximum, which rendered Howell unconscious. Alvy then placed his feet into the concrete past mid-calf and sat him in a chair. He also utilized straps and tie-downs so that Howell was unable to stand or remove his feet from the tub. He injected a tranquilizer into Howell's arm that would leave him asleep for at least four hours.

During the wait for the cement to set, he enjoyed the now-distant view of the shore. The pine trees made the coastline seem like a fuzzy green coat, and the sun glinted off the water.

X X X X X

Six hours passed, and the drug was beginning to wear off. Howell was groggy and semi-coherent. The concrete was fully set, and it was dark. The concrete had fully contracted and was painfully squeezing Howell's feet and lower legs, and he was whining and puling pathetically.

"Now since you are in great pain, I offer you a choice my parents weren't given. You may select how you die. I can toss you overboard alive, and you'll drown as you sink to the bottom of the pacific, or I will shoot you once in the temple before you go for your final swim. Your call. Choose quickly."

The sounds coming from Howell were not even words, just incoherent grunts and intakes of breath.

"Candy, I need your help for a moment. Mr. Howell hasn't enunciated clearly enough, but I believe he'll forego the bullet and just swim."

Candace and Alvy hoisted Vincent Howell over the side of the *Lucky Seafarer*. It took a good deal of effort, with the weight of the tub of concrete, but they had both been working out regularly.

They made a final heave, and he plummeted into the dark ocean.

Alvy gave Candace a passionate kiss, and they took the ship back to shore. Back on land, Alvy headed back north in the car, and Candace navigated the yacht back up the coast to its normal Seattle moorage. Candace ensured the yacht was hosed down and sparkling clean once back home. Alvy drove the rental car back after carefully washing the exterior and interior numerous times. He also destroyed the tape, tape player, and all other evidence.

X X X X X

A few weeks later, Candace and Alvy were making wedding plans. Candace called her boss, Captain Cletus Potts, to tell him about the wedding and to invite him. Potts told her to come down to the station because there was a matter they needed to discuss.

She wore her most professional suit and sat in front of the imposing captain and said, "Sir, I'm going to resign from the force. Alvy has asked me to marry him, and we won't need my salary. But we will be a frequent donor to the Policemen's Benevolent Association and other law enforcement charities."

Potts's deep, booming voice spoke clearly as he looked closely at Candace, "I'm sure you read in the paper that Vincent Howell is missing, and his empty car was located at a rest stop."

"Yes, sir. I know it's wrong to say, but I hope he's dead."

"No, you're right. The loss of his life is actually a bonus for society, but it is still a case I am supposed to solve. Not much evidence, looks like the perpetrator is a female. Have a look, see what you think. The rest stop had an old, poorly equipped video security system."

Potts inserts a scratchy videotape that showed a black Lincoln Navigator pull into the lot. A man exits and enters the restroom. Then from a separate vehicle, which was partially out of the camera's view, a female exited and pointed something at the man, and they entered into the vehicle that was obscured. It appeared that there was another occupant in the second vehicle.

"We've had the tape enhanced, analyzed, and even sent it to the FBI lab. A detailing shows the first vehicle is Howell's Navigator, and the driver is Howell. The second vehicle is probably a Cadillac, though it may be a Crown Victoria. The plate is completely obscured. The woman who points something at Howell is not readily identifiable, though body reactions make it a certainty that the object was a gun."

Potts explained that Howell had plenty of enemies, and many would have enjoyed him dead. Candace fingered her diamond promise ring that Alvy had given her three months ago, a platinum band with three diamonds. Potts rewound the videotape and stopped at a particular clicker spot he had preset. It showed a still shot of the woman with the gun.

It is too indistinct to tell much.

"You see in her gun-hand that glinting in the sunlight. She must have been wearing a diamond ring. Her gun hand is the left hand, so she probably is a leftie. You're left handed, Candace. So of course, if one was to rob or kill someone, they'd probably use their dominant hand. Right?"

Candace's palms were sweating, but she looked Potts straight in the eye.

"Yes, sir. I'm sure in virtually all handgun shootings; the perpetrator would utilize his strong hand."

Potts stood up to his full dominating height and said, "Well, I know the whole story of Howell and his background. No loss to society that he's dead. I won't have the department dedicate many man hours on this case. I pretty much think it will just be one more of Seattle PD's unsolved missing persons."

Potts walked around the desk and gave Candace a hug.

"We'll miss you around here, but you've got everything working your way. I expect some donations to some police charities from you rich folks, and I'll damn sure be at your wedding."

Candace walked out of the captain's office with a huge grin.

THE NEW WILD WEST

"I'd like a cold one, bartender."

Joanna, known as Jo, analyzed her thirsty patron. He was no cowboy, just a wannabe motorcycle type. His leather jacket and chaps were new and creaked when he moved. He also had the required leather bandana. Undoubtedly, a brand-new Harley was parked outside the bar and likely had less than a thousand miles on it. Probably was taken out only on weekends so he could ride from Scottsdale, Arizona, twenty miles up to the town of Cave Creek where Jo worked at one of a dozen bars with Old West–style themes.

The "biker" sat on a swiveling barstool and chugged his Miller Genuine Draft. Jo was a lifetime Cave Creek resident and had seen it transformed from a real Western mining and ranching area to a weekend tourist trap for the Phoenix, Scottsdale, and Paradise Valley rich. The old-time Creekers tolerated the city interlopers because they were the town's only source of revenue.

"Another brew, barmaid."

As Jo slapped down another beer, she thought of her job at Handle Bar Bill's, one of the town's dozen fake Western spots, with piano players and cowboy hats.

The bartenders said their "Yes sirs, and yes ma'ams"—all the while hawking overprized food, expensive beer, all to a backdrop of dancing girls, staged fights, and poorly played country music.

"Only two kinds of music here, pardner. Country and Western."

Jo was fifty-five years old and a historian of Cave Creek. She frequently went to the Cave Creek Museum and studied the region's history. It was a proud history of tough men and women on horseback, who eked out a living hunting, ranching, and panning for gold. The current breed of Creeker struggled for other financial reasons. Low-paying jobs, sweating to build mansions for California transplants, but despite the toil, they were unable to buy their own homes because housing costs were so high.

Jo was a tough and determined lady who had been an attractive cowgirl in her younger days. She could rope, hunt, fish, and was quite a dancer when she had the notion.

"How's about one more brewski, cutie?"

The leather-clad fake biker was beginning to wear on the one nerve she had left, but she laid his Miller Genuine Draft down with an overly broad smile. She would be finished with her shift in a half-hour, and then she went to her second job, where she led jeep trips out into the dessert.

She could keep her jeans and Western-style shirt and just throw on a duster and cowboy hat. The jeep trips were ridiculous: she would take a group out and stay in the desert overnight, where the city folk would eat steaks she grilled over a mesquite fire, accompanied by cowboy beans and corn on the cob. This was all done in Western costumes, and during the evening, she would tell tales of the old Cave Creek and when it was a real town and not the bastardization it was today. Then she made the tourists s'mores as they sat around a campfire.

There was always someone who would ask, "Do they really have coyotes out here?"

"Do the rattlesnakes bite?"

"How long does a saguaro cactus live?"

"Was that a deer in the desert?"

She had heard the questions so often the answers were a tape reel in her head,

"Of course we have coyotes, that's what you hear howling. Snakes bite if you startle them, but I brought an anti-venom kit, and I'm sure you all wore boots (most never did). A cactus lives a lot longer than you ever will. And of course, mule deer live in the dessert. What do you think that was you just saw, a big dog?"

As she was clearing the bar, Jo's replacement arrived, a large man of fifty, with shaggy gray hair. He was broad shouldered with a narrow waist and a sweeping and perfectly waxed moustache. This was Handle Bar Bill.

"Hey, Bill, just one customer now, he's drinking MGDs. I've got to take off; we're doing a desert tour tonight. It's out near Seven Springs."

The biker type perked up and said, "Well, hot damn, that is what I came here for. I'm one of the people going on the tour. My name is Julius. My friends call me Jules. I live down in Scottsdale. Never been on a jeep tour, and I'm looking forward to it. The desert, the sky, a few brews, awesome."

Before Jo could respond, Bill said, "Well, it will be nice to have you. We've got a full load tonight, so we'll be taking two jeeps. Jo will drive one, and I'm driving the second. I've got a back-up bartender to fill in for us here. We meet outside in ten minutes."

X X X X X

In addition to Bill, Jo, and Julius, eight other travelers joined the group. Two married couples from New York City, the men were investment bankers from Wall Street, and the women were obviously high-society types, one of which had a parasol to keep the sun off. The other four in the tour were male tourists from Japan. Fortunately, one of the Japanese spoke perfect English.

They piled into the jeeps, and as they started out, Jo laughed at the members of the pilgrimage. There were two old-time Creekers, a yuppie biker, four New York City preppies, and four Japanese with cameras around their necks.

They drove past Desert Mountain, the upscale community with Jack Nicklaus–designed golf courses; but no Creeker could live in "DM," where the minimum home costs two million, and every garage was filled with Porsches, Mercedes, and Humvees. Not that those Humvees ever went off-road like the jeep tour would.

They bumped along once off-road, and Handle Bar Bill spun tales of the Old West and displayed his shotgun and pistol.

"They are only used to kill snakes nowadays. But years back when Cave Creek was wilder, everyone carried a gun. They needed to."

The Japanese were furiously snapping pictures, and the one English speaker was translating Bill's tales of blood in the streets and gun battles. The New York investment bankers were complaining that their cell phones were out of their service areas.

"What, you don't even have roaming up here. We're still in the US."

One of the New Yorkers' wives was worse. "It's hot. I'm thirsty. The dust is all in my hair and eyes."

Bill was leading the brigade and sped up, knowing the ride would become bumpier and the dust would swirl more.

Less wealthy Cave Creek residents, like Jo and Bill, had begun to see a big change in the 1960s and 1970s. The older residents were displaced and relegated to working at tourist attractions and at the high-end eateries as waiters. All the while, the rich just bought more land and treated the original locals like desert dirt.

Julius, who had been awfully quiet, asked if they could stop for a minute. Jo said they were almost there, but Julius vomited a good portion of his Miller Genuine Draft out the open-sided jeep window. It was a bit breezy, and a small hunk of puke bounced off Miss New Yorker's parasol. To her credit, she just tossed the umbrella away from the jeep, checked her clothes, and when she found no stains, said nothing.

A few miles farther on, they stopped in a lovely glen, where a spring allowed greenery to flourish. They were hot and dusty. The Japanese clicked more photos, the New Yorkers sat in the shade, and Julius looked green and dehydrated under a mesquite tree.

Bill and Jo set up camp with a partial tent, brought out three coolers of ice, and started a fire for food. Jo came over to each guest and offered them water, sodas, beers, or wine. Everyone had some water, but after some rehydration, the New Yorkers drank wine, the Japanese accepted beers, and even Julius sipped on an MGD. After a hearty cowboy meal and more alcohol, Bill and Jo cleaned up, and then as the desert air chilled, everyone sat by the fire for coffee.

Jo spoke now because she is the historian. She described the hard life without air-conditioning, clean water, and vehicles; but she also emphasized the strength of the citizens and the beauty of the native lands as seen from horseback. Everyone was listening intently, but Julius began to get drunk again after switching to a flask he pulled from a pocket of his leather vest,

"It was not so tough back then. They still had bars, and using a gun is still a skill today. Cave Creek is no different than any other has-been, once-upon-a-time dump, like Tombstone. I need to take a piss."

Julius walks away in the dark to relieve himself, and the New York parasol lady says, "He's a distasteful man. He would have done poorly in harder times. My father grew up in Cheyenne, Wyoming, and he taught me to shoot and hunt. Even though I live in New York City, I have never forgotten the lessons from my father."

The one Japanese who spoke English said, "Our cultures are not all that far apart. Over one hundred years ago, Japan was very different. My great-grandfather was a samurai, a feudal member of the warrior class, and not terribly different than your gunslingers and sheriffs. I still have his sword as one of my most prized possessions."

It had been a long day, but everyone talked late while watching the starry night. Everyone talked except Julius. Not long after he returned from his restroom break, he passed out. The remainder of the group was glad for the silence.

As everyone was falling asleep, dreaming of samurai, gunslingers, or dancing girls, a heavy, dense, impenetrable fog passed through the glen. No one noticed, and all slept soundly by the campfire.

X X X X X

The morning dawned cold, and Jo made the entire group ham, sausage, and scrambled eggs. They had situated the tents and food away from the jeeps, which were over a small rise and out of view. Jo had left the morning coffee in Bill's vehicle, so she walked over the ridge to get it.

The jeeps were gone.

Jo went back to the campsite and expected to quietly tell Bill the bad news without the others hearing. She need not have bothered with discretion. Bill was physically restraining Julius and one of the Japanese men. Jo did not have to understand curse words in Japanese to realize a serious fight was breaking out.

The grandson of the samurai warrior attempted to translate in the midst of the argument.

"My friends' cameras are gone."

"Fuck your cheap Jap cameras. My Smith and Wesson .459 semi-auto handgun is stolen. So are all my money and the keys to my Harley."

While Bill tried to restore order, one New York banker started whining that their cell phones and their computers were also missing.

A final accounting showed a lot of things absent. Some of the stolen items were significant and valuable, others not.

Not a single person had a dollar, not a dime. Jo and Bill still had their pistols and rifles, but the brand-new semi-auto was gone. The women checked their purses. No identification, but lipstick and perfume remained. The men's wallets were the same: no identification, and just empty leather. They examined their camping items: blankets and clothing, but no neoprene tarps, and no all-weather gear. The Igloo ice chest was gone, and there were no beer, sodas, wine, or ice.

They had all stopped arguing because they were confused. Jo took the lead and said, "Let's pack what we can and carry it out to the location where we left the jeeps. If we find nothing there, I've got a canteen of water, and I'll hike back down the road and send help."

After walking back to the jeep area, stranger things had taken place. There were no jeeps, but there was transportation.

Eleven saddled horses, looking well-nourished and well watered, were tied to a wooden railing anchored into the desert ground. Each horse had saddlebags, and each saddle—except for one—was outfitted with a holster for a rifle. The rifles were pre-1900 models, and each had a large number of rounds. The saddles each had engraving in leather, identifying the owner: Joanna, Bill, Julius, Kevin, Sandra, Jill, Mike, and on three of the saddles, the writing was in Japanese characters. Obviously, these were the saddles for three of the Japanese travelers. Bill asked, "Why does the one horse have ringlets of armor, but no name tag?"

"Because I am to ride that animal, and a shotgun would be of little use to me. If you check on the left side, you will likely see a scabbard."

Inside the scabbard was a new and razor-sharp samurai sword. Emblazoned on the weapon was an inscription. The English-speaking Japanese explains, "The inscription, when translated, says, *I am the fire of Hausegawa.* My grandfather, the samurai, was Ihiro Hausegawa."

Everyone rapidly checked their own saddlebags, and while no one found other swords, each found items of importance.

There were cowboy hats, boot chaps, and spurs for those lacking them. For the ladies, there were denim jeans and blouses. Also in every female's bag, there was a fancy dress, corset, and hat for evening wear. Each and every saddle contained gold nuggets and currency from the 1900s in the amount worth perhaps five hundred dollars in that era.

X X X X X

After many questions, and few answers, all agree that they will change into horse-traveling clothes and ride back down to Cave Creek. The ride back is difficult, but the horses seem to know the way. They find water in a stream and allow the horses to rest briefly.

The couple from New York, Kevin and Sandra, whine continually.

"My back hurts."

"I cannot ride a horse."

Finally, Jill—the New Yorker with the family from Wyoming—says,

"Shut the fuck up. No one cares that your butt hurts. If we make it out of this alive, then complain. Otherwise, zip it."

Her husband, Mike, nods in silent agreement. Before his investment banking days, he had been a drill sergeant in the Marine Corps, and a sore ass was the least of his concerns. His behind would heal, but he did want some answers. He was also curious as to the actual date because he was a history buff.

They camp at nightfall and depart at first light the next morning. After another long ride filled with complaints, they crested over a rise and saw a smattering of dust and smoke. It must be Cave Creek.

It was Cave Creek—but it was Cave Creek 1900, not 2012. Somehow they had been transported back in time. The whiners no longer complained because they were much too frightened.

The residents of the town were surprised to see a group of eleven riding into town, especially with four Asians. But Chinese were building the railroads into the Western frontier, and the Cave Creek residents mistook the Japanese for Chinese laborers. While old Cave Creek was wild, it was not necessarily unfriendly, and prejudice was harbored mostly against blacks and maybe slightly against certain Indian tribes.

The local inn was also the tavern, and the cash and gold in their saddlebags made for something of a welcome. Each New York couple got a room, Jo and Bill bunked together, and the Japanese secured more limited lodging in the barn with the horses. It seemed Jules might have been out of luck, but the bartender offered him a room at her house, but at twice the price. As selfish as Jules was, he was too stunned to question the cost.

It was a Friday, so everyone cleaned up, and the women changed into their fancy clothes. It was rodeo days, so a big dance was scheduled.

It ended up as quite a party.

There was dancing, gambling, and a lot of drinking. Jules gambled and lost all his money and gold and got knocked unconscious when he grabbed the bartender's behind.

The bartender introduced herself to the newcomers as Tabitha, and she ensured their glasses were full. Except, of course, Jules—who she had laid out. He was sleeping it off in the corner. The New York couple, Sandra and Kevin, complained about the whiskey, but Mike and Jill seemed happy to drink and two-step the evening away. The Japanese remained quietly with the horses, except for Hausegawa. He joined the party, and everyone noticed the sword on his hip and provided him a wide berth.

× × × × ×

The evening had run late, and even following bar fights and drinking, no one seemed to be slowing down. Tabitha was handing out free drinks like there was no tomorrow. Perhaps there was not.

Tabitha took Bill and Jo aside, into a backroom away from the noise. "So did you have an interesting trip getting here?"

Bill and Jo looked at each other, uncertain of what to say, and so said nothing.

"The fog didn't scare you, did it? Actually, I really only wanted you, Jo, but my powers aren't quite that specific. If the other jeep hadn't come, I'd likely have only had a few extras and not a whole barn's worth of y'all."

Bill started to ask a question, but Tabitha interrupted and explained.

She was a witch, and she had taken the name Tabitha because she thought it was humorous, with *Bewitched* scheduled to air on television in a hundred years or so. She had moved west a hundred years before, came from Salem, Massachusetts. No reason to get burned at the stake. She explained that witches were not the all-powerful, celestial creatures mortals believed.

Powers must be utilized sparingly, and frugally, because each only had so much magic, though it varied from witch to witch, or warlock to warlock. There was also a consent or compatibility factor.

Bill spoke, "Tabitha, there's no doubt I believe you because I'm here, but could you try to summarize it, or I'm going to need a hell of a lot more whiskey."

Tabitha laughed, and the laugh was pleasant, but with an undercurrent of darkness.

"It's like this. Here is an ancient example. It would drain a tremendous amount of my magic, both white and black, to turn you two into toads. This is true because you're both nice people and not toad-like, and more importantly because neither of you desires to become a toad. Do you understand?"

Bill answered, "I do understand, but it is a little deep for me. As either bartender or witch, could you arrange another whiskey?"

Tabitha did not smile, but a bottle of whiskey and three shot glasses appeared on the table.

"I put it in an old-style bottle, but it's actually Seagram's 7 Crown American Whiskey from 2010."

All three clinked glasses, and it was Seagram's 7 Crown. The bottle emptied fast as Tabitha explained. The Japanese tourists were just a damn coincidence. What she wanted was to teleport forward to 2012 Cave Creek and replace Bill or Jo as bartender at Handle Bar Bill's. She could do it on her own, but the energy drain would be significant on her magic. Tabitha was aware that both Bill and Jo wanted a calmer, unhurried time in old Cave Creek, and this was really old Cave Creek.

Jo had always been attracted to Bill, and she knew the feeling was mutual, and she said, "Can we both stay and manage your bar here? And you can have both our 2012 jobs."

"Of course, you can both remain, and I'll leave you the bar and plenty of money to run it, but what about your companions, particularly that asshole Jules? It will cause a much-decreased power drain to me if I accede to their desires, but I use minimal power if those who want to stay stay, and if those who want to return to your time, return."

Unexpectedly there was gunfire and loud words in the street. A drunken cowboy was firing revolver rounds at Hausegawa's feet.

"Well, hop like a frog, you fucking slant-eyed bastard. Go build a railroad somewhere else."

This time the cowpoke shot Hausegawa in the leg and cocked and aimed the gun toward his head. Like a magician, Hausegawa drew his sword from its scabbard and thrust the blade into his adversary's chest. He spun just as quickly and withdrew the blade, holding it beneath his armpit. Then, making one final turn back to face the cowboy, he swung quickly and severed his head, which fell onto the dirt.

Everyone was watching, and this included Hausegawa's companions from Japan who had left the barn, Tabitha, Jules who had awoken from his drunkenness, the New Yorkers, and the entire town of old Cave Creek.

The townspeople's first inclination was to "Kill the Chinaman!" But explanations quickly showed it was self-defense, and damn talented self-protection at that.

The town's hierarchy, which included Tabitha, made the call. Hausegawa and his friends would live, but they must leave Cave Creek by nightfall. The white visitors were free to stay as long as they desired.

Bill, Jo, and Tabitha quickly gathered all the new-millennium visitors and explained the entire story about witches, time travel, fog, and current options. They had all gone through it, and so it did not seem fake or surreal. Each person's options were simple—stay or return to their own time. Bill and Jo were excited to remain, but they were surprised at some of the others' requests.

Obviously, Tabitha would travel to the future Cave Creek. She admitted she wanted a trip to Los Angeles so she could do some surfing.

The stuffy New Yorkers, Kevin and Sandra wanted back to present times ASAP.

"Hey, I've got millions of dollars in a convertible debenture deal ongoing," Kevin added.

Mike and Jill, the more open-minded New Yorkers, had a better idea, and Jill spoke, "We'd like to stay in this time, and Mike knows the West Coast. Gold rush is coming. We believe we'll buy a little land."

Tabitha smiled at their ingenuity and suggested a few particular acres that might prove very lucrative.

The Japanese businessmen just wanted back to the future and their cameras back. That is, with the exception of Hausegawa.

"If it is not too much trouble, Ms. Tabitha, I would like to stay in this time but return to my homeland of Japan so that I might be trained more completely in the way of Zen and the samurai."

Tabitha responded and said that he had showed great bravery in the battle of gun versus sword and deserved to return to Japan.

It was not exactly a *poof* but more like a cyclonic *whoosh*, and Hausegawa vanished. But just before his image faded completely, all saw a shadowy image of him in chain mail armor and full samurai regalia.

Finally, Julius spoke, "Well, I'm not staying here in this time zone, but while you're granting wishes, how about a new, better Harley when I get back? I'll give you a ride, and we could have dinner."

Tabitha looked disgusted. "Your bike will be there, but sorry, I rarely date mortals."

A sound like thunder exploded in the sky. No fog this time—just dense black smoke.

XXXXX

The three Japanese men were back at the Scottsdale Princess, with their cameras still slung around their necks. They flew to Seattle and then to Tokyo the next day.

Tabitha spent a few weeks surfing in Malibu and then returned to Cave Creek. The bar was just like before, and her name as owner was on the wall, but she got a surprise too. The bar had been renamed, and a plaque stood at the entrance.

> *"This establishment—formerly known as Handle Bar Bill's—is renamed on this date of October 31st, 1894, Halloween Day, as Tabitha's Hideaway."*

Tabitha enjoyed her new place and the clientele. Sure, some of the regulars were cocky and rich snobs, but they knew she lived in a nicer mansion than they did. She lived at Desert Mountain, so no one gave her a hard time. She had a view overlooking the Cochise course, and she and her cat "Familiar" watched the golfers shank it around.

One afternoon, she went to the Cave Creek Museum and saw the old photos. One in particular was nice: it showed a group in front of Handle Bar Bill's in March of 1894. When she looked closely, she could see Bill with his arms around Joanna.

As she walked back to her bar, Tabitha passed a newspaper bin containing the local rag, the *Cave Creek Sentinel*.

An article read: *"A Scottsdale man was killed yesterday in Cave Creek. The man, Julius Lutz, inexplicably veered in front of oncoming traffic and was struck by a semi-truck. Lutz was operating a new Harley Davidson Roadster, and the Maricopa County Sheriff's office believes he may have been unfamiliar with the motorcycle's operation."*

Tabitha smiled and laughed a deep, hearty laugh.

THE LORD IS MY SHEPHERD, I SHALL NOT WANT

It is the year 3432, under the old earth calendar, and Captain Jonathan Orlando Buenaventura is overheated, tired, thirsty, and a bit scared.

He emergency evac landed two days ago on this godforsaken asteroid, which orbits its sun, Delta Califa. His copilot, David Andreesen, had been killed in the crash. When he had checked David for vital signs, he had found none, and he also felt along the spine, which had wash-boarded, indicating multiple spinal fractures. It was good he died during the crash. Jonathan had morbidly wondered if David Andreesen's middle name might have begun with an O, like his own. Appropriate, because the copilot was clearly DOA—dead on arrival.

As Jonathan created dusty cloud-spewing footprints on the asteroid's seemingly never-ending plateau, he adjusted his air supply. He had two full days of air remaining, but his ship was no longer able to produce oxygen due to the crash. In fact, the ill-fated *Leviathan* would never fly again, nor could she produce edible nutrients or communicate with earth or even the closer human outposts. Basically, unless Jonathan found water, he would be a dead man on a dead world.

Help would never arrive if his final distress call had gone unheard, and even if outpost Alpha Zeta Seven received the wavelength communiqué, a rescue ship could not arrive for two months. All the while, Jonathan would never know.

The only good news was that a scan of the planet showed what appeared to be water, twelve kilometers away, over a low rise of mountains. The temperature on the planet was 118 degrees Fahrenheit, so if the liquid was water, Jonathan had the equipment to break apart the H_2O into hydrogen and oxygen. The oxygen could then keep him breathing.

Food was no problem; the pack he was hoisting had enough MREs for three months. That was long enough for the rescue ship to arrive—if it did.

Jonathan liked MREs—or "meals ready to eat" in nonmilitary, non-spaceflight parlance. MREs had been available since World War II in 1939. The food itself had not changed much in 1,500 years, though astronauts now had a device in their sealed suits that allowed them to eat by placing the food in an external pouch. The pouch then sealed inside the suit, a few buttons were pushed, and Jonathan was munching on half-decent turkey with cranberry sauce.

Jonathan reached the "lake." It was little more than a muddy three-inch-deep sinkhole, but it was water. He hooked up the analyzer and determined that—while tainted with zinc, arsenic, and lead—the primary ingredient in the sludge was water, H_2O. His oxygenator and purification devices could turn this cesspool into breathable oxygen and potable water. A quick glance at the size of the lake confirmed it would produce sufficient life-giving oxygen for at least six months. He had food, water, and a panoramic view of Lake Slime. What more could any good man ask for?

"Hopefully, a goddamned rescue ship in two months," he spoke aloud.

After he had set up all his equipment, he erected a tent shelter and lay down to sleep on his cot. There was no night or darkness on the asteroid, so he flipped down his darkest visor and tried to sleep, but he had an uneasy feeling as he eased into slumber.

He dreamed of a black-cloaked figure with horns like a big-horned sheep. Except these horns were longer, steel-tipped, and red; and they sprung directly from the thing's head. It was not a person; it was a demon, with black eyes and talons for hands. The creature moved closer, and his breath smelled sulfurous, and there was great heat coming from its body. Jonathan thought he glimpsed a pointed tail and cloven hooves.

He awoke screaming, and after he settled down for an instant, he realized his body was itching everywhere, and it felt as if his skin were burning off in chunks.

Jonathan was experiencing full-blown agony. Due to some goddamned technical glitch, his purification equipment had inadequately purified the water from Slime Lake. It was a certainty that the air he was inhaling and the water he was sipping were tainted by some plague his equipment could not adequately adapt to. Every instinct told him to tear away his flight suit and claw at the itching fire that held his entire body prisoner.

His rationality was still in control, and he knew this would be immediate, excruciating death because of the poisonous atmosphere.

He had brought a small medical kit with him to the swamp, but there was a more complete medical mobile infirmary unit back at the *Leviathan*. Perhaps medicines at the ship could relieve some of the discomfort and symptoms and might even provide a cure. The hike back to the ship was hell.

His skin was beginning to rise into open sores and boils. The sores themselves gradually became pus-filled sacs, and as the suit invariably rubbed these spots, the boils broke open. They seeped fluid, which itself seemed to be an allergic irritant. His suit gradually filled with pinkish blood-tinged body discharge. He felt like the Michelin man with a suit filled with acid rather than helium. Blessedly, the suit did have a purge feature. Without letting atmosphere inside, the internal air and waste could be forcibly expelled via a suction/discharge system.

Jonathan activated the extraction system and watched in disgust as greenish-red fluid ejected from the exit port. He vomited in his helmet as almost two gallons of vile, putrid liquid spewed from the port. After a few moments, he reactivated the system to rid his suit of his own disgorged bile and puke. He hated to even imagine how his body appeared without the protective space suit.

As an astronaut, he understood that death on far-flung worlds was a distinct possibility. In egotistical moments, he imagined his death during a pitched weapon battle with a far stronger creature. Or better, a hand-to-hand struggle with multiple aliens, where he ensured two or three monsters died and headed straight to their own hell even though his life was sacrificed in the cause. More realistically, he knew death would likely be due to a technical equipment malfunction that caused his spacecraft to fireball into a volatile, unstable atmosphere.

Never in his wildest nightmares had he envisioned himself rotting away alone on an uninhabited world, with his flesh sloughing away like a rotting toadstool. The affliction had not affected his mind or his vision; his eyes itched like every other portion of his body, but he could see perfectly.

Exertion tired him quickly, but the basic skeletal and muscle systems were largely operational. It originally had taken him ten hours to travel from his ship to the lake of slime, which he had now renamed Loch Ness. Now he was the Loch Ness monster. Due to weakness and the frequent purges of discharge from his suit, the trip back to the ship took over three days.

He entered the still-smoldering hulk of the *Leviathan* and immediately headed for the room in the ship dedicated to triage. The room had been designed as an area to treat injured victims and determine the priorities for action in extreme emergencies. Jonathan knew he was going to the head of the triage line, and any possible curative drugs would be tried. He injected himself with antitoxin, antioxidant, anti-everything. He also utilized every oral medication that might even conceivably diminish the itching. As he scoured the room for useful medications, he saw a thick dark-blue bound book hidden behind the drugs, syringes, pills, and potions. The copilot had been the medical expert, but since he was dead, he was of little use. Still, perhaps the medical book would describe his current condition in a manner a layman like Jonathan could comprehend.

He tugged on the book and examined the cover. What did it say?
Cures for Alien Infection?
Palliatives for Contamination?
Solutions to Viral Plague?
Hell no! It was his deceased comrade's personally inscribed Holy Bible. Jonathan opened the book to its first page, an inscription in gold leaf.

This

Holy Bible

is presented to

David Andreesen

*By Karen Andreessen,
your loving wife, on the
day of our marriage,
November 16, 3429.*

Love eternal.

Jonathan nearly lost his temper. A damned Bible—he needed medical information. Why would a medical man waste ship space with a Bible? The spot could be used for medicine or, at least, a medical encyclopedia.

Jonathan began to calm down through his discomfort and anger.

He remembered David Andreesen—a quiet, unassuming man. He did not wear his religion on his sleeve, but Andreesen was a believer. Jonathan had attended his wedding. It had been a moving traditional ceremony, and it was the first, and only, Christian wedding Jonathan had seen.

Long before the dawn of the third millennium, most of the major religions had diminished in size, score, and form. There were still small groups of the devout, mostly seen by many as zealots or—at a minimum—unnecessary. Still, there were core adherents to Islam, Buddhism, Christianity, Judaism, and other faiths.

Andreesen had been a Christian. If Jonathan remembered correctly, David and his wife Karen had been what were termed Catlics, *Chatholicks* or *Katholicks*. No, no—the terminology had been *Catholic*, Jonathan was certain. He hoped their faith would give David's wife Karen some peace after she learned of her husband's death on this lonely asteroid orbiting Delta Califa.

Jonathan casually tossed the Bible on the *Leviathan's* deck. He did not look down, but the Bible fell open to page 443, the Book of Job.

Jonathan examined the remainder of the spacecraft, placed all the medication in a large pack, and prepared to trudge back to Loch Ness. He took one final look about the cabin to ensure he had forgotten nothing, and he observed the Bible and folded it into his rear suit pocket. Hell, he would need something to read, especially if there was no rescue ship.

He began the slog back to the lake.

X X X X X

The way back was arduous, and he began to experience chills, fever, and headaches. He was exhausted once back at the "pristine" shores of Loch Ness. He unshouldered his pack, and it slipped and knocked him off balance. He fell heavily on his right wrist and heard an explosive crack.

"Oh, that's just goddamn beautiful. Jesus Christ, I'm on an asteroid hell, and now I've got a broken arm!" Jonathan screamed to a barren landscape.

He moved his arm and realized it was not broken or even twisted. A close examination of the wrist disclosed healthy movement but a shattered, supposedly indestructible government-issued watch. It was much more than a "watch."

It contained homing beacons, range-finding capability, and even a minute laser capable of slicing steel plate. Destroyed beyond any repair, typical of the shit they gave the space program. It was probably worth thousands of selenium credits at any pawnshop, but now it was useless. He was unfamiliar with the special constellations in this region of the Felis-Dromegan quadrant, so he was now incapable of accurately gauging the passage of time. What did it matter, anyway? Either rescuers came, or they did not. Jonathan fell asleep.

He dreamed again of the black-cloaked figure with red steel-tipped horns. The creature beckoned with a casual wave.

"Follow me to your correct path," the creature hissed.

Jonathan could see himself in his own dream. He was naked, covered in painful blisters and scars, and bleeding from various wounds on his wrists and legs. He begged the creature to free him, and the beast merely responded, "Free thyself!"

Jonathan awoke to the blisters, sores, and pain. He again drained the loathsome fluid from his suit. He was bored, so he removed the Bible from his pocket and read.

> "There was a man in the land of Uz, whose name was Job, and that man was blameless and upright, one who feared God, and turned away from evil..."

> "So Satan went forth from the presence of the Lord and afflicted Job with loathsome sores from the sole of his foot to the crown of his head..."

> "Why is light given to him that is in misery,
>   and life to the bitter in soul,
>   who long for death, but it comes not,
>   and dig for it more than for hid treasures;
>   who rejoice exceedingly,
>   and are glad, when they find the grave?
>   Why is light given to a man whose
>   way is hid,
>   whom has God hedged in?
>   for my sighing comes as my bread,
>   and my groanings are poured out
>   like water.

> For the thing that I fear comes upon me,
>   and what dread befalls me.
> I am not at ease, nor am I quiet;
>   I have no rest; but trouble comes . . .
>
> For the company of the godless is barren,
> and fire consumes their tents.
> They conceive mischief and bring forth evil,
> and their heart prepares deceit . . ."

Jonathan was interested in the troubles of Job. Jonathan had many days to read and study the Bible, and he came to understand some of the words as a signpost. Not to be taken literally but to be interpreted with a kindly spirit. He read the Bible constantly, and his soul was uplifted. His loneliness did not dissipate or leave entirely, but it did ease. His purification system must have been working more effectively now because the blisters diminished, and he found himself walking for the pleasure of it. He was stronger, and his heart lighter.

Every moment, he read the Bible. The pages were becoming worn, and every word he studied. He read the old books of Genesis, Exodus, Deuteronomy, and Ezekiel through to the new words of Matthew, Mark, John, and Revelation. He felt strength in the words, and that transferred to his own health. One day when Loch Ness was almost dry, it rained. It was pure, clean rain from a cloudless sky. But that was not possible; the asteroid's atmosphere was incompatible with such a storm. The previous water contained in Loch Ness likely seeped up from a long-held internal water core, but rain—that was impossible.

Jonathan was most enthralled with the Book of Job and his plight and subsequent resurrection. He read the chapter endlessly, thousands of times. Somewhere inside, he understood that a rescue ship would never arrive. His watch was gone, but much more than two or three months had elapsed. It did not matter; he was content with the words he had found. He was healthy and restored.

X X X X X

For a long time, Jonathan continued his studies in peace. One day, as he sits cross-legged at Loch Ness—which has strangely become a three-square-mile lake of crystalline, azure water—he hears the sound of an antigravity whirr from a landing system. For an instant, he imagines trumpets and angels; but it is only a mining ship, which scanned the asteroid and saw the water. The crew's astonishment is complete when Jonathan waves them a friendly welcome.

Soon he is on board with his flight suit removed, breathing without a helmet, and sipping a warm orange tea with a hint of mint. The captain of the mining ship remarks on Jonathan's miraculous health, vitality, and youthful appearance.

"It was lonely, but my faith helped me through. I am glad to be back with people. I'm certain things may have changed since I left, and I am curious as to the date since my chronometer is broken, and I never could tell time in this sector by the stars."

"It is the year 3637 under the old earth calendar. When did your ship arrive on the asteroid?"

"Quite a long while ago, captain. I am not certain of the exact year."

Jonathan was certain that they would have considered him insane if he admitted he arrived 205 years ago. He still had a long way to reach the biblical patriarch Methuselah, who lived to the age of 969. Jonathan silently contemplated his good fortune and thanked his god. He remembered the final lines in the Book of Job. While the quotation was not verbatim, the wording in his mind was clear:

And the Lord restored the fortunes of Job, and the Lord gave Job twice as much as he had had before. Then came to him all his sisters and brothers, and all who had known him before, and they ate bread with him, and comforted him for all the evil that had been brought upon him. And the Lord blessed the latter days of Job more than his beginning. And after Job lived a hundred and forty years, and saw his sons, and his son's son's, four generations. And Job died an old man, full of days.

G-STRING

Janet Columbo was a titty dancer. She preferred terminology such as *exotic topless dancer*, but *tit* was not a word she found offensive. Hell, she had paid a plastic surgeon two months of her income for her rack, and she believed they looked outstanding. They were full and firm, with slightly upturned nipples. They looked real, not the extra-oversized models the younger gals were buying these days.

With the exception of her chest, she was petite, with a slender waist and long wavy brunette hair. Actually, she was not completely sure what her real hair color would have been. The colorings had been many—from blond to jet black to red with curls. She even dyed it greenish during a punk phase she passed through. That, fortunately, passed rapidly. There were hints of grayish streaks recently, so she tinted often because gray stands out strongly, and negatively, under the black lights of any dancing establishment. Hanging upside down on a trapeze bar or spinning on a pole furthered the perception of hair discoloration, though she doubted customers took much note of her hair.

She lived in a cool loft in a funky section of Greenwich Village in New York. She loved the cafes, music, nightclubs, and energy of the place. It was also near her exotic dance club and her other side business.

Janet also worked as a somewhat-high-end call girl or prostitute. For this business, her partner—actually, her pimp—had an extremely tiny apartment where she turned tricks. The pimp leased the apartment, and she received a message by beeper when a paying customer was scheduled. She generally only did repeat clientele, and her pimp was careful not to schedule criminal lowlifes or weirdo psychopaths.

Claudio was her pimp. He was a reed-thin piece of sinew, topped by his ever-present fedora. Old-timers would have called him a sugar pimp. Claudio would have never hit, slapped, or even maliciously bumped into Janet. Janet probably could have whipped his ass if she needed to, but Claudio did his job and brought her quality johns. The oddest quirk about Claudio was his accent, not his looks. He was a black Jersey dude that looked like Snoop Dogg complete with the hat and feather, but he spoke King's English.

"Pardon me, perhaps you have the precise time of day."

She always expected him to add something even more ridiculous.

"Have we missed high tea, my dearest? I just love scones."

Actually, Claudio would not understand the difference between a scone and a stone, but it did sound like something he might say. Claudio had always been straight with Janet, and they both made a good profit, regardless of how strange he was. She was scheduled to meet him at a corner pub in fifteen minutes.

As she walked down one of the winding Greenwich Village streets, she began laughing uncontrollably, but since it was New York City, no one gave her a passing glance. Under her breath, she was giggling and muttering in her best British accent, *"I'm on schedule, my dahling Claudio. Kiss, kiss. See you ever so shortly."*

She entered the nouveau lounge and observed Claudio at the bar sipping a martini. He wore a black hat with a large pink feather and matching black cane with a pink tip. Janet thought Claudio looked like a cartoon caricature of a 1960s pimp, but it was the new millennium, and obviously he was as proud as a preening peacock. Janet sat down, kissed him on the cheek, and ordered an Amstel Light.

Claudio tipped his hat and said, "Shakespeare wrote in *Antony and Cleopatra*, 'To business that we love we rise betimes, and go to it with delight.'"

"That sounds good to me, you Don Juan. What did you need to see me for?"

"Such swift words. Take time and relax, Janet."

"Cut the bullshit."

"An old client of yours has reemerged and requested use of your charming services. A man named Monsieur Kevin Winthrop."

Janet's widening eyes failed to conceal her interest and excitement.

"When does he want to see me?"

"Tomorrow at 6:30 PM, and he has requested your services for the entire evening. Paid in advance, I might add."

"I will be waiting with bells on, or maybe a single bell around my neck. Perhaps nothing at all."

Claudio gave her five hundred dollars in cash, and she moved to exit. She is amazed at how pompous he can get and would love showing that some of her own prowess above the neck extended to more than just giving a blow job.

He touches his right hand, kissed his fingertips, and blew her a farewell kiss. She walked out the door.

Claudio was unaware that Janet graduated from Slippery Rock State Teachers College and understood more Shakespeare than Claudio would read in a lifetime. An excellent catchphrase for Claudio might be from *Macbeth*: "A walking shadow, a poor player that struts and frets his hour upon the stage, and then is heard no more."

She has the next two nights off from the dance club. She had one night to unwind and then an evening with Kevin Winthrop. Of all the customers she had ever known and serviced, Kevin was the most sincere. She wondered why he had not come to see her in almost seven years.

X X X X X

Janet returned to her loft in Greenwich. She curled into a ball on her eight-foot-high jester chair.

She had designed it herself. It was satin material, with two-inch-wide vertical stripes alternating between gold and maroon. The arms and back were so high she looked like Alice in Wonderland when she had eaten from the become-small side of the mushroom. The two other chairs in the room were of a similar material, but only gold in color. These chairs were shaped like women's high-heeled shoes. The spike of the heel and the sole of the shoe rested on the ground, and the chair's back was where Alice, in her large form, might have placed her Dr. Scholl's arch supports. The shoe chairs were comfortable, but the jester chair was Janet's relaxation central.

Janet arose and went into the tiny kitchen, which she had redone completely in stainless steel appliances and black granite countertops. As small as the kitchen was, it did feel like the entrance to a rabbit hole.

She loved good wine and had a collection that even snobby oenophiles would envy. There were perks to working in a cash business like fucking for money. No traveler's checks, no debit cards—just crisp Ben Franklins. Janet had a contact for wines in the SoHo district, and since she paid in cash, Luigi, the owner, gave her bargains on items going out of stock. She opened an Australian Penfolds Shiraz and poured it into a decanter to breathe.

A button was pushed, and a crystal clear re-mastered version of Frank Sinatra's "The Lady Is a Tramp" crooned through hidden speakers. Janet smiled at the song choice and poured some wine from the decanter into a tall-stemmed wineglass. The wine was smooth but substantial, and she returned to her chair and set the decanter on a triangular black-slate table. She relaxed and finished another two glasses of wine. The wine and the mood made it clear that she would spend the remainder of the evening thinking of Kevin Winthrop. In that region between consciousness and slumber that young Alice found so strange, Janet located both distinct and blurred remembrance of her Kevin.

Janet had met Kevin nine years ago, shortly after she came to New York. Before her arrival in New York, she had endured two years of instructing brat-like monster fourth graders in Des Moines, Iowa, after graduating from Slippery Rock. It had been clear from the second week; she was not cut out to be a teacher. Following the spring of her second year, she sold all her belongings and moved to the big city. She stayed in some dump apartment and started dancing at a moderately sleazy topless joint. She liked it. Her path had wound from a dead-end teaching job in Nowheresville to shaking her assets and moving up the New York feeding chain.

She had met Kevin at a beer joint one block down from the topless dance club. She had been winding down with a glass of wine after work, and he was drinking soda water. No one at that alcoholic dump ever ordered a soda, so she discreetly watched him.

His suit was a quality wool blend, black with charcoal pinstripes. She had learned to study a man's clothes to estimate net worth and, even more so, emphasize his shoes. Any cheap loser could have one decent suit, but this man's suit was accompanied by a white silk shirt, diamond cuff links, and a solid black silk tie. It was more than a decent suit; it was double breasted and either Giorgio Armani or hand-tailored. She was not sure she needed to consider his shoes, but she did, anyway. A smile curled just at the very corners of her painted lips.

He was wearing cowboy boots: hand-stitched black elephant-hide cowboy boots. They were likely worth over a thousand dollars. Since she knew his monetary potential, she decided it was worthy of her time to look at the rest of the cowboy businessman.

She looked at his face and was surprised that he was not even glancing her way. They were both facing the mirror behind the bar, and his look was intense but had no specific purpose. He looked back directly into his own eyes, appearing to see into himself. Janet could not help but be annoyed. People paid money to see her, and here was some country rube with a free chance to look, and perhaps catch conversation, and all he did was stare at his own stone face. Sometime during her slightly pouty disappointment, she looked more closely at her city cowboy.

"Handsome" is an amorphous and slippery term. To one person, it described high cheekbones, chiseled features, or an aquiline nose. Janet found Kevin handsome in a strong, masculine, earthy way. He was over six feet tall, with a body that has been built by sweat. He might have money, but this was not a man who paid for manicures. Even clothed by the three-thousand-dollar suit, his hulking muscular frame was on display. His face matched his body: a strong jaw that jutted below deep, sunken eyes that were blacker than brown. His most pronounced features were his hands. They were huge and heavily calloused. The palms were worn down, and the natural lines almost eroded away as if he sandpapered them into oblivion. The back of his hands were interspersed with cords of veins that merged into two or three rope-thick tunnels as they entered beneath his long tailored sleeves. His wrists were as large as the barrel end of a baseball bat. One wrist was partially concealed by his watch, an antique gold Pulsar. The clunky watch had been the first digital display ever made; its worth as a collector's item was invaluable. He noticed her looking at his watch.

"My uncle bequeathed me this watch in his will. It is one of my most prized and sentimental items."

His voice was deep and resonant, like the bass singer in a church choir. She was startled that he had spoken to her after such an extended period of silence.

"I'm Janet," was the only comment she could stammer in response.

Kevin extended his oversized paw and lightly shook her hand.

"My name is Kevin. It is a pleasure to meet you. I would have spoken to you sooner, but I believed you might desire your privacy."

Usually, Janet craved and savored every instant of private time, but she was intrigued by this man, and she anxiously awaited where their conversation—or anything else—might lead.

As Janet fondly remembered her initial meeting with Kevin, she realized she had finished her decanter of Shiraz. She was enjoying the reminiscence, so she opened another bottle and poured directly into her glass without using the decanter. She got comfy in her chair.

Their relationship had been an unusual one. Despite the immediate sexual tension between them, things started at a glacial pace for good reasons. She was making terrible money, dancing at the Kit Kat Club, and had soon thereafter met the strange humanoid known as Claudio Jones—also known as Claud Jackson, AKA Cletus Smith and other numerous aliases. Claudio had convinced Janet he could set her up dancing at a better "gentleman's establishment." She only had to do some side work for him.

The side work was that she would make good coin to fuck some of the clientele, as well as others Claudio would introduce. Janet had been low on cash, so she agreed to the deal and soon was making great money. She had rationalized it away easily.

Everybody fucked for money. Hell, the president of the United States fucked his citizens routinely, and he was paid handsomely and received a permanent pension. During their initial meetings, she explained the situation to Kevin.

"I'm careful, I am getting repeat clientele. No sex without condoms. I'm cool with it."

Kevin agreed and said that he understood that there are times when tough decisions have to be made for the good of all. Janet wanted out eventually and had tried other things, but now, this was her only ticket to freedom. She explained that she had done some porn flicks under the name Twyla Light, and she was proud of the movies. In one that never received approval, she was to have shared some scenes with Linda Blair, she of exorcist fame and the person who uttered arguably the most famous line in all filmdom: "Your mother sucks cocks in hell."

But Blair's handlers merely had her pose in some slutty magazine, and the movie deal fell through. Oh well, stardom is fleeting at best.

Kevin said he would like to see her and cared nothing about her past. He explained he had some history of his own, and burdens followed him as well.

He had been born and raised in Tulsa, Oklahoma, and played two years of college football for the Oklahoma State Cowboys. There had been a wild party, and a teammate was raping some townie teenager. Kevin had stepped in to stop it, and a teammate confronted him. Kevin threw him through a plate glass door. Somehow, a long glass shard punctured through the punk's eye and into his brain. Punk had died on the spot, and a local prosecutor that wanted to make a name for her charged Kevin with second-degree murder. She alleged there had been an exchange of threats between the two before the brawl. Kevin's mom and dad were poor corn farmers, so a good lawyer was impossible, and the public defender was completely incompetent. Because the charge was based on the fact that Kevin had just been involved in the felonious rape of the young girl, the case fell under the felony murder doctrine. This, even though the girl herself said Kevin was only trying to help her.

Kevin told Janet that his trial only took three days, and he was found guilty and sentenced to the state penitentiary outside Oklahoma City for ten years minimum.

His family sold the farm and hired a real lawyer and appealed. Two years later, he was released. The only good from the story was the prosecutor was subsequently disbarred for attempting to induce false testimony from the teen.

Both Kevin's parents had died while he was in prison. Janet asked him what he had done then.

"I tried to get work anywhere. Finally, got a job working a corn farm in Kansas. That's why my hands are like this. I made enough money to reenroll back at Oklahoma State. Could have gone anywhere to complete my degree, but I went back to prove I did nothing wrong. I graduated with honors. Later, I got an MBA. Then I came to New York to make my fortune—just like you."

They both admitted they had two interesting tales and started a friendship and relationship that lasted nearly two years. Every time he asked her out, he brought a flower. He brought a purple iris, a tulip, a rose—anything that highlighted Janet's beauty. Early on, he also made two prerequisites on their relationship.

He had become a successful banker, with an investment boutique that handled mergers and acquisition work of smaller capitalized businesses. Kevin received a small share of the company. He was not truly wealthy, but he was on the correct career track. Because of this, and wherever the relationship went, Kevin would pay Janet two thousand dollars per evening. She tried to demur, but he refused—it was a done deal. He would always pay.

Kevin's second issue was a more personal one.

"When I lived in Oklahoma, I married a young woman named Elise. She came with me to New York City. I only see her rarely and briefly now."

A slight tremor entered into Kevin's voice as he spoke of Elise. "She was—she is—a beautiful lady, but..."

For the only time in their days together, Kevin looked down and away from Janet's eyes. He paused and regained his composure.

"She was raped and assaulted outside Central Park. He shot her once in the head with a small-caliber revolver."

Now his eyes had filled with tears, and he broke down and sobbed. His shoulders heaved with the weight of the internal pain. He looked away from Janet again, and when he looked back, she was surprised to see hatred behind the tears.

"They never caught him, the DNA and physical evidence matched no known rapists. I spend two fucking years in maximum security for something in self-defense, and some evil soul in New York never spends an hour in custody."

Janet tried to comfort him, but appropriate words were hard to find, and her mouth was gritty and dry. No red wine would have helped her words that day. He had continued on and finished and explained that she had immediately entered a coma from her injuries. The brain damage was permanent and irreversible, but her Catholic family had demanded that every effort be made to save her. Some legal wrangling had gone back and forth, but eventually, she was maintained in a vegetative state on a respirator. Kevin visited her in Saint Mary's Hospital once every week. There was never any change. A blank stare or closed eyes and the intermittent sound of the respirator inserted permanently through Elise's trachea. When Kevin finished his story, he clenched his fists, and the muscles in his neck and forearms stood out.

Only once in two years of their money-exchange, flowers, and sex relationship had Kevin ever again spoken of Elise: after over a year between them, and following a sexual liaison that would have made gymnastic teams proud, Kevin said, "I'm not a well-spoken man, but I am falling in love with you, Janet. You are everything I have ever wanted. You are a caring person with beauty, class, but no pretenses. I would ask you to marry me, but Elise is still alive in the slightest sense. While she is in that state, I could never ask you."

From any other man, client, john, or trick, she would have been either insulted or amused. She was a prostitute and a part-time dancer.

"No one weds their whore, Kevin."

"You're not my whore, nor anyone else's. You're a lady that has taken one route that was an opportunity for you. No different than I have."

After that moment, their relationship grew close. It was not just sex. They attended Broadway shows—she particularly enjoyed The Lion King, he The Phantom of the Opera. They had intimate dinners at small out-of-the-way spots from Chinatown to Little Italy to Harlem. By this time, she had leased her loft in Greenwich, and he was the only customer ever allowed to be with her there. He was the one who selected, and purchased for her, the jester chair on a Valentine's Day. They would lie in her bed—a lace-canopied four-poster style—and talk, hold each other, and enjoy their moments alone. They shared their innermost secrets and disappointments.

Janet had nearly finished the second bottle of wine. Thinking of Kevin made her happy and wispy at the same instant. Yet as the glow of the past faded, she grew dark as she recalled the day seven years ago when Kevin disappeared.

Like a warm passionate storm, her lover and only friend was gone. In the jester chair one moment, then a wash of winter wind and complete disappearance. No good-bye . . . nothing. She had tried his apartment, his business, every nightclub and bar.

She had considered calling the police, but prostitutes do not call cops. No trace. She assumed he had been killed, except that a call to Saint Mary's Hospital disclosed that there was no longer a woman in intensive care with any name even similar to Elise Winthrop.

Where had Kevin been for seven years? Her Siamese cat that she overfed constantly curled up in her lap, purred, and contemplated Janet with slanted blue eyes. "Siamese, if you please." She fell asleep and dreamt of Yul Brynner as the king of Siam.

X X X X X

The next morning, the phone rang loudly. She was still sleeping in the chair, and her cat was napping on one of the shoe chairs. Groggily, she answered hello. It was her investment banker, Charles Schwab.

"Ms. Columbo, it's Carl from Charles Schwab. Both of your treasury bonds and your tax-exempt municipal bonds should be rolled over and sent to your money market fund."

A long and boring discussion ensued, where Carl suggested various allocation options for her portfolio, which now totaled almost two million dollars. She was a basic conservative investor: one-third stock funds, one-third tax-free municipals, and one-third taxable bonds and convertible securities.

Time on your back, or sucking cock, could be quite lucrative, and while she managed her money well, the process of dealing with brokers bored her. She always paid her taxes; no dishonesty in this whore.

"It sounds fine, Carl. Send me the paperwork. I'll review it, and I'm sure it will be satisfactory." She hung up.

She passed by the chair where her Siamese, Kitty Style, was curled up. Janet attempted a casual stroke, but as was Kittystyle's manner, he jumped from the shoe chair and headed to parts unknown. She used her espresso maker, and as the elixir hissed out, she grabbed a good-sized mug. The lingering tendrils of a hangover were present, so no small espresso cup would suffice. A full-sized mug of strong espresso should jolt her into full consciousness.

She took her supercharged caffeine into the bathroom and turned on the bronze knobs in the black marble stand-up shower. She was always told that ladies took baths and soaked away to relax. Janet had experienced too much grit and dirt in her life, and she preferred her steaming-hot triple-headed shower. Afterward, she looked in the full-length mirror.

Not much sag—tits looked great, legs and ass were solid from five days per week grunting at the gym. A closer examination of her eyes revealed crow's feet she hid with high-quality Lancôme makeup base and concealing powder. She slowly and efficiently rubbed her body with lotion and completed her detailing with a dab of Christian Dior Poison perfume behind each ear. She also added a few droplets somewhere distinctly below her navel. She decided against panties and instead chose a long black skirt with a white fishnet top, covered by a black fur-collared blazer. Kevin was a tall man, so she chose her highest black spike heels. She topped it with a beret that would have been ridiculous unless one was as beautiful as Janet Columbo.

It was only 11:30 AM, but Janet tweaked, fussed, and manipulated her hair, dress, makeup, and outfit until it was 5:00 PM. She had looked stunning getting out of the shower hours earlier, but by five, she was damn near Venus on the half-shell.

It had been agreed that he would meet her at a Brooklyn mainstay known for great steaks and loud conversation. The restaurant, Peter Luger, was famous for its steaks and its somewhat bleak and tawdry location in Brooklyn, just over the bridge. The rich and elite loved to eat there, but most would have been scared shitless to walk around the block to find an ATM. Though dressed with immaculate precision, it was unlikely the neighborhood would have intimidated either Kevin or Janet.

It was a Wednesday, and at 6:27 PM, Janet's cab pulled up outside Peter Lugers. Kevin was waiting just inside the door. His brown camel-hair overcoat failed to conceal the broad shoulders and athletic build. Janet thought that he did not look even a day older. Even with her high-heeled black pumps, Kevin's boots allowed him to bring a larger presence to their hug and kiss. The restaurant was loud and noisy, but either by gratuitous tipping, or luck, their table was somewhat secluded and offered them some privacy. She wanted to be angry that he had not contacted her in such a long time, but looking at him melted most residual animosity.

"I have missed you every single moment during these last years apart, Janet."

She wanted to slap him or kick him in his crotch, but what she saw in his eyes extinguished any animosity she clung to.

"I missed you too, you fucker. Where the hell have you been? And by the way, if you think you're getting any tonight, you're paying double."

Kevin ordered a bottle of strong French Bordeaux and a dozen oysters for them both and responded, "I will pay you whatever you want. My desire for you runs deep, but there are some important things I must tell you about my current doings, as well as my unexplained extended absence from your life."

Over a double porterhouse steak for two, another bottle of Bordeaux and during the limo ride back to Janet's apartment, Kevin explained.

Seven years ago, he had moved his unconscious wife from New York to Cleveland at her parents' request. Her parents were religious holy rollers who prayed to God five times daily. It would have been easier to purchase a prayer rug and bow to Mecca.

They had a vision, which through strength of conviction, and a legally binding living will, provided Elise's parents absolute authority to handle her affairs. The commandment to Kevin had been something like this: "Elise's life is in the hands of the Almighty Godhead, and yeah, as her husband, thou shalt honor God's request."

After preaching endlessly and quoting scripture from the holy word of the Lord, they decided she would move to the Cleveland center, and a "healer" would visit her daily to read scripture and cast the devil from her body.

Kevin had wanted to throw up. He had seen and heard sufficient Bible thumping during his tour in the Oklahoma State Penitentiary. Most inmates routinely purchased Bibles, not to read but to use the pages as toilet paper. It was much softer than the prison TP.

Further, the parents commanded that as the leader and man in the house, Kevin would burn in hell's fire if he failed to move to Cleveland to assist in the redemption and healing of Elise.

As significantly as he cared for Elise, he had known this was insane and, after only a few days, planned to seek a court-authorized divorce and return to New York, his job, and Janet.

This had occurred seven years ago, not long after he had first left New York. He had planned to beg Janet's forgiveness and ask her to marry him. Then a twisted God, or perhaps Satan himself, intervened. On the day he was saying his good-byes to Elise, and as her parents hurled epithets at him, Elise regained some minor coherence. As her parents sang Hosannas, prostrated themselves on the floor, and praised everything from God to the Holy Spirit, to the patron saint of popcorn, Elise spoke, "Kevin thanks for waiting. Promise me you'll take care of my parents until the instant of my death. I know I am weak and will pass on to God's country soon."

At that moment, the parents rose from their knees and continued their fiery rhetoric against Kevin. They described how he had sinned with another woman in New York and wanted a divorce. They made signs of the cross and called him a servant of the devil. Amidst their proselytizing, perhaps coincidentally, Elise threw up on her mother's upturned face.

Elise weakly spoke again, "I understand, Kevin. You're a handsome man, and you never believed I'd awake. But please honor our love and our life together, and until I pass, be true to me. See no other woman. Afterwards, enjoy all the pleasure and joy other women can bring you. I love you and am sorry this happened."

He kissed her softly and promised to do as she asked. Moments later, she slipped back into her coma. While her father was kissing his crucifix and her mother was wiping vomit from her face and hair, Kevin slowly wept.

She never again regained consciousness, and her death was far from quick. The doctors were very wrong. She "lived"—if that term was used loosely—for almost seven more years. She gradually lost weight and became little more than a drooling body, surviving on her feeding tube and respirator. Two weeks before their dinner at Peter Luger, she finally died. He had stayed for the funeral and suffered through the pathetic tears and "Christ led her to the Promised Land" cries of the family. As soon as he could leave, he packed up his belongings and took a train to New York.

While in Cleveland, he had lived in a cheap converted warehouse in the flats section of town. He had paid almost nothing in rent, and he had worked for a securities brokerage firm on the shores of Lake Erie. He had no social life, and he could barely tolerate seeing Elise's body rot away in the hospital. Therefore, for the last years since he left New York, he worked seven days per week, twelve hours a day. He has made millions—tens of millions, actually.

The limo arrived at Janet's apartment, and Kevin said, "All I ever did away from work is lift weights and stay in shape, so when I came back to see you, I hoped you might still find me attractive. I still love you. I never stopped."

During the recount of his life in Cleveland, Janet had been unusually quiet. Even the fine wine did not seem to cheer her. He was still as handsome as before, possibly more so with the dusty gray temples. She considered her life and her options. She loved the loft and New York City and her cat Kittystyle, but she was lonely. No one had gotten close to her since Kevin left, and she had enough money in the bank to retire. She would spend time with Kevin, and if he was the same man as before—hell, why not? There had been enough time on her knees and on her back, sharing moments of either grueling or incompetent sex with nobodies. A retirement might be perfect.

For the next few months, they reestablished a relationship. She still danced at the club and did her side-prostitution work overseen by her pimp, Claudio. now, multiple times per week, the prostitution was Kevin hiring her for an entire evening, and Claudio did not care because he was still making the same percentage. Initially, Kevin had stayed at a hotel across from Madison Square Garden, the Hotel Pennsylvania. It had a gym, and it was adequate.

After a month, it was ridiculous for him to stay in a separate hotel, and Kevin moved in with Kittystyle and Janet in her loft. She had guaranteed Claudio that Kevin would pay two thousand dollars per week to her and one thousand dollars per week to Claudio. She had told Kevin soon after he moved in that he need only pay Claudio, but Kevin adamantly disagreed.

"A deal is a deal. Being with you is worth ten times that price."

So the circle began again. She would dance and turn a few tricks each week and pay Claudio his cut, and she would save the remainder. The extra money from Kevin easily made up for any other clientele she lost. She took the opportunity to drop some of the johns she did not particularly enjoy and told Claudio to send someone else. Claudio's response had been, "As you wish, my lovely one, your monetary return to my coffers is substantial as they now stand. As Shakespeare, said in Cymbeline, 'Fortune brings in some boats that are not steered.'"

"Do whatever, Claudio, just send somebody else, except my selected clients who we discussed."

In their free time, Kevin and Janet toured the city. Both admitted that neither had even been to the Statue of Liberty. On a windy day they visited the most famous icon in the world. Kevin argued that the Eiffel Tower and the pyramids in Egypt were better known. Neither had been to any of these famous sites, nor the Taj Mahal, nor the Great Wall of China, nor the rainforest of the Amazon. They looked back at the city from the viewing level of the most famous lady in all New York. Kevin held Janet in his arms, covering her from the wind and chill.

She fit comfortably there. He held her inside his jacket and rested his chin on the top of her head and looked at the view, and she peered up into his eyes. Nothing needed to be said.

× × × × ×

They began to make longer-term plans, while Claudio lined his pockets with a sizable amount of Kevin's money. They were in love and lust, too, for that matter. But the time together in New York clearly proved that love was the driving factor.

They lay in bed, snuggling, one cold winter day. Sleet was falling on the window pane at the loft. It was then freezing into a maze of crystalline shapes, like a child's version of folded-up, and then cut-apart, paper snowflakes. Kevin pulled her closer, believing a little body heat might be generated by some active physical romance. Janet was more than willing, and Kittystyle, who had been curled up in a ball at their feet, knew where the routine was headed. Kittystyle bounded off the bed, and the couple produced body heat with activity that completely steamed over the icy window.

As Kevin held her afterward, Janet spoke to him with intensity he had never seen in her.

"It is time for me to retire. I love you, and the only cock I want to see from now on is yours. A Midwestern gal like me knows high-quality beef when she gets it. And you got it, Kevin. Can it be you and me forever?"

"It's all I've ever wanted, Janet. We have more than enough money. We'll pick up and go somewhere warm and sunny. Then I can enjoy seeing you in a thong bikini."

Janet admitted that she had always harbored a fantasy to move to an island in the Caribbean. She had also done extensive research and found that the US Virgin Islands allowed them to maintain full American citizenship. Kevin agreed it sounded wonderful. She brought out a cardboard box that contained flyers, condominium prices, and real estate listings. It contained voluminous, detailed, and specific data. The prices to purchase were easily within their finances. Janet said, "I already have a real estate agent there to handle our requests. The US Virgin Islands are perfect, and the most laid-back island is St. John. I, a lifetime prostitute, retiring to an island named St. John, in the Virgin Islands. That is absolutely fucking poetically perfect."

They decided the issue right then: she would speak to Claudio, terminate that pimp relationship, move her furniture by container ship, and they could fly over by the end of the month. She was on a month-to-month lease, and she had already contacted a local islander who explained there was a way to sneak Kittystyle over without an extended quarantine.

Janet turned on some calypso music, and they made love again. After, Kevin slipped off to sleep, and she made a phone call to Claudio. She told him in limited detail that she was getting out of the business and asked him to meet her in an hour to finalize everything. She went back into the bedroom and whispered to Kevin that she was going to see Claudio for the last time, and she would return shortly.

✕ ✕ ✕ ✕ ✕

Kevin began to get very concerned because, five hours passed and Janet had not returned. He called her pimp, Claudio, on his cell phone; instead a deep-voiced man answered.

"Claudio is a busy man. Maybe I help you."

"I am looking for Janet, and . . ."

"You must be Kevin, the ho's true love. You come down and meet me and Claudio and Janet at the fuck apartment. The one you probably used before you got all fuckin' sweetie sweet on the ho' and took her at her apartment."

"I know the location. I'll be there in twenty minutes."

✕ ✕ ✕ ✕ ✕

Kevin grabbed a few items of clothing and a long leather trench coat to diminish the chill. He also wore black gloves to keep his hands warm.

Kevin arrived at the fuck apartment and knocked. A large white man with a whitish scar on his left cheek answered. The room included a large bed and a single cheap end table and lamp. Handcuffed and gagged on the bed was Janet. Her face was purplish red on the right cheek. Blood oozed from that wound, as well as a large gash on her shoulder. Kevin noticed a three-foot-length of loop chain lying on the floor. It would have been the type of chain one might use to padlock a gate at a corral. Obviously it had been used for a more violent purpose here in the apartment. The pattern of welts on Janet's face matched the chain on the floor. Kevin looked more closely at the chain and saw blood and strands of hair attached to it.

The white monolith of a man pointed at Kevin and said, "Welcome home, you fuck. What makes you think I'd ever let a good earner like tight-pussy Janet off my payroll."

Kevin looked at Claudio, the sugar pimp, who while not wounded or restrained, seemed much more scared than either Janet or Kevin.

"Don't look at that fucking pussy Claudio, he's nothing. He works for me as a front. He's just a little fag, anyway. He does what I tell him to."

Kevin edged closer to the bed and said, "I had always been certain Claudio was not running this show. I also do not give a fuck about Claudio, but I do love Janet. How much would I need to pay you to buy Janet out of her so-called contract permanently? A cash deal between you and me, and after the exchange, Janet is free and clear, and you have no control over her."

"Yeah, a deal is possible to buy out the whore. You got fifty grand, motherfucker?"

"Yes and no. I do have fifty thousand dollars, and I never fucked my mother. No one but my dad slept with her, and she died of cancer before my dad died later in the same year."

"Sad story, sorry 'bout your family. I know they died while you was in the can on a murder rap. But I ain't scared of you. I just want remuneration, as you college-educated gentlemen might say."

"I'll either pay you the fifty K and you can accept my offer and give me Janet back, or I will break your fucking neck, and your fag buddy Claudio's too, and pay you nothing. It's your call."

At this point, the scarred man introduced himself by saying, "I'm Mo, and as they said in *Scarface*, this is my little friend."

Mo points a 10mm MP5 machine gun at Kevin's chest. Kevin had previously noticed Mo's long jacket and suspected some danger was concealed within.

"Mo, you kill me, you get nothing. What the fuck good does that do you?"

Kevin heard soft sobbing and quick intakes of breath from the bed. He turned, expecting to be angry because Janet was injured. Instead, he was surprised that it was the sugar pimp, Claudio, huffing, bleating, and whimpering with terror. Janet sits steely eyed, the anger and venom virtually shooting from her eyes.

"That's a nice weapon, Mo. You're no weak tit like Claudio. You remember me?"

Mo lowered the weapon and agreed that Kevin did look familiar. They had done time together at the Oklahoma State Penitentiary. Mo had been in for extortion and attempted murder.

Mo said, "We were in the same cell block. Fuck, I completely forgot. You were in for killing that guy that was ass-raping that teenage girl."

"Yeah, Mo, the dude I killed was in for butt-fucking that fifteen-year-old chick. And opposed to what was said at trial, I did kill him on purpose."

Claudio was openly crying now, loudly, knowing violence was likely soon. Janet sat quietly.

Kevin stated that he had over fifty thousand in cash in a safety deposit box at a Citibank branch in Manhattan. He agreed to go with Kevin and get it. Claudio could watch Janet. They agreed that if he returned with the money, Janet is free, no ties, and all is forgotten.

"Everybody lives fucking happy ever-fucking after."

Mo and Kevin exited the fuck apartment, and Mo's MP5 stayed with a still-whimpering Claudio. Kevin was certain Mo had other firepower hidden in his coat if needed.

They took a cab to the bank, and Mo waited outside while Kevin opened his safety deposit box and removed sixty thousand and separated it into packets containing fifty thousand and ten thousand.

Kevin displayed the money to Mo, who smiled a dark grin. His teeth were perfect and in contrast to his scarred skin. Kevin noticed that one of Mo's eyeteeth was gold capped.

"Nice tooth, homes. If times were a little different, I think we might have been pretty tight."

Mo replies, "You don't act much like an investment banker either. That's what that bitch Claudio said you was now."

"I've dabbled in lots of trades. Let's stop for a quick drink before we return to the apartment."

At this moment, Kevin hands Mo the fifty thousand. He also showed him the extra ten grand. Once inside the noisy bar, Kevin offered a simple addendum to their already completed deal.

Kevin explained that while he was angry that Janet had been injured, this side of the law had certain drawbacks. Kevin would be leaving with Janet, never to be seen again. Mo would be making fifty thousand. It was all a happy ending except for one weakness. Kevin spoke forcefully after he chugged his last swallow of beer.

"That sugar pimp Claudio is a weak link. Any cop could squeeze him like a zit and make him pop. He'd talk about you, me, and Janet. I've done some questionable things in my life, so has Janet, so have you. Don't forget, I know what you did before to get sent to jail in Oklahoma. You were running some high-quality blow into the jail. You were moving major product weight before jail—thirty to forty kilos per month. You said your contact was . . . I believe the quote was . . . let me remember. 'A lace-panty nigger who probably took it up the ass.' I imagine that might have been our mutual friend Claudio."

Mo was very quiet, but his eyes were shifting from side to side. After a moment he spoke, "I could use a partner, you want back into the business?"

Kevin declined, saying he had enough cash stuck away for both he and Janet, but he was worried that Claudio might weaken and go to the cops now or sometime later. Their plan was to retire to the Caribbean. Perhaps Mo could ensure nothing every came out concerning the relationship between the four of them. Kevin handed Mo the other ten thousand dollars and said, "I'm sure you can find another sugar pimp."

"Yeah, I bet I can."

They returned to the fuck apartment and removed the handcuffs from Janet. Claudio was apologizing profusely and crying as he held onto Kevin's hand. Kevin pushed Claudio's hand away as if it were covered with a virus. Kevin helped Janet out to a cab after covering her face with a scarf. They returned to Janet's flat. Janet slept much of the next few days, and Kevin played the role of caretaker, doctor, and travel agent.

X X X X X

Three weeks passed, and all possessions were being packed away to be sent via container ship to St. John. The last item packed was an antique stand-up piano. As it was being moved from the apartment for its personal Caribbean cruise, Kevin asked if Janet knew how to play,

"No, I just liked how it looked with the other furniture. I would not know the difference between G-flat and G-stacked, though I'm quite familiar with a G-string."

The apartment was now completely empty, and Janet and Kevin were sitting on the floor, reading the *New York Times,* waiting for the car that would take them to the airport. She was reading the sports section to find out if the Knicks had won the night before.

Kevin was casually perusing the local events section and wondering what the weather was like in St John. As he was ready to toss the local section into the trash, he noted a small article.

"Fifth homicide this month in Greenwich Village, the body of a 43-year-old black male was located in a dumpster. The body was subsequently identified by NYPD forensic analysts as Claudio Cletus Jones. Jones had an extensive criminal record for offenses related to prostitution and narcotics. The cause of death was a 10 millimeter round fired into the posterior region of Mr. Jones's head. Any information concerning this homicide should be forwarded to NYPD Homicide Detective Ronald Flynn.

The apartment doorbell rang, and their limousine driver was waiting downstairs. They only had two small carry-ons, and as they prepared to enter the limo, they passed an empty city trashcan. Kevin threw away the *New York Times*. Janet said, "Kevin, I haven't finished reading the paper."

"No worries, honey, nothing of interest in it. It's just the usual garbage. Let's wait until we land in the Virgin Islands. We'll get a local island paper there, and I'm certain the news is more enjoyable. Like where to find a good piña colada."

FINALLY, FLOWERS

Malcolm's business is rocking. Dozens of customers enter or call in to order birds of paradise, tiger lilies, tulips, or any combination of floral arrangements. The phone has been ringing nonstop for hours, and it is a Tuesday and nowhere near Valentine's, Mother's Day, or the traditional big-sale days.

Love just must be in the air.

Malcolm Jurgenson is a solidly built second-generation Norwegian, with whitish blond hair, hands the size of a heavyweight prizefighter, and shoulders linebackers would find useful during a crushing quarterback sack. He is a gentle and kindly giant even if he does look like Thor or Conan the Barbarian. He loves his job. Selling flowers is his life's joy. The shop is in Santa Monica, California, so he has access to the freshest and most beautiful flowers in the world. The growing regions near Santa Barbara produce most of the flowers for the entire West Coast. Los Angeles, the City of Angels, may not be full of angelic types, but halos of floral arrangements are available on demand and at a good price.

Everything is expensive in Los Angeles except flowers; every movie executive, actor, and businesswoman can outfit their homes and offices with bouquets of every imaginable color and type. Every romance can be sparked with a dozen roses in red, pink, yellow, or white. Flowers bring joy to both giver and the receiver. Flowers are the gift of beauty on earth from the Lord himself.

Malcolm arranged a mixture of marigolds, geraniums, and baby's breath into an emerald-colored vase, and the phone rings.

"Finally, Flowers, this is Malcolm. How may I help you?"

"This is Pixar Animation Studios. We are hosting an event at the Los Angeles Convention Center on the seventeenth of May. We will need a floral arrangement for each table. Approximately one hundred will be required. It will be very high profile, with many stars, and studio execs. The movie is an animated Western, so the theme of the flowers should fit into a similar concept."

Malcolm responds, "That is not a problem. I already have some ideas. Vases could be Stetson cowboy hats, hay straw around the displays. I will make it beautiful."

It is agreed they will meet tomorrow, and Malcolm will bring a few examples. He is to arrive at the studio at 2:30 PM and ask for Charlene Relingrad, who is coordinating the event.

Malcolm is excited; Pixar Studios is a major business and one of the largest entertainment operations in all Los Angeles. It is run by the notoriously obnoxious Marley Weldensteinberg—a fat, overbearing swine known throughout the industry for his ever-present Cuban cigar, crude language, and desire for women half his age.

Malcolm plots ideas for floral arrangements for the Pixar soiree. While thinking, he creates for himself a blood-red miniature-rose boutonniere and pins it to his lapel and smiles.

X X X X X

At 2:30 PM, exactly, Malcolm arrives at the Burbank offices of Pixar and asks for Charlene Relingrad. Relingrad is a scrawny redhead, attired in an ultraconservative black suit. Her age is indefinable, and her hair is pulled back so tightly in a bun that it is unlikely she could smile if she so chose. Malcolm's quick assessment of Charlene—who prefers to be called *Ms. Relingrad*—is that she probably never smiles anyway.

Malcolm displays the arrangements he has brought. Ms. Relingrad examines them closely and pronounces them "satisfactory." She then speaks seemingly without moving her lips, "You have probably heard of Mr. Marley Weldensteinberg, the president of Pixar Studios. He is a very hands-on manager and considers the upcoming Convention Center party important because influential actors and executives will be on hand. Everything must be like clockwork. Nothing missed. This includes the floral arrangements. He has asked to speak to you briefly today to ensure absolute compliance with all details."

Malcolm is shown into the waiting room for Mr. Weldensteinberg's office. There is a secretary that takes Malcolm's name and says she will notify him.

She could be a duplicate of Ms. Relingrad, and Malcolm is reminded of the movie *The Stepford Wives*. Perhaps they actually can clone people in the Los Angeles movie business. At least in Stepford, the women were attractive. Ms. Relingrad and this secretary had faces, and demeanors, that could chill the sex drive of a sixteen-year-old.

After a few moments, the clone ushers Malcolm into Weldensteinberg's enormous office. Modern art hangs on the walls, and the rug is a hand-loomed silk array of colors that matches the artwork. Malcolm knew quite a bit about rugs and art and estimates that their value exceeded his entire net worth. Weldensteinberg sits behind a mahogany desk that almost fills the room. It is a certainty that the desk had been assembled in the room because it could never have fit through the door.

"Good afternoon, Mr. Weldensteinberg. I am here to show you some floral examples."

"I know why you're here, florist. Everything must be perfect for my event at the convention center. No fuckups. You make one mistake, and you'll never sell a single carnation in the state of California. Catch my drift, flower child?"

Malcolm displays his examples and explains potential alterations that might be made.

"They look satisfactory. But don't screw up a single thing. By the way, you don't look like a fag. I thought all male florists were queer. You know that TV show *Queer Eye for the Straight Guy*? It was my idea."

"Actually, sir, I'm quite heterosexual. Most florists are. They just enjoy the sight, touch, and aroma of flowers."

"Whatever. Get out of my office. I have more important business to attend to."

As Malcolm exits the office and leaves the Pixar building, he vows to ensure every detail is perfect. He also makes a mental note to complete an in-depth review of the personal and business background of Mr. Marley Weldensteinberg.

Weeks later, on May 17, the event is a tremendous success. The floral arrangements contained in black-and-white Stetson cowboy hats are a hit. A number of the guests ask if it would be permissible to keep the bouquets, and of course, they are allowed. Malcolm received a call from Ms. Relingrad, who advises that Mr. Weldensteinberg was very pleased and would consider Finally, Flowers for subsequent events.

Malcolm is quite happy that his shop had done well for Mr. Weldensteinberg's party, but Malcolm has learned many sordid details regarding the man himself via Internet queries, review of court documents, and a search of newspaper articles. Malcolm determined just what a scum he is.

In his early teens, he had raped and killed a thirteen-year-old Pasadena girl. The trial would have been quite a sensation, but the charges were eventually dropped when an uninvolved teen claimed to have been the perpetrator. The physical evidence was conveniently lost by the Pasadena Police Department. The teen who admitted to the crime served two years in a juvenile facility until he was released on his eighteenth birthday. More interestingly, upon his release, he received $2.5 million from the Weldensteinberg family. It stunk, but eventually, the furor died down. Money can buy anything—even media silence. Eventually, he went to UCLA, got his degree, and then bought his way into the entertainment business.

Finally, Malcolm discovered that Marley Weldensteinberg owned a villa in Costa Rica, which he frequented multiple times per year. Coincidentally, Malcolm had a close childhood friend who had relocated to San Jose, Costa Rica. Malcolm made a few inquiries and discovered that Weldensteinberg had just transferred his sick predilections outside the US. He paid girls, ranging in age from twelve to sixteen, for sex at the villa. Most recently, he had shifted in his desires and was sodomizing young boys. Malcolm checked and rechecked. It was all true. Weldensteinberg was a sick, perverted pedophile, and he was getting away with it. Malcolm made a decision.

Malcolm had recently been diagnosed with a type of pancreatic cancer. It was a relatively slow-growing cancer, but virtually all pancreatic cancer is fatal. His doctors had given him six months to live, perhaps less. Malcolm believed that should be enough time to do the world some good.

Malcolm had been a Navy SEAL prior to his retirement from the military. He had also been one of their best-trained snipers. He had all his weapons at the flower shop. He also had some .308 glass-piercing rounds. More than sufficient to shoot through the glass of Weldensteinberg's office window, and there was a building in Burbank directly across from Pixar.

It was a perfect sniper position.

XXXXX

Three evenings later, Malcolm is carefully concealed on that roof, with a high-powered night-vision scope trained on the office window of Marley Weldensteinberg, who is at his desk. Malcolm slowly and gently squeezes the trigger, and the sound of the shot surprises him. It had been a long time since his duty in Vietnam when he had last taken a killing shot. Malcolm calmly looks through the night-vision scope and sees Weldensteinberg slumped over his desk, dead. Malcolm repacks his rifle, returns to his car, and then drives back to the flower shop.

The funeral was two weeks later. It was not particularly well attended, but Malcolm was there, and as the rabbi said a few words, Malcolm saw the floral arrangement he had sent—African violets, leopard flowers, snapdragons, tulips, and more.

XXXXX

The killings became easier as Malcolm committed them with increased frequency. He is detailed in his research: people from all types of life that had committed egregious crimes but, through some miscue, had been released. He had considered searching out O. J. Simpson, but it did not seem worth the hassle, and Simpson did have kids.

After each killing, he would later place a lovely bouquet at the cemetery site. He did this at night to avoid detection.

After six months, he had killed ten individuals. He went from Wichita to Los Angeles to Seattle and everywhere in between. Each grave site either received flowers or a living plant. Bluebell, begonia, forsythia, dahlia—each received a different type of flower.

XXXXX

He knows his work is almost completed, and his pancreatic cancer is worsening dramatically. He has no more than a few weeks to live.

Malcolm is certain that what he is doing is right. His last duty was the most difficult. Malcolm drove to his final destination.

XXXXX

Inside a bar called Bully's, Malcolm drank one of their famous Bloody Marys and read the *Washington Post*. Malcolm is uncertain if his nausea came from the Bloody Mary, the cancer, or the *Post* article.

PRESIDENT JUSTIFIES TO CONGRESS WARS ON THREE CONTINENTS

In his State of the Union Address, the President detailed the continued necessity for US troops to remain in Iraq, Korea, Afghanistan, and Russia. While expressing extreme grief that over 10,000 soldiers had been killed in these conflicts, and tens of thousands more wounded, he vowed that the battles would continue. He stated that the US has a responsibility to foster and protect democracy worldwide...

Malcolm laid the newspaper to one side and contemplated what he came here to do.

In the last months, Malcolm had killed many evil people and lost little sleep over it. What he needed to do here brought him deep cause for reflection.

Malcolm pays his bill and returns to his hotel room and loads a handgun with .45-caliber rounds. He opens a briefcase that contains a rubber surgeon's glove and special glue that would adhere to the glove. From a vase, he removes thirteen red roses and carefully clips the thorns and stems.

He holds the gun in his shooting hand after he places the rubber glove on and then carefully glues roses on the exterior of his hand and to any areas where the .45 shows through. It is a long tedious process, but when complete, it appears he is holding a large bouquet of roses. Still, Malcolm's finger is poised and ready on the trigger.

The president is scheduled to make a brief public appearance outside the Lincoln Monument to trumpet his case for expanding US involvement in conflicts around the globe. As the president begins his speech to the multitudes at the steps of the memorial, there is cheering, there is yelling, and then suddenly, a large man carrying roses uses his large frame to push through the masses.

Even the president sees the flowers and smiles, thinking at least he has a few advocates on his side. Suddenly, two quick .45-caliber shots ring out, and the president lies bleeding on the lowest step. Hundreds of hands and arms grab Malcolm, and he is thrown to the ground. The flowers scattered at the weapon's firing and had left an airburst of rose petals. The gun is still in his hand, and a secret-service agent wrestles it away.

The president had been mortally wounded, but he was strong. With two .45 rounds—one in his shoulder and one in his head—he lived for ten more days.

The cancer took Malcolm's life just one day after the president's death.

Malcolm Jurgenson had not been a rich man, or perhaps a good man; possibly, he was even evil. Yet he was conscientious.

Before his trip to Washington DC, he had set up a trust under a fictitious name, which would generate at least $100,000 per year. The purpose of the trust was simple and clear in its intent. Each and every day, a different type of flower would be placed at the burial site of the deceased president. This would be done every single day. Forever.

THE STORY TELLER

"So, Mr. Dantonio, do you believe this next novel of yours, *Vial of Blood*, will be another *New York Times* best seller?"

Paul Dantonio closely looked at the interviewer's face for the first time. He had not seen her face because, prior to that, he had been carefully examining her long legs, which were clad in fishnet nylons. She wore an ultra miniskirt of black leather, complemented with spike heels. Her cashmere sweater was tight, and her huge—and decidedly fake—breasts were bursting out at the top. Her face was attractive, as well. The plastic surgeon did a good job with the slightly upturned nose and her high cheekbones, and Paul figured, if the interview went well and she appeared interested, he would take a swing at some night duty with the young lady.

"I believe the story has some quality, but it is the public, and you analytical reviewers, that determine marketing and sales success. But I do believe it is innovative and interesting. Give me your honest opinion after you read and analyze it, Gloria."

Gloria the critic looked at Paul when her name was spoken. She had pretty blue-gray eyes that glinted in the bright lights of the camera and interview stage. To date, the medical capability was unavailable to change the color of someone's eyes. At least, some part of Gloria was not store-bought. She smiled what appeared a genuine smile. The likelihood of a nighttime rendezvous seemed increasingly likely.

"I look forward to reading it, Mr. Dantonio. And please tell our audience something about the novel."

"I don't like to give away a book's content because every reader's opinion is different. What I may see one way, a singular reader may approach completely differently. But here is a copy for you, Gloria. I autographed it. And please don't call me *Mr. Dantonio*. Call me *Paul*."

He handed her the copy of *Vial of Blood*. She opened it and read the inscription aloud to the camera and audience.

To Ms. Gloria Camarena,
I hope you enjoy the story. You are a reviewer of enormous quality and one of the few we authors respect and look forward to interacting with.

With admiration and respect,
Paul Dantonio

"Thank you, Mr. Dantonio. I guess that should be 'thank you, Paul.'"

He ended up taking her to dinner at Ocean, a good seafood restaurant not far from the pier in Santa Monica. Paul was impressed that she actually completely consumed her mixed seafood platter with linguine. He hated the model types that were rail thin and ate like birds or, worse yet, purged their elegant meals by vomiting into expensive restaurant toilets.

She has graduated from USC with a communications degree and a minor in Spanish.

"Of course, like every blond-haired female from Los Angeles, I thought the world would court me as the next coming of Marilyn Monroe. I found that there are many potential Marilyns, Cameron Diazes, and Julia Robertses in the actress contingent. Instead, I went to work for a local news station, then the Entertainment Channel, and now CNN. I enjoy my work."

Paul had been dutifully impressed by their conversation. She was not some vapid bimbo. When she arrived for dinner, she wore a conservative black pantsuit and pearl necklace. The more revealing interview attire was obviously relegated to a closet and donned only when the cameras of CNN were rolling.

They discussed the current situations in Iraq and Afghanistan, as well as lesser-known pockets of hell such as Korea, Bali, and Spain. She spoke knowledgeably about the Taliban, Al Qaeda, and the government's struggles in Saudi Arabia and Palestine. She was familiar with the internal civil strife in Colombia involving the terrorist groups and paramilitary organizations of the FARC, ELN, and the AUC. Paul had spent his own time overseas in spots like Nairobi, South Africa, and Mogadishu. He had assisted the CIA periodically, with his access based on his press credentials.

The evening went quickly and smoothly, and while her conservative attire somewhat concealed her physical beauty, Paul had not forgotten her substantial physical attributes. Following after-dinner drinks, he invited her to his home—his estate, actually—in Malibu.

She looked him directly in the eyes. "Not tonight, Paul. I enjoyed your conversation and company, but I'm a two-date girl. However, you're very attractive and just my type. Ask me out again, and I'll make you dinner at my condo overlooking the yachts in Marina del Rey.

Paul did not need much convincing, and it was agreed he would meet her at her place in two weeks. Paul said he would have liked to meet sooner, but he was headed out of town for a week or so.

"I don't mind waiting, Paul. I'm sure you're busy. I will be thinking about you."

She kissed his cheek, provided a more substantial hug, and had picked up her Corvette from the valet before Paul could even choose a romantic good-bye phrase. He smiled as she drove away and contemplated that a semi-famous writer should become wittier and romantically well spoken.

X X X X X

The next morning, he left on the United Airlines flight from LAX to O'Hare in Chicago. His publicist wanted him to provide some interviews about his new novel. He also had some more important personal matters that would be attended to during the same trip. When he landed, he was picked up by Chicago Police homicide detective Corwin Jackson.

Jackson arrived in an unmarked, nondescript police-issued tan Chevrolet Sedan. Paul thought that every law enforcement agency—federal, local, or state—must purchase their vehicles from the same batches that rolled off the Detroit assembly lines. Whether gray, light blue, or tan, they screamed *cop*. Jackson was waiting curbside, in a parking spot designated *law enforcement*. Jackson had placed his official Chicago PD placard on the dashboard in the unlikely event someone questioned his identity.

Paul tossed his carry-on into the backseat and said, "Howdy, how is Midwestern law enforcement these days? Have you had to kill any 'shines or WOPs on the South Side recently? The Windy City is moving up the homicide list, though still far behind Washington DC and Detroit in percentage terms."

"Fuck you, Paul. And just 'cuz you only Italian and aren't fortunate enough to have no black pride in your family, just makes you unlucky."

Corwin Jackson sped away from the airport after vigorously shaking Paul's hand. His grip was like a vise, which was not surprising.

Jackson was half-black. "On my daddy's side, hence the name Jackson," he liked to say.

"My momma is Italian, so I can cook well too," he frequently added.

Bottom line was, whatever his ethnic mix, he was a tough man who dressed in fine suits and made the Chicago description "City of Broad Shoulders" an understatement.

Paul had known Jackson for years and periodically assisted him on a child abduction investigation and homicides. In return, Jackson schooled Paul on new investigative techniques and provided tidbits on current cases. Many of the characters in Paul's novels had been based on information he gleaned from Jackson. It was kind of a symbiotic relationship, and each helped the other. Paul's insight into a criminal's mind seemed almost psychic to Jackson, and he often pointed an investigation in the correct direction. In return, Jackson took him to autopsies, allowed him to watch interviews, and be in on active cases. No one that Jackson worked with cared much—partly because Paul was a rich and famous author, and partly because Paul always paid the extensive bar tabs when Jackson and his cop buddies joined up after an arrest, search, or shooting.

Jackson began to describe a rape and homicide investigation he was working:

We found a Caucasian female's body which had been raped, decapitated, and left in a dumpster. DNA tests, hair-follicle, fingernail-scraping, and semen tests were all negative. There was vaginal penetration, but not a damn bit of physical evidence. We still cannot find her head. Victim's name was Clara Barnes, twenty-eight years old, no criminal history, lived in an expensive area on the seventh hole of an exclusive country club. Damn thing is, no physical evidence. Not a fucking hair or fiber.

Paul pondered for a moment and asked where they were going to eat.

"It's too early for Morton's The Steakhouse, so we are headed to the best restaurant in Chinatown."

Being a cop, Jackson knew all the best spots for food. The place was nondescript, and the sign was in Chinese, so Paul had no idea what the place was called. The seating hostess was an attractive older Chinese lady who addressed Detective Jackson by name.

"Would you like your usual table, Mr. Jackson?"

"Yes, please, and two Red Label scotches."

"We just received a bottle of the exclusive Blue Label, if you want that. I won't charge you extra."

Paul was impressed; Blue Label was the top of the line. The police department, or Jackson himself, must be providing security for the restaurant.

After each had finished two glasses of excellent scotch and quickly eaten an appetizer of pork and dim sum, they awaited a noodle-and-fish platter. When the main course arrived, it was steaming, delicious, and could have fed two-thirds of the Chicago Police Department. Cops always knew where to get a good meal.

After eating, as was common, Paul started to pay.

"Not this time, buddy. This one's on me. I need your help and ideas on this headless body in the dumpster case. She was a pretty important lady here in Chicago, and the department is taking heat until it gets solved."

Paul was surprised. Jackson must really need help—and be getting administrative pressure—if he was willing to open up his wallet.

"Did they autopsy the body yet?"

"They did what they could. It's tough to do a full autopsy without a head. I had them save the body and keep the report for you to see."

They went down to the Cook County Coroner's Office, and Jackson filled some paperwork, and within a few minutes, what remained of Clara Barnes's body was lying on a slab.

The coroner also provided Jackson and Paul with his report. Paul carefully reviewed the report and then looked at the body. They had completed the traditional Y-shaped incision, and obviously there was no need to open the skullcap and analyze the brain because Ms. Barnes did not have a head.

Paul slowly and silently walked around the body, analyzing every inch of skin and every detail. He paid particular attention to her feet, vaginal area, and the extremely precise and clean line on her neck where the head had been severed.

After approximately twenty-five minutes, he asked only one question.

"In the toxicology report, what drug did it show had been utilized to render her unconscious?"

Both the coroner and Jackson were startled at the pointedness and accuracy of the question. The coroner responded, "It was a mixture of substances—Xanax, alcohol, Percocet, and a strong animal tranquilizer. Something a veterinarian could probably knock out a rhinoceros with."

"Or a twenty-eight-year-old lady named Clara Barnes," Paul replied.

Paul had seen enough, and he and Jackson left the office as Clara Barnes was replaced on her gurney and wheeled back to the "meat room," as the coroner so delicately called it.

They drove in silence to a dingy bar on the South Side. Paul had not seen a white face on the street in quite some time. The lounge did not have a name on the exterior or the door, just a neon sign that said "Cocktails." As they entered the dimly lit tavern, every head turned and eagerly eyed Paul's white face. Paul was a tough man and had been a decent amateur fighter, but he doubted his fists could win out against the knives and guns many in this classy establishment undoubtedly possessed.

Yet Jackson had brought him here for some reason, and Jackson had a gun. Actually, Jackson had lived in Chicago his entire life, and he always carried two guns. A .45-caliber semiautomatic in a shoulder holster with an extra magazine loaded with fourteen rounds, giving that weapon a total of twenty-eight if needed. Also, on the inside of his left ankle, he had a five-shot Chief's Special, just in case. Even in this unfriendly environment, Paul felt fairly safe.

They both slid into a wood bench seat that had a view of the bar and the door. Paul noted that while the occupants of the bar had been seriously eye-fucking him, they stopped immediately when they observed he was accompanied by Jackson. Presently, a haggard-looking black woman who looked fifty (but was probably only thirty-five) came to take their order.

"Two scotches, Felicia."

Paul doubted these drinks would be Johnnie Walker Blue, Black, or even Red Label.

When Felicia brought the drinks back, the heroin track marks were easily visible on both of her arms. She was mainlining directly into her veins, not skin popping it between her fingers or toes. She was not hiding anything. From her look and demeanor, Paul doubted she would make it another five years. Maybe not another five months.

"I like your choice of establishments, Jackson. I'd wager this is the first time two people sat in this booth wearing thousand-dollar suits."

"Actually, mine is a two-thousand-dollar suit, but I didn't bring you here for the ambiance. If I wanted that, I'd have taken you to some fancy place on the lake shore. I brought you here because this was the last place Clara Barnes was seen alive. Six hours before her body was found—headless, in a dumpster, ten miles from here."

Paul was completely silent as he sipped his bad scotch and thought of what Jackson had just told him and what he had seen at the Cook County Coroner's Office. Jackson waved at Felicia, and she brought over two more scotches.

"Who was she here with?"

Jackson explained that was where the mystery really began. She was by herself. Had never been there before, ordered one beer, asked for a Heineken, which got a laugh out of the bartender. She drank one Budweiser, acted nervous as hell, and left alone. Everybody in this bar—and they are all regulars—verified the story.

"What did the victim's husband or boyfriend say? And let's get the hell out of here."

Jackson left sixty dollars on the table, which—based on the swill they had been drinking—included a sizeable tip for Felicia to go buy her next heroin fix. Felicia must have been an informant for Jackson.

As they drove away, Paul asked that they view Clara Barnes's residence.

"I was already on my way there, my inquisitive friend."

Clara Barnes had lived in an upscale apartment in downtown Chicago. An area that was expensive, had a security guard in the downstairs lobby, and was, in every respect, high class. Originally, the police had obtained a search warrant for the unit after the body was found and identified, but now, with Barnes dead and the unit vacant, legally it could be treated as abandoned property and searched and researched whenever law enforcement desired. This was especially true since Barnes had lived alone and paid her rent for six months in advance.

Jackson confirmed that the forensic teams had been through the apartment thoroughly and identified no signs of struggle or physical evidence.

"Go through anything you want, Paul. Just wear these rubber gloves in the unlikely event you find something."

Everything seemed in order. This was exactly what you would expect to find in a rich, younger, single woman's apartment. Nice artwork on the walls, a neo-modern curving sculpture on the living room table. Wine coolers in the refrigerator nestled next to a few bottles of white zinfandel. The refrigerator also contained low-carb meals, and among her reading material, she owned *Women's Fitness* magazines and a well-worn copy of *Body for Life* by Bill Phillips, describing how to transform any fat slob, or slobette, into a fit marvel of sculptured flesh.

The bedroom had a white four-poster bed with a canopy. The sheets were crisp linen in a white-and-powder-blue motif. There were a half-dozen stuffed animals on the bed, mostly teddy bears, with a poodle and a tiger thrown in for contrast. Her closet contained tasteful suits, casual jeans and tops, and some trendier but classy going-out-on-the-town clothes.

A review of her underwear drawer revealed a nice lace thong that Jackson felt compelled to display. He was even more enthralled by the slender vibrator.

"She's obviously a white chick. Black girl would need something a lot meatier."

"Did you note that opinion in your official police report, Jackson?"

As Jackson was emulating Zorro, slicing and stabbing the air with Clara Barnes's vibrator, Paul said, "There are no photographs. None of Clara or anyone else."

Jackson realized that Paul was correct, replaced Clara's vibrator in the drawer, and searched the apartment in earnest. Both looked everywhere conceivable—the kitchens, the restrooms, the entire space. Not one photograph of Clara or anyone else.

"Jackson, you have that copy of Clara Barnes's DL photo?"

Jackson pulled out his small notebook from an inside jacket pocket and located a police copy of her driver's license photo. Both looked at it. Even in her DL photo, which is notoriously awful, Clara Barnes had been a great-looking lady. "A downright fox" were the words Jackson used.

"What woman who works out with *Body for Life* and has a face like that doesn't have even one photo of herself? Answer that, Jackson."

Jackson had no response.

After a moment of silence, Paul asked if Jackson had spoken to Clara Barnes's parents.

"Hey, I graduated from the FBI National Police Academy. I received more training than you. You're just a hack author who writes crime books."

"No need to insult me. Besides, I make ten times your salary being a hack."

Both were laughing now because, despite the mutual insults, they had finally found a clue. Jackson explained that Clara Barnes's mother was deceased, but the father was a rich retired investment banker who lived in Shaker Heights, Ohio—a wealthy suburb of Cleveland. They agreed it was time for Jackson to use his FBI National Academy contacts to conduct an in-person interview in Cleveland. After he Okayed it with his own supervisors, Jackson called his friend that worked for Cleveland PD.

"Tommy, I need to come to a suburb of Cleveland to conduct an interview on a homicide case. The murderer left her headless body in a dumpster."

"I read about that one. I'll clear it. No problems."

They continued their conversation, and it was agreed that Tommy would confirm the father's physical address in Shaker Heights and schedule an interview. He also said it was no problem if Paul came along, but only if he would autograph a copy of *Vial of Blood*.

Less than ten minutes later, Jackson's cell phone rang, and it was Tommy O'Keefe from the Cleveland Police Department. He had already spoken to Clifton Barnes III, Clara's father, and he was anxious to do anything to assist. They would meet at the Shaker Heights house at 3:00 PM tomorrow.

X X X X X

The flight to Cleveland was bumpy, which Paul took as a negative sign.

Assistant Chief Tommy O'Keefe picked up Paul and Jackson at the Cleveland airport. Jackson introduced Paul, and O'Keefe received his autographed and personalized copy of *Vial of Blood*. On the way out to Clifton Barnes III's house, O'Keefe was filled in on the details of the investigation.

The residence was not a house at all but a multistory mansion. It had twelve-foot-high security gates, and O'Keefe had to buzz in and receive a verbal approval from the owner before they were able to enter.

Everyone—cops, authors, everybody—has preconceived notions. They all expected Clifton Barnes III to be old and resemble and talk in a voice reminiscent of Thurston Howell on *Gilligan's Island*.

Preconceptions can clearly be misconceptions.

After driving through the gates and around a circular driveway that contained a statue and fountain, Mr. Barnes was waiting outside. He was blond, handsome, and looked twenty years too young to have a daughter as old as Clara had been.

"Please come in, gentlemen, and I'm very pleased to meet you in person. I also want to thank you, Mr. Dantonio. I'm a fan of your books, though sorry my daughter's murder may be fodder for your next novel. However, that would be well worth it if you can assist in solving the crime."

The house was a work of art. Tapestries hung on the walls; Persian rugs partially covered dark wood floors. On the most prominent wall, there were three magnificent life-size paintings. One was of a beautiful auburn-haired beauty, obviously Mr. Barnes's deceased wife. The other paintings were lifelike representations of Mr. Barnes and Clara. Barnes noted that all were looking at the paintings and said, "You can see how beautiful my wife was. That was clearly where Clara got her looks from, and now they have both been taken from me. I'm sorry, I don't mean to mope and feel sorry for myself. Most of my life has been quite blessed. Please come into the library. There is plenty of room."

The space was enormous, and there were thousands of books. Paul noticed that a newly purchased copy of *Vial of Blood* lay on the massive oak desk.

"I read it last night. It was very suspenseful. In honesty though, I believe *Thrill of the Chase* was even better."

Paul smiled.

"I agree. If I ever wrote a good one, it was *Thrill*."

After more pleasantries, Mr. Barnes called for the butler, who brought coffee and iced tea.

O'Keefe spoke and said that because it was a Chicago investigation, he would defer to them for their questions.

Jackson began, "Mr. Barnes, we just have a few questions, but anything you can tell us may be of help."

"I will answer anything you like, but only if you call me Cliff."

Jackson conducted a typical interview while Paul and O'Keefe merely listened.

"Did your daughter have enemies?"

"No."

"Did she feel she was in danger?"

"No."

And so the interview went and developed no information of value. Cliff Barnes answered every question, but it just did not seem he had any information of importance.

Paul became somewhat lost in the drone of the endless questions and answers and looked around the room and saw numerous photographs of Clara and her mother and of the family together.

It was a lifetime of photos. One particular photo on Cliff Barnes's desk did catch his eye. The photo was quite recent and was of Clara with her arms around a dark-skinned, brown-haired man of approximately thirty-five.

Jackson was finishing up his interview and thanking Cliff Barnes. Somewhat suddenly, Paul spoke, "On your desk, Mr. Barnes, who is that man with Clara?"

Cliff Barnes hesitated for just the slightest instant, but long enough for Paul to notice.

"That is—I mean, was—her fiancé, Ashton Clark. They were to have been married in a year or so. He is a wonderful man who worked with her in Chicago."

Other matters were touched on, but within two hours, O'Keefe, Dantonio, and Jackson said their good-byes and headed back to the airport. O'Keefe asked if they felt they learned anything of importance, and Paul spoke, "Probably not, but I will be convincing Jackson to have a conversation with one Mr. Ashton Clark."

"Hell yeah, my white brother. I believe we may be on the trail like a couple hound dogs. Though you'd be Scooby Doo, and I'd be Snoop Dogg."

Paul laughed. "I wonder how much time twenty-to-life is when it is in Snoopy Doggy Dog years."

X X X X X

The next morning, after another turbulence-interrupted flight back to Chicago, Paul and Jackson paid an early-morning visit to Ashton Clark.

Even at 6:00 AM, with a Chicago cop and a famous author knocking on his door, Ashton Clark seemed neither frightened nor surprised.

"Please come in. I was just making my morning cappuccino and sampling a scone. I'm aware cappuccino is truly an evening drink, but I like it in the morning. You're welcome to either, I have plenty of both."

Jackson glanced at Paul with a what-the-fuck look. Jackson explained they were there to inquire about the murder of Clara Barnes.

"It was awful. We were to be married. We worked out at the local fitness center together, and she worked with me also. One day, I just realized how much I adored her and was honored when she accepted my wedding offer. She—one so lovely. I miss her every second."

At this moment, two things occurred simultaneously. Ashton Clark began to cry uncontrollably, and a white Persian cat appeared and jumped into Clark's lap. As he wailed pitifully about his little Clara, he stroked the cat's back, and the Persian purred.

"Would it be possible for us to look around your apartment, Mr. Clark?"

"Of course, but please try not to do the traditional episode of *Cops* and trash all my stuff. I'm quite particular. I must go to work regardless. If you wait one moment while I shower. I'll leave the entire place to you so long as you'll lock up."

Jackson told Ashton Clark to feel free to shower, and they would wait. Clark left the room, and they heard the shower begin. Forty minutes later, Jackson asked Paul if he thought Ashton had slit his wrists.

"No, I believe we'll be seeing him shortly."

After another five minutes, Ashton emerged shaved and scrubbed in a dark blue suit, spread-collar shirt, and rep-patterned tie. Jackson realized the suit must have cost at least five thousand dollars and was an original Armani. Paul noticed the suit but focused on the silver-tipped wingtips.

"So sorry I took so long, but I have an important meeting with the partners today, and so I am required to look my best. I must go. Have a scone and cappuccino. Please lock up."

And like that, Ashton Clark was gone.

Jackson and Paul put on rubber gloves to conduct the search. Searching was easy because the place was spotless. The closet had the clothes organized by type. For example: suit jackets, then by color, then by style (single-breasted or double, narrow lapels or wide). All other items of clothing were similarly oriented to their specific kind. One drawer contained socks, underwear, and T-shirts—again broken down by color and style.

Jackson commented, "The guy irons his T-shirts. He irons his fucking T-shirts. What a retentive son of a bitch."

Paul noticed a framed photograph on the dressing table, carefully positioned between rows of cuff links itemized by color and type of jewel. Green cuff links, emerald and jade; red cuff links, garnet and ruby; and blue cuff links, diamond and opal. The photo was the same one as the one on Clifton Barnes III's desk: the smiling face of Ashton Clark snuggling in the arms of Clara Barnes.

"This time, I choose the bar, Jackson."

It was not the lounge at the Ritz-Carlton on Pearson Street, but the place was decidedly nicer than Felicia the heroin addict's spot on Chicago's South Side.

Paul ordered the drinks from a stunning blond waitress. "I'll have a Bombay emerald martini, and my Italian friend will have the Johnnie Walker Blue Label."

"I'm sure you must have found a clue, if you're dissin' my momma."

"I've met your mother and love her, and we must visit her soon for some linguine and clam sauce. And yes, I believe you and I have discovered something."

As they guzzled their high-octane drinks, they talked cop shop talk. Both agreed the headless corpse was linked somehow to the wealthy Clifton Barnes III, but both believed he was not the killer.

"Man like that never kill his daughter, much less mutilate the body," said Jackson.

"Yet he knows something," countered Paul.

"What does he know?"

"He knows who killed her and chopped off her head."

"So we go back to Cleveland, and we squeeze him with Cleveland PD's help, and he pukes out the murderer."

Paul ordered them two more drinks and said, "We don't have to return to Cleveland to find answers. They are right here—in Chicago."

Jackson and Paul returned to Clara Barnes's apartment and completed a neighborhood questioning. To each apartment occupant in the vicinity, Jackson identified himself as being with Chicago PD and asked questions about Clara's friends and visitors.

All described her as a wonderful, quiet neighbor that they passed casually in the halls and lobby. When Jackson displayed the photograph of Ashton Clark, a few of the neighbors recognized him but advised that he had only been a frequent visitor to her apartment in the last few months or so. All agreed that, mostly, she just had friends over to the house, and they watched TV or movies. An elderly male occupant of unit 146 provided the dynamic information that "She told me once that she was a huge fan of the TV show *Survivor*."

As they walked away, Jackson snarled. "She was a *Survivor* junkie. Well, that pretty well identifies her killer."

Paul suggested that the doorman for the complex would likely have a list of approved visitors for Clara Barnes.

"Already checked it, Sherlock, and I have a copy of it should you be interested."

"Boy, are you testy, Jackson. You need another drink or something."

Jackson replied, "Why not get a beer because this is a waste of time?"

Paul countered with, "I'll buy, but let me look at the visitor list first."

Jackson handed the list to Paul, and the list read:

Jaqueline Creamer
Adam Scott
Carol Johanson
Margaritte Harned
Traci Valponi
Melissa Jackson
Valencia Forbes
Angela Holmes
Ashton Clark
Clarisse Adams
Sandra Cook
Marissa Jones
Karen Savage
Amanda Blake
Terri Smalls
Casandra Simpson

"I presume you ran backgrounds on all these folks—right, Jackson?"

Jackson nodded. Paul offered his guess that "Adam Scott would have been a coworker of Clara's."

"You're wrong, super sleuth. Scott was her accountant and money manager."

Paul responded, "That is just the same. I believe we have our killer on the list."

Jackson seemed startled, but excited, and said he was glad that it was Ashton Clark.

"I detested that little fag from the instant we walked in his perfectly organized apartment. Let's get an arrest warrant."

"We are close to an arrest, but it won't be for Clark. He clearly is a homosexual though, but I don't think you're his type, Jackson."

Paul headed back to the lobby and asked Jackson to display his badge to the apartment lobby attendant and indicate Paul was his partner. Then Jackson was to be silent and take notes.

The lobby security officer was a gray-haired relic who smelled like a mix between Brylcreem, Aqua Velva, and bourbon. After the introduction, the interview was turned over to Paul.

"These matters are always so sensitive, but our first duty is to solve Clara Barnes's murder. You see who comes and goes. She had many friends, and I know Ashton Clark had visited frequently. Yet he never stayed overnight?"

"No sir. You're correct. Before her death, last few weeks, he was here almost every night, but he never spent the night."

"Thanks. That's valuable information. But before that, prior to her death—say, in the last nine months—who was her most frequent visitor?"

The guard hesitated and said that she had had a few visitors. Paul fired a malevolent look and said, "I do not have time for any niceness. Chicago PD must solve this homicide, and we know she was a lesbian. Ms. Clara Barnes was well known to law enforcement as a homosexual. Prior to the last few months, who was her most frequent sex partner? Not her one-night dike sleepovers, who was here most of the time?"

While Jackson looked downward, Paul stared at the bourbon-swilling, slick-haired Aqua Velva security officer.

"Tell me who, you useless fucker, or I'll charge you as an accessory because you didn't come forward."

The security guard looked sick but stammered, "I-I wasn't sure, and I didn't want to injure her memory. Ms. Barnes was nice to me."

"Tell me, or you're going for more questions—handcuffed in my patrol car."

"It was Valencia Forbes. Valencia, that was her lover—at least, her full-time frequent one."

"Thanks for your final gift of honesty. We'll be leaving now, but I'm sure some others from the department will be speaking with you later."

Once inside Jackson's vehicle, he called dispatch and obtained the home address for Valencia Forbes. He requested a marked unit to act as discreet backup and also reached down to his ankle. Jackson removed the five-shot weapon and handed it to Paul.

"This is for you, just in case!"

✕ ✕ ✕ ✕ ✕

Valencia Forbes's apartment complex was not nearly as fancy as Ashton Clark's or Clara Barnes's. It was not in downtown but in a decent suburban area, clean and probably fairly safe. There were no security guards here, so Jackson just knocked on the door of her unit.

A short, dumpy brown-haired, ferret-faced female answered.

"Are you Valencia Forbes?"

"Yes."

"We are with the Chicago Police Department—"

Before Jackson could finish, Valencia Forbes said, "I've been expecting you, but it took an awfully long time for you to figure it out."

Jackson cautioned her to silence and then read her Miranda rights. She immediately waived all rights and agreed to speak. A uniformed officer was also brought in to listen to her confession.

Paul sat quietly in the corner and listened to a story he had already figured out.

Valencia Forbes had been the longtime lover of Clara Barnes. As with any relationship, they had difficulties, and each had had affairs with others. She stressed that the affairs had only been with other women. That was the one ironclad rule: men were dirty, disgusting vermin who were absolutely off-limits.

A few months before, Clara had come to her and said that her father was placing enormous pressure on her to marry and have children. Initially, she believed that appearing to have a relationship with a clearly gay man like Ashton Clark might alleviate the strain and remove her father's pressure. Valencia Forbes did not find any difficulty with that arrangement.

Then things began to go awry when she found that however gay Ashton might appear, he was actually bisexual, and he made advances on her. While she had initially been repulsed, Ashton was in some ways more of a woman than Clara's female lovers, and his house was cleaner at a minimum. They began a low-grade heterosexual relationship. It worked perfectly for them but was absolutely unacceptable to Valencia Forbes. Her anger overflowed, and she decided to kill Clara rather than allow her to reenter any type of dirty relationship with a male.

Valencia Forbes then explained how the murder took place. She had contacted Clara and asked her to meet at the ghetto bar. She did not enter but watched as Clara went in. Forbes knew the bar would frighten Clara, so she watched the entrance, and the moment Clara exited, she drove by. Clara was relieved to get in her car. They then went back to Forbes's apartment. They had a good-bye drink, which was dosed with Xanax, Percocet, and tranquilizers. Once she was completely unconscious, Forbes used a guillotine-like device and severed her head.

"No one should ever see that beautiful face marred by death's hand."

She then placed the head in a canvas bag weighed down with stones and had thrown it into Lake Michigan. The body she had driven back to the vicinity of the bar on the South Side and left it in the dumpster. The marks on the feet had been from her dragging the body on the pavement.

The next day, Forbes had utilized her key to Clara's apartment and removed all the pictures. Many she removed because they showed her and Clara together, the others she took to maintain remembrances of her "only true love." She also took the photo of the spineless fag Ashton Clark and burned it.

Jackson said he had no further questions, but Paul interrupted him.

"I'm sorry. This is a bit of a personal question, but did you have physical relations with Ms. Forbes on the night you killed her?"

"Not while she was conscious, but after I drugged her, I used a huge vibrator on her. Figured I should give her one last good fuck. She wanted to go back with guys, so let her enjoy one last big one before she died."

That explained the vaginal tears Paul had seen in the autopsy room.

There were plenty of lesbians in prison; Valencia Forbes might even enjoy the life sentence she was destined to receive.

X X X X X

X X X X X

Paul returned to Los Angeles and realized that he liked the ocean more than he had imagined. Even the shores of Venice Beach seemed clean after the filthy experiences of Chicago and Cleveland.

He had been seriously dating the CNN reporter Gloria Camarena for six months. She was just as good at making love as she was as a reporter. He also determined that he was not as keen eyed as he always imagined. She proudly proved to him that her ample chest was real and God-given, but she did admit that she had had her nose bobbed.

"Hell, I used to look like Bozo the Bimbo Clown."

Paul was headed to pick up Gloria to take her to Spago. He reached into his pocket and fondled the small wrapped package—a diamond engagement ring. A jaded guy like him asking a beauty like her to be his wife . . . He had a feeling she would probably say yes. He respected her savvy and knowledge. In his other pocket was a new draft manuscript for her to critique and provide ideas on. He was not 100 percent sure what he would title it but knew the dedication would be to her. He spoke out loud to no one in particular, "I think I'll title it *The Headless Torso*."

WHAT DO YOU CALL A COPYCAT WHO COPIES COPYCATS?

John preferred redheads. Ideally brownish auburn–haired women with fair skin and freckles, but this was a guideline and not an absolute rule.

His current object of lust had black hair and white translucent skin.

Bitch probably dyes her beautiful red hair black—fucking cunt.

John moves closer to his object of desire and can smell the strong scent of alcohol on her breath. It is scotch, not a ladylike cocktail in the slightest. Her short miniskirt and spandex top are tight, and John can see the stains from her previous customers.

It is dusk, and the temperature is extremely cool, which is a nice change from many of his other sweat-soaked exchanges. He speaks quietly, "There is a quiet spot back in the alleyway, here's two hundred dollars. Not bad for just a blow job on a romantic night such as this. Après vous, mademoiselle."

For two hundred bucks, she would have sucked his cock at high noon in Times Square.

John follows her down the alley and suddenly seizes her by the throat and strangles her.

When unconscious, he slowly lowers her body to the ground behind a dumpster. Once on the ground, he severs the majority of one of her carotid arteries by reaching over her right side and, with a scalpel, cuts the left side of her throat. In this manner, the spurting blood is directed away from John and his clothing.

As is his just reward and trophy, her carefully makes an incision lower in her body and removes her kidney and places it in a Ziploc plastic bag and stashes it in his pocket. In this situation, there is no need to have intercourse with the whore; his work is successfully completed. He casually glances around, sees no one, and leaves.

× × × × ×

Even in jaded New York City, the giant worm-riddled Big Apple, the police and the press take note of a slasher that surgically removes kidneys.

NYPD detective Calahan got the case. Within one hour of being assigned the investigation, he receives a call from a Newark, New Jersey, homicide detective.

"It's a serial killer. Out in Jersey City, just outside the tunnel, we found a body two days ago. Younger female—sexually assaulted, strangled. Cut her throat and removed her sexual organs with one clean knife stroke."

It was agreed that NYPD detective Calahan and the Jersey City officer needed to talk. Even people who work in Jersey City think it is a dump, so they agree to meet in Manhattan.

× × × × ×

The interstate cop meeting is very informative. While there was no physical evidence of semen, body hair, DNA, or fibers at the New York City crime scene, the Jersey crime was sloppy, and evidence was already pointing to a subject.

DNA and semen provided a 99 percent probability that that crime had been committed by a former nuthouse inmate named Larry Darlington.

Previously, Darlington had done four years for sexual assault on a minor. One year after his release, he had been charged with forcible rape, but a technical glitch led to the case being dismissed. Darlington lived in New York City, on the streets, and in drug halfway houses.

Calahan clears the way for the New Jersey officer to be on hand in New York for the arrest and adds, "Scumbag killed your New Jersey girl first, so you can slap him around first too. Then I get my shot."

Fifteen officers and beat cops locate the halfway house near a seedy section of the projects by the river.

Darlington makes a halfhearted attempt to flee, and Calahan cracks him full force along the rib cage with his night stick. The sound of the shattered rib is clear and sharp and reminds the other officers of the sound a tree branch makes when snapped off.

Darlington curls on the ground in a ball, whimpering in pain.

There is a mistaken impression in law enforcement that men always frisk men, and women always pat down female criminals. In practice, safety is the primary concern, and this day, Janice Darlow completes the frisk of Darlington. All went well until she checks his pockets. Darlow is a young, smart, attractive gal who would likely be named detective soon.

Even Calahan—the oldest and most jaded member of the arrest team—is stunned when she steps back, throws Darlington down to his knees, and begins kicking him in the face. Once she is out of breath, Calahan drags her off and says, "Something get your panties in a wad, Janice?"

Calahan is forced to bodily restrain her from resuming her kicking Darlington's teeth in, but she does have time to hand Calahan the plastic bag she had found in Darlington's pocket.

The bag contains the recently severed sexual organs of the New Jersey victim.

X X X X X

There are videos in the rear seat of NYPD vehicles, and all interrogation rooms have video and audio recordings. But cops are not as stupid as they are depicted on television. All precincts have closets, coatrooms, and vacant offices.

Clarence Darlington receives significant interrogation. Some are on tape. Some are not. Some are violent. Some are tame. Yes, the New Jersey officer got his shots in and his questions answered too.

Unsurprisingly, Darlington confesses quickly. He had killed the one girl in Jersey City, raped her before and after he killed her, and then kept a souvenir of her sexual organs. Calahan said, "That's what Jack the Ripper did in London in 1888, you copycat scum."

"Jack the what? I never even heard of him. I cut her because she was a dirty whore."

"What about the girl in New York City you mutilated in the same way? No semen there, what happened? Couldn't get it up?"

"I never did nothing to no gal in New York. Just the bitch in Jersey."

"You lying motherfucker. Janice, at your convenience, please help Mr. Darlington back to his holding cell."

Officer Janice Darlow stares at Darlington with pure hatred, but also anticipation. She would get a few shots at him away from the prying eyes of the cameras.

Darlow found her swing and a set of pliers too, once the cameras were off, but Darlington refuses to admit to the assault on the New York victim. Finally exhausted from torturing him, she said to Calahan, "Fuck him. He admitted the Jersey torture and killing. Any jury will convict him of the New York mutilation."

"I'm sure you're right, Jan. I am proud of you tonight."

Two days later, the *New York Times* ran an article.

"Lawrence Darlington, age 35, was charged with the sexual assaults and murders of two New York area females. The names of the victims are being withheld at this time, to allow full, and discreet, notification to the families."

The tabloid papers in New York ran garish and detailed articles of the homicides and graphically detailed the mutilations and systematically pointed to comparison with the travesties committed by the notorious Jack the Ripper.

John sat, carefully reading the tabloid accounts as he polishes off a protein-powder-infused pineapple smoothie near Greenwich Village. The drink is filling, so he decides some exercise is in order. He walks and watches the citizenry of New York. John believed New York the perfect hunting grounds. In the city, everyone is always looking at their wingtips or fancy high-heeled pumps. Few were even casually watching their surroundings.

John thought of his chosen career and is quite proud. His accomplishments are legitimate, and he muses on his beginnings.

John had been a slightly pudgy youth and often the brunt of other children's pranks. His father also frequently beat him with an oar handle. Most often, these beatings were because John was a constant bed wetter and had done so until he was fifteen.

One day was deeply ingrained into John's mind. That morning, he had wet his bed, and his father had beaten him mercilessly while his mother watched. She had cried, but the tears were somehow forced and faked. That evening, John was depressed and angry, and the family cat, Tigger, had jumped onto his lap. John absentmindedly stroked the animal, but inexplicably, the cat scratched and bit him. Fifteen-year-old John had grabbed the cat around the throat and found a large plastic garbage bag. He suffocated Tigger and buried him in the backyard.

Exultation and power ran through him. Tigger deserved to die because he was weak, like John had been until moments before.

The next morning, John went into the basement and found his baseball bat. His father had returned home drunk and threatened him. John used the bat and broke both of his father's legs. His dad never bothered him again.

John had grown up in Chicago and, by eighteen, had moved out of his hellish birth home and was living on the streets. Yet he was able to get a job as a framer for building construction and as a painter. He lived in a small apartment with a heroin addict for a roommate. John had minimal formal schooling, but he was able to read and became an avid reader.

The year was 1980. The first book he read cover to cover was Killer Clown: The John Wayne Gacy Murders by Sullivan and Maiken. The book detailed the life of John's subsequent hero, a fellow Chicagoan who often dressed up as a clown and lured young men to his home, where he drugged and raped them. John found kinship in that they had the same name and the same urges.

At first, John had been confused at his identification with an antihero like Gacy who—it was confirmed—had tortured and raped over thirty young men and buried many in his basement. But the lure was too strong, and John, while periodically conducting normal heterosexual relationships, realized he was at least partly a pedophile like Gacy.

It was essential that he not be caught like Gacy, so he had developed an ingenious plan. He would become the best serial killer and sodomist of all time. His legend would ring like the church bells he had heard as a child.

He would research previous stars from the darker side and emulate and reproduce their crimes. Except he would not be caught; John would become the expert undetectable copycat.

Of course, he had begun with his hero Gacy. He lured young men into various places, drugged them with chloroform, and then sodomized them. He would be smarter than his mentor, and he developed a handmade latex skintight bodysuit which he wore during all assaults. No physical evidence, hair, fiber, or semen would remain. These acts must be committed in Chicago. And so, with these methods, seven young men were "brought into the fold"—as John conceived it. The first *choice had been his heroin-addicted roommate. He had buried the bodies beneath a vacant house in nearby Gary, Indiana.*

John liked to challenge himself during his actions, so he completed more detailed research into serial killers of the past. Jack the Ripper he had just finished in New York.

Another had been: "Lizzie Borden took an axe and gave her mother forty whacks, and when she saw what she had done, gave her father forty-one."

This quote was written in an untraceable note left by John at the scene of a double homicide he committed in a suburb of Boston, Massachusetts. He had killed a pastor and his wife. Utilizing a razor-sharp axe, he had struck thirteen blows into the wife's head and eleven into the husband. John believed them all strokes of genius.

×××××

John had travelled to Milwaukee to idolize the memory of Jeffrey Dahmer, the cannibal. There he killed four black victims, mutilating their bodies and eating certain body parts. At the crime scenes in Milwaukee, he left a severed penis and a human head in a freezer.

Again clad completely in his head-to-toe latex condom, there was no physical evidence. John did not particularly like the cannibalism, so he had moved on quickly to the West Coast to replicate a most audacious killer.

×××××

Richard Ramirez, the night stalker, committed his acts in California, and John left satanic markings at crime scenes there. He killed four people and sexually assaulted two dozen other elderly females and, at his final scene in Los Angeles, left this chilling note:

"You don't understand me. You are not capable of it. I am beyond your experience. I am beyond good and evil."

John is happy, and things have been going so well. He has been able to end the suffering of numerous types, both good and evil. As the marines say, "Kill them all. Let God sort them out."

John knows he may one day have a moment of reckoning. Yet he is unafraid because he has done so much good work already.

Besides, there is still much to be done. He thinks of the movies *Red Dragon* and *Silence of the Lambs*, but his own story is better. He will understand the mind and soul of every significant killer. One must learn from the best if one is to become the best. He will do even better by learning from their mistakes so he will not be caught.

He glances at the airline tickets in his hands. A circuit of American cities: Salt Lake City, Seattle, Denver, and Tallahassee. Nice locales, all beautiful and unique in their own ways. They have little in common historically or geographically: West Coast, high plains, mountainous, and eastern Sunshine State. There is, however, a strong linkage in John's mind.

A man named Ted Bundy.

CONCLUSION

Hopefully, some of the stories in this book made you laugh, created dread, or at a minimum, entertained you. I believe authoring fiction is the most interesting type of writing. Particularly in horror and suspense, I have the opportunity to play God a bit.

I can kill off the heroine, let a murderer go free, or conversely see that justice is served. This is true even if my type of justice is twisted or perverted.

The genre of short stories and novellas is becoming limited in the arenas of suspense, sci-fi, and horror. This is a shame. It may take a reader only ten minutes to read these types of tales, but in this short period of time, strong and lasting messages and feelings can be imparted.

I encourage you to read other books that contain similar material. As I wrote in the Introduction, I have always been enthralled with the short works penned by Asimov, King, and Bradbury. Seek out some of these works if you want more stories set on other planets, in morgues, and dead-end jobs (excuse the pun). Find fantasy places to explore, and perhaps you will want to write some of your own tales from the darker side.

It is okay to be scared once in a while, but it is better if you can scare others. Think of the classic example of ghost stories told around a campfire beginning to die into just glowing embers. Help keep the art of storytelling alive, even when you are talking about the dead. Boo!

SALES AND MARKETING

C-Rex Marketing
Carla Rexrode
crexmarketing@aol.com
PO box 271796
Fort Collins, CO 80527

www.FredericDonnerBooks.com
or by phone
XLIBRIS 1888-795-4274 ext 7879

WWW.FredericDonnerBooks.com

Look for other books published and for sale by Frederic Donner

- **Zen and the Successful Horseplayer**
  How to win and find calmness in Horse wagering

- **A Broken Badge Healed?**
  The F.B.I., A Special Agent, and the Cancer within both

- **White Cats Can Jump!**
  But Black Cats are scarier on Halloween
  short stories of intrigue, horror, humor and mystery

- **TO DIE, TO SLEEP, PERCHANCE TO DREAM**
  (A Tale of love and mystery)

- **The Queen of Hearts**
  (Is Murder A Mystery Or A Game To Enjoy?)

- **365 Daily Inspirations**
  A Five Year Reflection Journal
  a collection of quotes and self-observation growth journal

Sales and Marketing Inquiries

CRexMarketing@aol.com
Carla Rexrode
PO Box 271796, Fort Collins, CO 80527
970-682-2251
CRexMarketing@aol.com

CPSIA information can be obtained
at www.ICGtesting.com
Printed in the USA
FSOW01n1957220116
16124FS